I0648121

THE PAPER DETECTIVE

OTHER BOOKS BY E. JOAN SIMS

The Paisley Sterling Mysteries
Cemetery Silk
The Plague Doctor
The Paper Detective
The Cradle Robber

THE PAPER DETECTIVE
A PAISLEY STERLING MYSTERY

E. JOAN SIMS

WILDSIDE PRESS

THE PAPER DETECTIVE: A PAISLEY STERLING MYSTERY
Copyright © 2004, 2005 by E. Joan Sims.
Cover design copyright © 2005 by Garry Nurrish.

ACKNOWLEDGEMENTS: Thanks to all the good folk who took the time to educate me about deer hunting, coyotes in Kentucky, and other forest lore: Mary and Benjie Cronic, the Lear family, and Mary Louise Joiner.

Wildside Press
www.wildsidepress.com

Dedicated to my one true love—my husband Luis—
todavia "te amo muy mucho"

"It is all very well to sneer at the paper detective, but a principle is a principle, whether in fiction or in fact. Many of the great lessons of life are to be learned in the pages of the novelist."

—Sir Arthur Conan Doyle, June 1929

CHAPTER ONE

I lounged back against the comfortable arm of the red chintz sofa in the library and gazed out the double French doors at the snow. Flakes as big as goose feathers had fallen softly and steadily all night long. Deep pillowy drifts piled up next to the orchard fence and around the base of the fruit trees, and according to the weatherman, more snow was on the way.

Three mating pairs of cardinals hunted and pecked on the sparkling diamond-white surface where Cassie had tossed out some bread crusts earlier. Only a few crumbs remained.

The bright red birds on the glistening white snow made me think of a fairy tale my Grandmother Howard used to read to me about a princess with snow-white skin. She had pricked her finger with a needle. When that drop of red blood appeared on the fairest of hands, a whole kingdom had fallen to sleep for one hundred years.

I yawned and turned back to the crackling fire that burned merrily in the big hearth. My bowl of buttered popcorn was almost gone, but I lacked the energy to go back to the kitchen for more. I was considering a serious nap when the phone rang.

When you have a beautiful, unattached, twenty-year-old daughter, there is only the remotest chance that you will ever have to answer the telephone. The possibility of the call being for anyone other than her is even smaller. Therefore, I was surprised and even a little annoyed when I heard Cassie yelling at me from the hallway.

"Mom! Telephone! It's New York Pam."

Ordinarily, I would have loved to hear from Pamela Alison Winslow. She was my agent and more than a little responsible for making sure that the whole wide world read my mystery novels. Unfortunately, she was also the one who insisted that I use the pen name of Leonard Paisley and let that imaginary schmuck take all the credit for my hard work. I did realize, however, that a rough, tough, hard-boiled detective could make more money selling books than a middle-aged woman who is afraid of spiders—at least for the time being.

Nobody seemed to mind when it was just little old me writing children's books. *Bartholomew the Blue-eyed Cricket* had gotten me and Cassie through the lean years after my husband—her father—had disappeared from our home in San Romero. We had escaped the worst of the revolution in that beautiful, but politically torn country and gone to Manhattan to live. It was there that Pam, who had been my college roommate, suggested Bartholomew might be our meal ticket instead of simply an entertaining bedtime story for my little daughter.

Ten years of insects and small, furry rodents was about all I could squeeze out of my imagination, and once again, Pam saved my bacon by suggesting I write mysteries. I, excuse me, *Leonard* was a big hit from the start. We had just published our third book.

My new source of income had allowed me to move back to Meadowdale Farm in western Kentucky where I grew up. My elegant and stylish mother, Anna Howard Sterling, was delighted that I was home to stay, even though we had our confrontations from time to time—mostly about my being neither elegant nor stylish.

It was three weeks before Christmas, and I was taking a well-deserved vacation in order to be able to really enjoy having Cassie home from university for the holidays.

"Damn it, Pam!" I said as I picked up the phone. "I thought we agreed I could take some time off? I told you to tell everybody I've gone fishing."

"Fishing?" she protested. "According to the weatherman, it's sixteen degrees there!"

"Ice fishing. You cut a hole in the ice, warm the worms in your mouth, and . . . "

"Paisley, you know I wouldn't bother you unless it was absolutely necessary."

"No!" I insisted.

"Now, Paisley, you're being childish."

"No. No. No." I shook my head vigorously even though she couldn't see me.

"You don't even know what I'm going to ask you," she wheedled.

"Pam, I recognize that tone of voice. It's the same one you used in college when you wanted . . . "

"That history term paper was mine from start to finish. I didn't use *any* of your notes. Come on, Paisley. Just give it a listen, please?"

"Okay, okay." I conceded. "It is almost Christmas. I haven't had time to shop. Consider this your gift."

"Great. Now, don't say 'no' right away. Be reasonable and let me finish. Promise?"

"Oh, boy. I knew this was going to cost me. I should have gotten you something from K-Mart."

"The feature writer from *Pen and Ink* magazine has contacted me. They want an interview with Leonard."

"You've got to be kidding!"

"I asked you not to interrupt," she said.

"Are you out of your tiny little mind?"

"Ten thousand dollars worth of out of my mind," she chortled.

That did put a new light on things.

"You want me to grow a mustache?" I asked.

Pam laughed. "It wouldn't hurt; but then again, it won't help.

No, we'll have to find someone else to be Leonard. Got any ideas?"

"Pam, this is the craziest . . . "

"Oops, another call. Gotta go. Let me know when you find 'Leonard.' And remember, it's not just the money. It'll be terrific publicity."

Cassie came in as I hung up the phone. Aggie, her temperamental Lhasa Apso, trailed despondently at her heels. The puppy knew her mistress was all dressed up to go somewhere without her, and when Cass plopped down on the sofa opposite mine, Aggie hopped up in her lap as if trying to anchor her down.

Cassandra looked beautiful. Hair the color of mahogany framed her perfect oval face and fell straight and shining past her shoulders. A light touch of eye shadow over her brown eyes made them appear even larger and more mysterious against her porcelain skin. The ankle-length burgundy velvet dress clung to her tall, slender body more than I would have liked it to, but I knew better than to say anything.

"Wow! You look terrific. What are you all dolled up for?"

"Nothing much. Danny's taking me to a Christmas concert in Morgantown."

"Hmm, Danny," I muttered, as I tried to see him in Leonard's skin. "What?"

"Has Danny ever done any acting? High school play, community theater?"

"Sure. His stepfather showed me some pictures. He said Danny was the best Peter Pan ever.

CHAPTER TWO

When Danny arrived, I inspected him with Leonard's imaginary physique in mind, but Danny didn't pass muster. For one thing, he was too young, and for another, he was too good looking. Tall, blonde, and handsome, he barely escaped being pretty. I would have to look elsewhere, but seeing Danny gave me an idea of where "elsewhere" might be.

Danny Hall was the new police chief of a neighboring county. He was the youngest to hold that office since Robert "Pee Wee" Atherton, in 1909. I only knew that little piece of trivia because Pee Wee had been a distant relative. Danny had taken over temporarily when his stepfather was wounded in a robbery attempt. After Bert Atkins took early disability retirement, Danny was officially appointed to his office.

Bert Atkins would be the perfect "Leonard." He was as tall as Danny but his looks were craggy and worn. His steel-grey hair was cropped close to his skull, and his dark blue eyes could burn into yours like a laser. When they stood side by side, Danny appeared inches taller because Atkins affected a casual slouch. Some said it was from his early days in the Marines, when his height made him a bigger target. Mr. Bert Atkins looked lean and mean, I realized with a delighted shiver—lean and mean like Leonard.

Atkins had been shot in the hip by a sixteen-year-old bank robber wanna-be almost a year ago. The last time I saw him was two months before that, when he came to us in search of answers about the death of a young woman in his jurisdiction. Cassie met his stepson that night, and they started dating shortly afterwards. Danny was serious. Cass was not. She had turned down at least two of his marriage proposals and dated several other young men in the meantime. Danny said he would keep on trying. I knew he didn't stand a chance. I warned Cassie against giving him false hope, but she assured me they could remain friends. I think Bert was angry with us because of Cassie's rejection of his stepson. He had refused several invitations to dinner and was just short of abrupt when either Mother or I called.

Somehow I had to get past that gruff and angry façade. I had to convince Bert Atkins to be Leonard Paisley just for the interview. I had my work cut out for me. It wouldn't be easy. Nothing about Bert Atkins was easy.

When Cassie left, Aggie transferred her affection to me. The rough translation of that was: she hopped into my lap so I could keep her warm. Aggie hated cold weather. She especially hated snow. It stuck in between her paw pads and froze her toes. She was even more nasty-tempered in the winter, but she did treat me with a smidge more respect. I had told her when nobody was looking that if I kicked her lily-white ass out into the white snow no one would ever find her.

When Mother finished watching her one television show of the week and came to join me, I told her about Pam's call and asked her what she thought about my idea.

"I've always thought you and Bert Atkins should get to know each other better. This is a perfectly lovely excuse to call on him, dear."

"I'm not looking for romance, Mother. This is serious business. Pam won't let me off the hook this time. She's tried to get me to produce a 'Leonard' before, but I've always managed to weasel out of it. *Pen and Ink* is too important a magazine to ignore."

"Then let her find someone in New York, dear. Leonard was her idea. There must be hundreds of actors up there who would be glad to do the job."

I had to smile. Mother thought less of New York than she thought of Siberia. "Up there" to her was as bad as saying "in hell" for anyone else.

"Pam knows me better than that. She knows I would scream like a stuck pig if she picked somebody without me. I have to give her credit for that. She's letting me call the shots on this one."

I pushed Aggie gingerly off my lap and went to look out at the cold winter night. The bare branches of the tall trees swayed and clacked against each other in the freezing wind. The top layer of snow swirled from ground to air and back again. I wondered if the owls and squirrels and other little creatures had a warm place to hide from old Jack Frost. And I wondered what in the world I was doing writing murder mysteries when I still had the mind-set for children's books.

Mother went to bed, but I waited up for Cassie. She came home at twelve on the dot. Danny walked her to the library door and when he leaned over to kiss her he saw me pretending to sleep on the sofa. He straightened up quickly and hugged her instead. Cassie tapped lightly on the door as he was leaving. I stretched and yawned like I had just awakened, then pretended to lurch sleepily over to let her inside.

"Is that why you were asking about community theater, Mom? Are you thinking of taking up acting? Because if you are, forget it. You didn't fool either one of us."

She took off her long woolen cape and sat down on the hearth to warm herself by the fire. "But thanks, anyway," she sighed. "The last thing in the world I wanted was that kiss. I think you're right. I'd better stop seeing Danny once and for all. I really hate it because he's so much fun." She sighed again. "I love being with him. I just don't love him."

She looked at me for a response. I had none. Long ago I discovered it was best to stay out of my daughter's love life. I did have to ask one thing, though.

"Would it be a problem for you if I asked Danny's stepfather to impersonate Leonard for an interview with a very important magazine? I won't do it if it is."

"Don't be silly, Mom. It's not a problem for me. They haven't seen each other much since Bert retired. Danny probably won't even know."

"I thought Danny lived at home."

"He does. But Bert moved out as soon as he recovered from his hip surgery. He's living way out by Jackson Lake in a cabin he built several years ago. Really roughing it from what Danny says. He doesn't have electricity, or running water, or even a telephone."

"Did Danny and Bert have an argument? They seemed so close."

"I honestly don't know, Mom. Danny doesn't say much about his personal life."

She looked up with a sad little smile.

"That's one thing about him that bothers me. You know how I feel about family."

"Well, if you really don't mind, I think I'll try to get in touch with Ex-Chief Atkins. He would make the most perfect Leonard. Don't you think, so?"

"If you say so, Mom," she sighed as she gazed sadly into the flames. "Although I really don't think there is a perfect man anywhere."

I smiled. This was an old discussion and I could comment.

"Remember what we said before? 'Perfect' would be boring!"

CHAPTER THREE

The next day dawned beautiful and clear and even colder. The sun sparkled brightly on the snow, but wasn't nearly warm enough to melt it. I called Danny at the Hall County Courthouse and asked him the best way to get in touch with his stepfather.

"You have a four wheel drive, don't you, Mrs. DeLeon?"

"Yes, a Jeep Cherokee."

"Dad's cabin is about twenty-five miles out the Sandlick Road. He's on the far side of Jackson Lake. It's a rough ride in the best weather. I don't know if I would recommend you trying to get out there in this snow." He laughed. "But if half the things Cassie says are true, that won't make a bit of difference to you. Just be sure to take your cellular phone, plenty of blankets, and a couple of flashlights. I'll be listening out in case you have any trouble. Cassie has my private phone number. Call me direct if you have a problem."

"Thanks, Danny, I really appreciate it. Is your stepdad all right? I mean, was the surgery on his hip successful?"

"Yep."

Try as I might, that was the only information I could get out of Danny regarding the personal health and well being of Bert Atkins. I hung up the phone feeling as if I were going out in the snow looking for a grizzly bear.

"Come on, Cassie," I pleaded. "It'll be fun! Just you and me and Watson."

"I don't think a sports utility vehicle named after Sherlock Holmes's sidekick qualifies as a person, Mom."

"Okay, then we'll ask your grandmother."

"I don't care if you ask the Atlanta Braves—I'm not going. This afternoon I'm telling Danny we can't see each other anymore, and 'anymore' means starting right now and includes his whole family."

"Okay," I grumped. "I understand. And you're right. Maybe Mother will go."

She looked at me with raised eyebrows.

"I don't quite see Gran in a mountain cabin. Now if Christian Dior's latest was something in a red plaid flannel and denim, you might have a chance at convincing her."

Cassie was right. Mother refused my invitation before I even finished asking. She, also, had a perfectly good excuse. Horatio Raleigh, her dear friend and companion, was suffering from a cold. She was taking him some homemade soup and a copy of my latest book, *Virtual Violence*.

Horatio was the retired director of our town's sole funeral home. He only went in to the "shop" when someone of note, or wealth, passed away and he was needed as a bereavement consultant. He had served in that capacity last weekend. The family had chosen the super deluxe casket, so he had even attended the burial. It had been a cold and rainy day. His doctor said he would be in bed at least a week.

I would have to go out the Sandlick Road alone.

Watson was warmed up in no time at all, and by the time I had loaded some blankets and old quilts and extra flashlights in the back I was actually looking forward to our little adventure. Danny was probably exaggerating. A little snow never hurt anybody.

Sandlick Road was about twenty miles out of Rowan Springs at the junction of the highway that led to the big lakes in the area. The lakes were there thanks to a big TVA dam project. The area was a great tourist attraction and even in the winter there was a fair amount of traffic. When I turned off the main highway, however, the traffic quickly thinned out. After a short time, I was all alone on the road.

I set my odometer at zero so it would count the miles for me. The road had been cleared, but the snow from last night had formed an icy new surface, and I had to watch carefully for glassy spots. Even with Watson's four wheel drive, I could feel the tires slipping and sliding in places.

The banks on either side of the road were a combination of new drifts and old snow pushed off by the snowplow, higher in some places than the car. It was like driving down a long white tunnel.

Wynonna was telling me in her own beautifully melodious way about the perils of country love when the big buck came out of nowhere. I saw his heels as he jumped over Watson's hood, and I did all the wrong things instantly. I panicked and slammed on the brakes to avoid smashing the deer's hindquarters just as I hit a spot of black ice. Watson spun around two or maybe three times before careening like a billiard ball off the mountains of hard-packed snow on the shoulders. We finally came to a jolting stop after bursting through the last barricade of snow sideways. The horn blew loudly as I slumped forward on the steering wheel.

The blow to the car was on the passenger side, so my air bag didn't deploy, and at some time during the wild ride, I hit my head very hard against the side window. I might have even blacked out for a moment or two until the blaring horn woke me up. That's my only excuse for the stupid things I did next.

I would like to think that if I hadn't been woozy I would have thought twice before leaving the car without a flashlight or my cellular phone. I didn't even remember to check the mileage on the odometer. If I had, maybe I would have known better than to try and walk the last five miles to Bert's cabin.

Danny had told me that Bert had a big black mailbox with his name, "B. Atkins," on it. That was all I could think about as I walked and walked. I suppose I would have walked forever before I realized that the snowdrifts at the side of the road had buried any and all mailboxes. Fortunately, I still had enough sense to follow tire tracks leading off the main road and down a narrow track.

Cold and exhausted, I had been walking a little over two hours when I began to lose it. The sky darkened as the afternoon sun passed behind big clouds that heralded more snow, and I began imagining scenes of warm fireplaces and bowls of steaming hot soup. My fantasy was so strong that I could smell wood smoke.

I had lost the feeling in my feet and legs. The only thing that kept me going was my desire to be with Mother and Cassie, and even Aggie, again. They were there in front of me, but with every step I took, they moved farther away. I started crying in frustration. Didn't they know how badly I wanted to reach them? I sank to my numb, unfeeling knees and sobbed in frustration.

Aggie relented and came bouncing up to me. She covered my face with big, wet, warm doggie kisses and licked away my tears. I struggled to regain my feet, but my legs wouldn't cooperate. Cassie joined us. I tried to tell her she looked really silly with a beard, but my mouth wouldn't work either. Cass reached out and grabbed me roughly by the scruff of my neck and hauled me up. She threw me easily over one shoulder and walked down the trail while I bounced against her wide back and made ridiculous cooing noises at Aggie, who trotted along behind.

As the smell of wood smoke and cooking food got stronger and penetrated my mental haze, Aggie began to look a little strange to me. I wondered vaguely why she had grown so large. Her face was almost as big as her whole body had been yesterday. And when did she get to be a redhead like me?

CHAPTER FOUR

A delicious warmth moved slowly up my body and into my mind. I was as cozy and comfortable as I had ever been. I stretched and opened my eyes, expecting to see my beloved bedroom on Meadowdale Farm. What I saw instead were the four walls of a rustic log cabin haphazardly decorated with disembodied antlers and stuffed big-mouth bass. A large red dog lay sleeping on a handmade rag rug in front of the big stone fireplace. I could hear his soft doggie snores over the crackling of the fire.

I tried to raise up on my elbows to see more of the room, but a heavy hand on my head pushed me back down.

"Stay still!" barked Bert Atkins. "I'll bring you some soup."

I opened my mouth to make a sharp and witty retort to the effect that I was a modern independent woman and didn't take orders from men, but all I could manage was a hoarse croak.

"Quiet!" he barked again.

I retaliated by childishly sticking out my tongue in his general direction, but even that didn't work. My mouth and throat were so dry I couldn't even work up a spit.

Atkins came back and pulled a footstool up to the big old sofa I was lying on. He tucked a rough towel under my chin and then ever so gently spooned a warm mouthful of broth between my lips. The soup trickled down my throat and warmed the cockles of my heart. I eagerly opened my mouth for more.

Bert laughed. His laugh was big and hearty and infectious. I grinned broadly back and immediately split my dry lips. The pain was intense and brought swift tears to my eyes. Bert got up and fumbled around in a first aid kit until he found what he was looking for, then sat back down and pulled my chin toward him. He dabbed the soothing ointment generously over my mouth. As an afterthought, he put some in the outer corners of my eyes and then grunted with satisfaction

"Should have done that first," he acknowledged gruffly. "Sorry."

He resumed my meal, and in no time at all I had emptied the bowl. My lips felt much better, but I couldn't keep my eyes open. I tried to concentrate on the bright flickering flames of the wood fire, but the warmth from within and without put me to sleep like a lullaby.

I woke up later because I was cold again. I had dreamed I was back in the snow—lost and alone. Bert was putting more logs on the fire. When he finished, he hunkered down awkwardly on his game hip and rearranged the coals with a poker.

My thirst had returned with a vengeance. I called out to him for something to drink, but he didn't respond. At first I thought I had unwittingly done something to anger him. But when I called again and he didn't even flinch, I knew why a proud man like Bert Atkins had sought this isolated refuge in the woods—why he had refused all of our invitations. He was deaf as a post.

I slept deeply and without further dreams until a full bladder woke me up. I lay there for a moment wondering how to tell a deaf man I needed to pee without embarrassing us both. I needn't have worried. As soon as he saw that I was awake he came over to the sofa and picked me up, blankets and all. Before I could protest, he opened the back door and carried me down a path through the snow to an outhouse.

My blood went cold at the thought that I would have to share the freezing toilet with spiders and heaven only knew what else. When we had moved out to the farm, we had an outhouse. Of course, my father and grandfather had already seen to it that we had functioning facilities as well, but the outhouse held a fascination for my sister, Velvet, and me. Fascination, that is, until one day when the door got stuck and I was faced, in my child's mind, with the possibility of being trapped in the stinking latrine forever. That ended my thrill of peeing outside for good. A few days, later Vel and I risked the wrath of my parents and grandparents by setting fire to the offending outbuilding. Our punishment was swift and severe, and something I never forgot. Forever after, I hated outhouses.

Bert opened the door and deposited me inside. I looked around in amazement. It was much larger than the boxlike structure that had imprisoned me when I was six, and thanks to a small stove, it was toasty and warm.

"I'll be back in twenty minutes," Bert announced abruptly, and closed the door.

A small chair in the corner seemed a likely place to unload my cocoon of quilts and blankets. I shuffled over and started unwrapping myself layer by layer. When I got to the innermost core, I found I was minus about two layers of my own clothing. Bert had shucked me out of my jeans, sweater, flannel shirt, and long underwear. At least he had the decency to leave me with a long-sleeved camisole and panties. My face went hot with shame. No one but Rafe had ever seen me this undressed. Mr. Bert Atkins had some explaining to do.

The little camp stove that warmed the bathroom also provided a basin full of hot water for a quick bird bath. The towels Bert had left for me were scratchy and rough, but they smelled clean and fresh. He obviously dried them outside on a line because the fold over could still be seen in the bath towel. I shook them out to make sure no little bugs were hiding anywhere. Once assured, I had quite a pleasant toilette.

The mirror above the dry sink basin was much too high for me to see myself. All that was visible was a mop of totally out-of-control auburn curls, two green eyes, and a couple of freckles. I scrubbed hard with the soap and hot water in the hope that cleanliness would substitute for loveliness, and rewrapped myself in two of the quilts. I felt much better. I was only a little dizzy, and I was starving.

Bert returned right on time. When he tapped lightly on the door, I opened up and was about to say I could walk back when he swung me up in his arms and carried me to the cabin.

He had set a small table for two in front of the fire. He plopped me down on the sofa and pulled the table over in front of me. A steaming platter of pancakes, scrambled eggs, and bacon beckoned. Without a word, he poured my coffee and his, and we set to work. When nothing was left of our breakfast but an "Ummm," he cleared the plates and brought the coffeepot back for refills.

Bert sat back and looked me up and down until I blushed. I was wondering how to communicate with him when he spoke.

"I can hear some, you know. And I'm fairly good at reading lips."

"Oh, I didn't . . . "

"Yes, you did. I saw you last night when I put fresh logs on the fire. You don't play possum very well."

I laughed. "So I've been told."

I sat bolt upright, almost losing my envelope of blankets. My head swam as I remembered.

"Cassie! She'll be worried sick. And Mother! I have to let them know I'm all right."

Bert pointed to a big oak desk back in the corner. There was some sort of equipment on it. It looked like a stereo with lots of fancy dials and lights.

"Radio. Runs on batteries. I called Danny last night and told him you were here. He radioed back while you were asleep. Mrs. Sterling and your daughter know where you are and that you're just fine."

"Oh, thanks, Bert. Er, Chief Atkins."

"Bert's fine. Remember," he laughed. "I've seen your skivvies."

"About that! Was it absolutely necessary to undress me?" I tried not to, but I knew I was blushing.

"Your clothes were soaking wet. You would have gotten pneumonia if I'd been fool enough to leave you to your modesty. They're almost dry, except for the sweater. You can get dressed after you take a nap, if you want."

"Nap? Don't you think I've already slept enough? A nap is the last thing . . . "

The yawn caught me unawares. "Well, maybe just a short one."

CHAPTER FIVE

The next time I woke up, the fuzzy feeling in my head was almost completely gone. The strength was back in my arms and legs, and I no longer felt shaky. I was ready to get dressed and go in search of Watson.

"Sorry," said Bert firmly when I informed him of my intentions.

"What do you mean, sorry?" I asked as I gave him the benefit of my haughtiest look.

His response was another deep and hearty laugh. I was getting pretty sick of being his stand-up comic, and I told him so, although something somewhere inside was pleased that he was laughing. I had always thought of him as a very angry and morose man. This Bert Atkins, the man with the steel-wool beard and the laughing blue eyes was not the taciturn cop who stormed the fortress of our home last year and wouldn't take "no" for an answer. This was a man who was happy, or at least gave a good impression of it. And I was beginning to realize that he was very attractive.

"I've got to go home. Mother's expecting me for dinner," I decided abruptly.

"No she's not. Danny told her you might not get back for two or maybe three days."

"Watson! I can't abandon Watson."

"Your jeep is fine. I walked down this morning early to check on things. I locked the door and turned off the engine . . . "

I was horrified at my stupidity.

"I . . . I left the engine on?"

I sank back on the old sofa wishing the soft cushions would swallow me up.

"Paisley, you have a slight concussion. You did nothing to be ashamed of."

He came over and sat down beside me.

"As a matter of fact, few *men* I know would have been tough enough to do what you did."

"I was stupid," I answered in a voice that was smaller than I wished. "I left the warmth and safety of the car and started walking in the freezing cold like a dummy."

"And a good thing that you did. The exhaust pipe was embedded in the snow bank. If you hadn't gotten out, you might have died of carbon monoxide poisoning."

My new-found strength vanished as I realized how close I had come to never seeing my beautiful Cassie again, and I started crying. Bert put his arms around me as the gentle tears turned into great hiccoughing sobs. When I was spent, he tucked the blankets back around me and urged me to sleep again. This time I didn't fight it.

I finally got dressed late that afternoon right before Bert fixed dinner. He let me sit on a stool by the dry sink and peel potatoes while he gave a hilarious account of his running battle with a family of thieving raccoons who lived in a hollow tree nearby.

I cried again, but this time they were tears of laughter. After dinner we played gin rummy while listening to a soft jazz station out of New Orleans. It had been a long time since I had so much fun and I told him so.

"Me, too, Paisley," he said softly.

"You're very different from the way I imagined. You're obviously not that uncomfortable with your hearing loss. Why did you come out here by yourself? Why leave Danny alone?"

He smiled. "Wow, just like a woman. So many questions."

"Forget that 'just like a woman' crap. This is a question from me to you, as friends."

"Are we friends, Paisley?"

"Well, sure, of course," I answered brightly, avoiding the intent look in those deep blue eyes.

"I have to confess I've thought a lot about you since we first met," he said. "I've wanted to call you a half a dozen times."

"Well, for heaven's sake," I sputtered, trying to defuse the situation. "Why didn't you come to dinner when Mother and I invited you? We thought you were angry about something. I know Danny and Cassie have an on-again off-again relationship, but that shouldn't keep the rest of us from being friends."

Bert's seemed suddenly uncomfortable with the conversation, yet determined to have his say.

"I like your mother, Paisley. She's a very admirable woman, but I'm not talking about a relationship with her. It's you who's been on my mind for the last few months. I know this must seem very sudden to you, but I've wanted to be close enough to say these things to you for a long time, and I can't waste this opportunity."

Bert reached across the table and took the cards out of my hand. He covered my smaller palm with his big one. My backbone melted like sweet, warm beeswax. I had never felt so delicate in my life. And I was terrified. I wasn't ready for this.

"Is there a chance that we could be more than friends?" he asked with a crooked smile.

I jumped up and practically ran to the window. The night outside was clear, with a bright, ice-cold moon shining on the snow. I could see his dog's tracks around the cabin and his own big footprints leading out to the woodpile.

I turned around and faced him.

"This is not why I came out here. I . . . I don't need this kind of complication in my life right now."

I was close to tears again. I hated crying. I hadn't cried this much in the last twenty years. Damn concussion, I thought.

I watched Bert's face close off. His lips narrowed and the light left his eyes. His irises turned from sky blue to the color of steel as he turned in on himself. I wanted to crawl in a hole and hide.

"Look, Bert, I'm sorry."

"Don't be. My mistake," he said abruptly.

He stood up and put on his jacket. He called the dog, and they went out into the winter night.

I sat in front of the fire for what seemed like hours until the man and his dog came back home. I heard him stomping his feet to shake off the snow and ran to open the door. At that moment I think I would have done almost anything to return to our previous state of growing intimacy, but one look at Bert's face told me that opportunity had gone for good. I sank back down on the sofa feeling like I had killed something young and innocent and infinitely promising.

He hung his coat up and fed the dog before he joined me in front of the fire.

"So," he said, "why *did* you come all the way out here looking for me?"

His voice was steady and very calm, almost without inflection or feeling, just tinged with a mild curiosity.

"Leonard, I needed a Leonard," I answered miserably. "But that was a stupid idea. Forget about it."

"Leonard. He's the one who's supposed to be writing your books, isn't that so?"

"Yeah, he's the one, all right."

"Well, go on."

I was getting questioned now, by the police. My new best friend had gone outside and the ex-cop had come back in his place.

27

"My agent called," I sighed. "There's a very important magazine in New York, and they want to do a feature story on Leonard Paisley. Pam wanted me to find him, and you came to mind."

"Why?"

"Why not? You look just like him, or almost. And you're familiar with murders and criminals, and . . . well, Leonard's kind of thing," I explained. "I thought you would be perfect. I didn't know you had turned into jolly ole Paul Bunyan."

Bert laughed for the first time since dinner, but it had a different sound. There was an edge to his humor now. The softness was gone

"So Raggedy Ann is calling me Paul Bunyan!"

"Raggedy . . . why, that?"

"That mop of funny looking hair, that's why. That's how I knew it was you in the snow. I held my gun sight on you for two hundred feet before you fell to your knees. I was getting ready to fire a warning shot when your hood slipped off and all that curly red hair spilled out. Lucky for you, too, otherwise I might have left you to cool off in the snow some more."

"You wouldn't!" I protested. "I could have frozen to death."

"Maybe just a little frostbite," he grinned.

"But why?"

He gazed into the crackling fire for a long time before he answered me.

"Not everyone is a friend."

"Look, I said I was sorry . . . "

He cut me off with a slash of his hand.

"I have quite a few enemies, real enemies—the kind who would like to see me dead. You asked me why I left Danny and came out here by myself. Well, that's the reason. I don't want any innocent bystanders getting in the way if somebody with an old grudge comes looking for me."

I tried to see his face, but like a good cop he had arranged it so he was in the shadows and I was in the light of the fire.

"Does Danny know?"

"Of course not. And I don't want him to. Understand?" he demanded gruffly.

I nodded in agreement as I pondered the vast range of human emotions. I had gone from giddy happiness, to bleak misery, and now cold fear in the space of less than two hours. It was exhausting.

"What's in it for me?" he asked after a long moment.

"Being Leonard? Well, the magazine is offering ten thousand. Pam gets fifteen percent. You can have the rest," I offered meekly.

He turned angry blazing eyes on me.

"I don't need the whole damned thing. You didn't come out here with that offer in mind, did you?"

"No," I admitted humbly. "I was going to split it with you."

"That's more like it!"

In spite of the fire, I was cold. I shivered and pulled one of the quilts up around my shoulders. Bert noticed and put another log on the fire. I was grateful for his kindness and told him so. He acknowledged my thanks with a curt nod. I knew we would never be able to talk as easily as we had before, but I was still curious.

"Have you taken any precautions to protect yourself? I mean, do you have any surveillance cameras, or . . . "

Bert dropped his head back and laughed. This time it was the same deep, truly genuine laugh he'd had before. I smiled tentatively in return. When he finished, he wiped his eyes and answered me.

"My God, woman," he said still chuckling, "haven't you noticed my rather primitive lifestyle? Where do you think I would get the power to juice up those cameras? Train the raccoons to run a generator?"

He walked back to the kitchen still chuckling to himself.

"Want some fresh coffee?" he asked, turning to watch for my answer.

"Sure. I don't think I'll ever be able to sleep again, anyway."

When his eyes sharpened, I hastened to add, "I've slept so much, I mean. I guess the blow on my head," I finished lamely.

He came back with two mugs of hot coffee laced with cream and sugar.

"I would have added a little Jack Daniels, but I don't think a doctor would approve so soon after a head injury."

We sipped our coffee in silence. He was much better than I at adjusting to the new distance between us. I think he was more at ease with himself, and maybe more honest.

"You've changed a lot out here in the woods," I ventured.

He was back in the shadows again, and I couldn't tell much from the tone of his voice.

"Maybe."

"Don't you get lonesome?"

"I have Murphy. He's all the company I need. My cigars and my books are a dividend."

The dog heard his name and thumped his tail on the floor in sleepy acknowledgment.

"I've read all your mysteries," he continued. "You made a few mistakes, but they're amusing. By the way, Leonard's an asshole."

"Then you are more like him than I thought," I retorted angrily.

Again his laughter was genuine and wholehearted. I felt like a naughty schoolgirl. I turned over on my side and pulled the covers up.

"I am sleepy, after all," I muttered. "Good night."

He sat there in silence until I almost screamed. At long last, he got up and put another log on the fire.

I lay awake long after I heard the steady breathing coming from his bed in the far corner of the cabin.

CHAPTER SIX

The next morning I was awakened by the sound of the county tow truck pulling Watson into the drive in front of Bert's cabin. I grabbed my clothes and ran barefoot to the outhouse where, thanks to my host, my warm bird bath was waiting. I washed and dressed quickly. I couldn't wait to get home.

Danny and Bert were on the front porch drinking steaming mugs of coffee and sharing a joke when I walked out. They cut their laughter short when they saw me. My cheeks burned when they avoided looking my way, leaving me little doubt as to the target of their humor.

"Good morning, Danny," I said a little too brightly. "Thanks for rescuing Watson. How is he?"

Danny cleared his throat, "Seems fine, Mrs. DeLeon. You may want to check the alignment some time soon, but nothing's bent underneath. Good thing you got out when you did. That exhaust was clogged up tight."

"Yeah, so I've been told."

I turned and looked directly at Bert for the first time. Despite his joking around, he looked tired and drawn. It was obvious that he hadn't slept well.

"Thanks again for your hospitality, Bert. I'll be in touch about our arrangements as soon as I call my agent."

I turned to go down the steps and heard the dog whine.

"Bye, Murphy." I said as I ruffled his furry ears. "Thanks for coming to my rescue."

I slid twice on the icy path as I hurried to the car, but the tears didn't start until I banged my knee against the door trying to get in. I averted my face as I backed out of the drive so Bert wouldn't see me crying yet again. When I stopped to make the turn, I thought for a moment I heard my name in the cold crisp air. I looked back at the cabin, but the two men had gone inside. I spun the tires in the snow as I made my getaway.

"Damn!" I shouted as I banged on the steering wheel. "Damn, damn, damn!"

It was almost noon when I got home. Mother was in the kitchen making fruitcakes. The strong, sweet smell of cinnamon and nutmeg made me want to puke. I stormed through her domestic domain with barely a, "Hello, Mother, I'm home." Her only response was an elegantly raised eyebrow.

I slammed my bedroom door and threw my clothes in the corner as I stripped down for my first whole bath in two days. Steam filled the bathroom as hot water filled the tub. I doused the water liberally with some of Cassie's flowery bath salts and sank down in the fragrance and the heat. I didn't turn the faucet until my limbs floated off the bottom, and even then I let the water continue to trickle to keep my bath hot.

Slowly, the hurt and anger began to disappear as my muscles relaxed. I deliberately avoided investigating the reasons for my feelings. They were better off tucked away. Out of sight, I decided, out of mind.

I had almost fallen asleep when I heard Cassie calling at the door.

"Mom, are you decent? Can I come in?"

I laughed. "I am in the bathtub, you know. Never mind, come on in, pumpkin"

The door opened, letting in a slight draft of cold air.

"Shut the door, for Pete's sake!"

"Wow, Gran was right. She said you were in a mood. What happened out there in the woods with your mountain man?"

Cassie sat on the chair by the vanity. She looked at me curiously through the mist when I didn't answer right away.

"It's like a steam room in here," she said wiping the perspiration off her upper lip. "Are you all right, Mom? I mean, he didn't take advantage or anything, did he?"

The tears started up again, and before I knew it I was crying as hard as I had all the way home.

"I don't know what's wrong with me," I sobbed. "I can't stop crying."

"Oh, Mom, maybe we'd better call the doctor. Danny said you hit your head pretty hard. Bert thought you had a concussion. Maybe you need x-rays or something."

I sniffed and blew my nose on the washcloth. "No. No doctor. I'll be fine." I tried smiling to reassure her, but my heart wasn't in it. I really was a very poor actress.

"Have you had breakfast?"

This time my smile was genuine.

"You sound like Mother," I chided. "No, come to think of it, I didn't. And I am hungry. Think maybe you could bring me some soup?"

Cassie fixed a tray for me while I dried my hair. Two days without a comb had made the curly auburn tangles almost impossible to brush out. Once again, I made the decision to get a haircut as soon as possible.

I looked in the mirror at my reflection. My face was flushed bright pink from my bath. Green eyes stared solemnly back at me over a ridiculously pert little nose. I swore softly as I realized once again how unfair it was for a forty-two-year-old woman to still have freckles.

I combed furiously at a tangle, and the pain almost brought the tears back to my eyes. The scissors in the cabinet were too much of a temptation. I decided impetuously that I could probably do as good a job as anyone in Rowan Springs. Holding up a twisted, tangled lock, I took an experimental whack. It was easier than I thought. The scissors were sharp and made a whispery little sound as I continued to snip away. The sink slowly filled with hair as my head got lighter. When I had finished, I ruffled the short, tousled cap of curls that remained with satisfaction.

"Goodbye, Raggedy Ann," I whispered.

Cassie loved my new haircut.

Mother was appalled.

"Paisley, darling, why in the world didn't you have the self-control to wait for a decent hairstylist?"

"Well, Mother, let's see. Number one, I have no self-control. You've told me so a hundred times. And number two, there is no such animal in Rowan Springs."

"Gennie does a very competent job on my hair, thank you very much," she huffed.

"Yes, she does," I agreed. "But that's because you have beautiful silver-white hair, and you've spent years making her perfect that French twist."

"Well . . . " she smiled, pleased with the compliment.

"Besides, I like the way I cut my hair. It feels great."

"If you want to look like Shirley Temple . . . "

I interrupted her angrily. "I'm not Shirley Temple, and I'm not Raggedy Ann! I'm me, Paisley Sterling. And if I want to shave my head and paint it blue, I'll do it."

I stormed out of the kitchen and grabbed my jacket from the hall closet. It would take a bracing walk in the snow to cool me off. I was more than a little surprised that my boiling point was so low.

The fields and the lane were covered with snow and prohibited a walk in the woods behind the farm. Instead, I went around to the front of the house and down the driveway. Off in the distance I could see smoke from our neighbor's chimney. Dora Nick was ninety years old. She had been a friend to the women in my family for four generations. We all loved and admired her for different reasons. Her house had been a quiet refuge during my years as a confused and rebellious adolescent. She and her porcelain doll, Phoebe, had listened patiently to my interminable tales of woe over endless cups of hot chocolate. Now, I thought, was the perfect time for another cup.

I trudged gamely through the dirty snow and ice on the shoulder of the road until I reached her driveway. She had already had it cleared by some enterprising soul, and the going was much easier as I walked up to her house.

Nicholas and Dora Nick had begun to build their big, beautiful home while they were still on their honeymoon. It had taken three years. Nicholas had been killed by a young German soldier before he got to carry his bride over the threshold. Stalwart and brave, Dora had moved in and made a life on the pattern they had planned, minus the six children.

She answered the door shortly after my first knock. "Paisley, love! Come in before you freeze to death." She looked up at me over little gold-rimmed glasses as I stepped inside her entry hall.

"Your nose is red!" she protested. "How long have you been outside?"

She hurried past me, her tiny figure still trim and neat, firing a barrage of questions without waiting for a single answer.

"When did you cut your hair? I love it. I've been thinking about cutting mine but Nicholas wouldn't like it. Oh, no, he loved my hair long."

I followed her into the cozy warmth of her parlor and shrugged off my jacket. A toasty seat on the hearth beckoned.

"Just a minute dear while I ask Rosie to bring us some chocolate. Would you like a sweet? Of course you would. You always loved my shortcake. I'll insist she put some on a tray."

She came closer and whispered loudly, "She's been threatening to put me on a diet because she's gaining weight! Imagine that!"

Dora hurried out to the kitchen and left me to gaze around at a room that hadn't changed since my childhood. Above the fireplace, a beautiful hand-carved oak mantle showcased several ornate picture frames with photographs of a handsome young man—in and out of uniform. Cheerful red-and-white striped taffeta drapes surrounded the big bay windows and brought out the red hues in the oriental rugs that covered the polished wood floor. Two big sofas upholstered in navy velvet sat in the center of the room, with a square mahogany table in between.

When the fire had warmed me sufficiently, I moved over to one of the sofas and sank back in the soft cushions. My eyes went to my favorite painting, a seascape of the New England shore with a sailing ship in the distance. Nicholas had been from Maine. When I was a child I had never tired of looking at that seascape, and it brought peace and calm to me even now.

Dora came bustling back in the room with Rosie in her wake.

"You still love that silly picture? Why of course you do. Look at your face. You could be ten years old again!"

Rosie Cummins was as rotund as Dora was slender. Her face was as round as a biscuit, and the spotless white apron she always wore barely met around her ample middle. She had lived with and cared for Dora for the last thirty years. They fussed and bickered constantly, but I knew that they were as fond of each other as sisters.

I helped Rosie put the heavy tray down on the table as she babbled on.

"My, my, it's good to see you, dear. Stay for dinner. I'm making pasties. You used to love them, I remember. Dora loves them, too. But she really shouldn't . . . "

Dora's thin little shoulder squared for the beginning of one of their pitched battles. I leapt in to head it off. I wasn't up to any controversy.

"I'd love to have dinner with you, but Mother and Cassie will be expecting me."

"Invite them, too, dear," urged Dora.

"Yes, do!" chorused Rosie with a grin.

I smiled at their genuine affection.

"Some other time, I promise."

"Well," sighed Dora, "at least you can have some cocoa with me."

Rosie apologized for having to get back to the kitchen. "I've something in the oven that needs watching. Come back," she murmured in my ear as she gave me a hug. "Come back when she's taking a nap, and we'll have those pasties."

Dora made a face at her retreating back and turned to offer me a piece of shortbread.

"Paisley, I haven't had a chance to tell you how much I loved your friend's last book. My, it was thrilling!" she said, her eyes shining with excitement. "I do hope you will introduce us sometime."

I had explained to Dora many times that Leonard Paisley was my *nom de plume,* that he really didn't exist, but I think she honestly preferred to believe he was real than to accept the fact that little Paisley Sterling had written such wild and wooly tales of murder and mayhem. I took a tender, buttery mouthful of shortbread and steered the subject in another direction.

"Tell me what you know about Bert Atkins."

"The ex-Police Chief from Hall County? Yes," she said answering herself. "He's a fine man. His wife was a lovely girl. I knew her grandmother. What a shame she died so young. Burt's never been the same, they say." She shook her little head with its coronet of white braids. "Made a lot of enemies. Death threats and all. Blackberry jam?"

"What kind of enemies, Dora?"

"Oh, I don't know. Wicked people with grudges, I suppose. It's hard being the law in a little town. You grow up with boyhood friends and then have to turn around and arrest them."

Try as I might, I could get her to say no more. We spoke pleasantly about Cassie's accomplishments at Emory and Mother's new wardrobe. Dora told me that she and Rosie had planned to go to Florida that winter but decided against it at the last minute. They wanted to have a white Christmas.

"Well, it looks like you're going to have your wish. If this keeps up for another three weeks, that is."

Dora laughed and topped off my cup with some more hot chocolate.

"Why don't you tell me why you really came, dear?"

I laughed and started to protest, but the words wouldn't get past the lump in my throat.

Dora patted my hand and then held it in her tiny little one. Her wide gold wedding band gleamed in the firelight. It had been on her ring finger for the last seventy years. She would understand about commitment, and vows, and wanting to believe someone was still alive somewhere. She would know why I rebuffed Bert's advances. She had probably felt the same fierce desires and yearnings and known the same guilt.

I looked at her frail old-woman's body and imagined the beautiful young girl made a widow too soon. Dora would know better than anyone why I'd cried all the way home. And why I was crying now.

I told her everything.

CHAPTER SEVEN

My step was lighter as I walked back home under a sky brilliant with the cold fire of winter stars. The wind was sharp and cold, and I realized that my new haircut meant I would now have to wear a hat to keep my head warm.

Cassie and Mother were in the kitchen, laughing and talking. I hurried to join them, eager to share in their fun and put aside my selfish, moody introspection.

"How are Dora and Rosie?" asked Mother. "I hear they're not going to Florida. Maybe they'll join us for Christmas dinner."

"Mom, Pam called from New York to see if you had found Leonard yet. I told her I thought so. She said call her if you had and get busy if you haven't."

"Paisley, will you set the table, dear? Cassandra, please hand me the soup tureen."

Quite easily, I was caught up in the comfortable, ordinary things that make up the whole of a happy life.

I called Pam after dinner to tell her that she could go ahead and set up the interview.

"Does this guy know anything about your books?"

"He's read them all," I told her.

"And?"

"And he thinks they stink," I admitted.

"Great!" she shouted.

"Look, Pam, I couldn't do any better, and I don't think you..."

"No," she insisted. "I mean that's terrific. Just the right attitude. The real Leonard would think they stink, too, but he wouldn't care. He'd just take the money and run. This man, I like. When can I meet him?"

"He lives in a cabin in the woods. His son visits from time to time. I'll send a message to him when you have everything set up."

"Fantastic! Thanks a lot, sweetie. This interview will be a big boost to your career."

"Yeah, I guess so," I answered with a sigh.

"What's wrong, Paisley? You haven't fallen for this guy, have you?"

"Of course not," I protested. "Although, he is a hunk," to satisfy her, and "How's your love life?" to get her off the track.

"Laura's in Europe with her family for Christmas," she mourned.

"Come down and spend the holidays with us. Cassie and Mother would love to see you."

"I just might, pet. I just might." And she hung up.

After dinner we played cards in the library. Aggie sat under the table and rolled her rubber ball back and forth around our feet with her nose. After an hour of her fruitless efforts to get us to play with her, Cassie and I relented and had a wild game of throwing the ball for the puppy. When she was panting and exhausted, we lay back on the floor in front of the fire to let her rest.

Mother turned off the lamp and moved over to the sofa. For a long while we didn't talk. The silence was warm and comforting and full of the unspoken knowledge of each other's moods. This, I thought, is what I missed in New York. This is why I came back home. All the rest—fortune and fame—mean nothing if you cannot share special time with the people you love.

"Ummnn, this is so cozy," murmured Cass. "Gran, that soup was delicious."

"Thank you, darling. Horatio enjoyed it, too."

"How much did you make? You've fed half the county," I teased.

"He also enjoyed your book, dear," she continued, ignoring my question. "But he says Leonard is getting a little mean."

"Leonard is mean," I muttered under my breath.

"And Bert Atkins has agreed to be Leonard for a day," she mused. "I have to admit I am somewhat surprised that he is going along with Pamela's scheme."

I turned over on my stomach and rested on my elbows.

"Why? It's a perfectly straightforward arrangement. He pretends to be Leonard. We split the money, and he goes back to the woods. What's wrong with that?"

"He doesn't seem like the pretend kind of man to me, that's all."

"You've only seen him once, Gran. And that was in an official capacity. You don't really know him," protested Cassie.

"Maybe not him, but later on I realized that I did know his mother. We spent a lot of time together when we were in high school."

I rested my chin on my open palms and looked at her elegant profile. In the firelight, she looked as young and beautiful as Cassie. I could imagine it had taken a very self-assured young woman to be the lovely and popular Anna Howard's friend.

"What was she like?" I prompted.

"Eva Anderson was one of the sweetest girlfriends I ever had. She was almost too good to be true. Some of our friends even called her St. Eva. She wasn't really what you would call pretty, but her face shone with a radiance, a happiness, that was very compelling. Harvey Atkins fell in love the minute he laid eyes on her."

"Where was he from, Gran?" asked Cassie. She loved a tale of romance.

"He was in the military. Harvey was stationed at the Army base outside of Morgantown. He was tall and handsome, and he swept Eva right off her feet. They were married as soon as she graduated from high school. They were very happy until Harvey went overseas. He was killed in action when Bert was just a few months old. Eva never remarried. She worked wherever she could to supplement Harvey's pension and raise her son. I lost touch with her when they moved to Lanierville. Eva died while Bert was still in school. I didn't even know when we met last summer that he was Eva's son until Horatio told me. She was such a lovely girl," she finished sadly.

I pulled a pillow off the sofa and lay back down to ponder Mother's words. The men and women in Bert's family seemed to have a habit of leaving the scene early. That explained a lot of his desire to live alone and isolated. When you're all alone, you can't be abandoned.

The next afternoon I got a call from Pam's secretary. The interview would take place in Nashville in two days time. Pam would fly down with the feature writer from *Pen and Ink*. She wanted me to come with Bert and fill him in on Leonard's character on the drive to Nashville. I could come to the interview if I wanted to, but I must remain in the background. I could pretend to be the pretend Leonard's girlfriend, she said. I gritted my teeth when I heard that, and vowed to get even if it took me the rest of my life. Pam's ass was grass.

I called Danny and asked him to relay the message to his stepfather. Some wicked little part of me hoped that Bert would chuck the whole idea so I could relax and enjoy my vacation with Cassie. Pam would be furious, but it would serve her right. Leonard's girlfriend, indeed!

Bert called the next night from Danny's house. He said he would drive over to pick me up first thing in the morning. We would be in Nashville by noon.

After tossing and turning half the night, I finally got up and took a shower at 4:30. I quietly made some tea and grabbed an apple for my breakfast. By the time I had decided what to wear, my bed was piled high with rejected clothes. I stood in front of the mirror and gazed hopelessly at my reflection. I had worn nothing but jeans for so long—in anything else I looked like I was playing dress up. I slumped down on the edge of my bed in a funk. Leonard's pretend girlfriend pretending to be a girl. What a riot!

"Mom? Why are you up so early?"

Cassie tapped lightly on the door then pushed it open and bounced in with Aggie right behind her. The puppy was chewing on the trailing belt of Cassie's housecoat, but we both knew better than to try and get it out of her mouth. Her bite was worse than her bark.

"Wow! Are you having a rummage sale? What's with all the clothes?"

She cleared a space on the bed and then noticed my outfit for the first time.

"Mom? Are you wearing a dress? Stand up and let me see. I've forgotten what you used to look like."

I stood up and turned around for her enjoyment. I knew she would get a kick out of seeing me look so silly.

"You look beautiful!"

"Don't tease me, Cassie. I'm not in the mood. Just help me find my jeans again. They were over there under that pile of sweaters earlier. But now I can't seem to . . . "

"Mom, you look great. I do remember that dress. It used to be too tight. You always wanted to wear it. Now's your chance."

"You don't think I look like an idiot?"

I re-examined my reflection in the mirror. The chocolate-brown knit with the high neck and flared, ankle-length skirt had been one of my favorites. And Cassie was right. I had never been able to wear it before. My city persona had been fifteen pounds heavier—thanks to luncheons at "21" and cocktails at eight. Farm living had slimmed me down, and firmed up what was left. Maybe I didn't look so funny after all.

"Okay, I'll wear it. But what coat can I use? I left my fur in storage two years ago."

"Take my cape. And wear those knee high boots, so you don't have to wear panty hose."

"Good idea. Maybe that will keep me sane."

"Relax, Mom. Even your hair looks good. Naturally curly covers a multitude of sins. Have a ball, Cinderella!"

CHAPTER EIGHT

Bert Atkins arrived right on time driving his Jeep wagon, a beat-up version of Watson. I said goodbye to Cassie and Mother as if I were going to the gallows and picked my way carefully down the walk. Somewhere in the back of my mind I was sure I would make a complete and utter fool of myself before this trip was over. I didn't want to start out by falling flat on my overdressed behind in the snow.

By the time we were out of Rowan Springs and on the road to Nashville, Bert had succeeded in putting me completely at ease. He was cheerful and easygoing and kept the conversation strictly on the matter at hand.

"So Leonard looks like me now that I shaved my beard?"

"You've read the books, what do you think?"

He laughed.

"How many men do you know who are really aware of their looks?'

I didn't want to say that I didn't really know that many men, but instead I asked, "How come you knew what to wear?"

"That was easy. In *Bodies in the Boneyard*, Leonard buys a tweed jacket and wool turtleneck to wear to dinner at some rich dame's house. The jeans were my idea. Mainly because I don't have anything else anymore."

"I know what you mean," I said under my breath.

"What did you say?"

"You heard that? How come?"

I turned and looked at him.

"I don't see a hearing aid, but you're wearing one, aren't you?"

He grinned and glanced over at me.

"Did I tell you I like your hair?"

"When did you get it?"

"The hearing aid? Oh, I've had it for a while. I just never had much occasion to use it."

"I should think being worried about someone sneaking up and killing you would be enough of an occasion!"

"I have Murphy for that. He's all the ears I need at the cabin."

"You put a lot of trust in a dog that sleeps so much."

Bert laughed again. I could tell he was enjoying himself. I relaxed a little more.

"So, pretty much all I know about Leonard is he's supposed to be a real detective writing about his own exploits. Tell me how you get the ideas for his stories. I'm sure that will be one of the questions they'll want to ask."

"You're probably right. And the answer is complicated but simple at the same time. The ideas come from everywhere. I read a lot, mostly scientific journals. You'd be surprised how much goes on in the world of academia that can be translated to mysteries. But Leonard's latest had a different birthplace."

"Where?"

"In a pawn shop in Morgantown. My laptop computer was stolen last year. I got it back but it was, er, . . . out of commission. Cassie bought me another one. She saw it in the window of the shop one day when she was over there with Danny. The price was low enough for her to be able to write a check on the spot. It was my birthday present."

"I asked how you got the ideas for stories, not what you wrote them on."

"But that's just it. When I turned on the computer, I found all this funky personal information on the hard drive. At some time, the power had gone off and the information on a disc had been saved to a backup file. Whoever owned the computer probably wasn't even aware it was still there. I'm sure he wouldn't have sold it if he had known. The stuff was too revealing."

"Laptops are the most frequently stolen item nowadays. Whoever pawned it wasn't the person who owned it; I'd be willing to bet on it."

"I hadn't thought of that, but you're probably right. Anyway, there were private letters, business statements, even a love poem, all waiting to be read. With a little imagination it was easy to weave a story around them. I changed the names, of course. I don't want anybody else suing me. I had enough of that last year. But the computer wrote the book in more ways than one."

"Where did you get the idea for *The Neighbor from Hell?*"

"Pretty much from something that actually took place in our family. That's another story that ended up writing itself."

"Things seem to happen around you, don't they?"

"You make me sound dangerous," I laughed. "I'm no *femme fatale*, that's for sure, but I guess you're right. Ever since I came back home, life has been very interesting."

Pam was waiting downstairs in the hotel lobby when we arrived. She was all decked out in one of her "hey look me over" outfits.

"Wow, Pam," I said as I gave her a hug, "chartreuse suede and crimson satin?"

"Isn't it divine, darling?" she answered with a wink. "And take a gander at the back."

She turned around and glanced coquettishly over her shoulder as she slowly lowered the suede bolero jacket. The shiny red satin blouse underneath was backless and revealed a tiny tattoo on her left shoulder. At first I thought it was a mole, but when I looked closely I saw eight little legs and the red hourglass.

"Wouldn't Cassie just love a tatt . . . . " she began.

"Pam, I swear I'll hack you up in pieces so tiny they'll never even find that spider if you . . . "

"Okay, okay. Spoil sport! But it looks great on me, huh?"

"Let's just say it suits your personality."

Bert had let me off in front of the hotel and parked the car himself. When he came in the revolving lobby door, I pointed out his tall, lean figure to Pam.

"Oh, but Paisley, he is yummy!"

She turned and watched me closely as Bert walked over to join us.

"Um hum," she whispered.

"Um hum, what?" I hissed.

"Um hum, you've got it bad, that's what."

"Pam, if you don't behave yourself . . . "

In an instant, Pamela turned on her business mode. She shook Bert's hand politely when I introduced them, then guided us expertly through the crowded lobby to the penthouse elevator.

"I've reserved a conference room on the top floor. The gal from *Pen and Ink* is waiting up there for us. I also took the liberty of ordering a light luncheon. I do hope you like grilled salmon, Bert."

She took his arm as they entered the elevator and left me to follow in their wake. From that point on, I was a fifth wheel.

Pen and Ink had sent a thirty-something, six-foot-tall, blonde bombshell with the brain of an Einstein and the vocabulary of a James Joyce. Blondie was provocatively posed and waiting as the elevator opened directly into the executive conference room. A silver knit dress slithered over every curve from her shoulders to her calves, and from the way the dress was molded to her body, it was obvious to one and all that she considered undergarments to be unnecessary. Short platinum curls framed her high Slavic cheekbones, and her almond-shaped grey eyes gazed indolently at Bert from under artificially thick eyelashes. Bert was entranced.

My former best friend aided and abetted Blondie all the way. Pam fed her lines and plots from books that I had slaved and sweated blood over, and together they coaxed and encouraged Bert, alias Leonard, to tell all. The platinum goddess batted her long sooty eyelashes and thrust out her bosom as she asked questions loaded with double entendre. It was a thoroughly disgusting spectacle.

I sat at the same table as the others and ate the same food, but I had on a cloak of invisibility like the young boy in *Grimm's Fairy Tales*. Not one word was addressed to me in three-and-a-half hours.

I buttered every roll in the bread basket until one shot out of my hand and landed on the floor. I plucked the petals from all the radish roses on my salad and cut my salmon steak into pieces tinier than Pam's black widow tattoo. I had hardly eaten a thing, but I wanted to throw up. Finally, when I could stand it no longer, I decided to take desperate measures.

"Leonard, honey," I whined. "I'm real tired. Don'cha think we can go back to our room now? Baby will rub Snookum's wittle back."

The three of them turned and stared at me as if I had suddenly transported from the planet Zarcon.

I stood up and sauntered slowly towards Bert with the sexiest walk I could muster. Unfortunately, the buttered bread I dropped on the floor earlier had rolled out from under the table and lay in the path of my right foot. The next few humiliating minutes of my life probably provided the two women with several months of amusing dinner party conversation. It afforded Bert a knee-slapping belly laugh right on the spot.

My right foot shot out in front of me, but the left lagged a few seconds behind. I was never very flexible, yet somehow I found myself doing something I had only seen twelve-year-old gymnasts do. In the process, my dress hiked up over my hips and exposed the Winnie the Pooh underwear Cassie had given me last Christmas.

I tried desperately to get to my feet, but the butter on the bottom of my boot, coupled with the highly polished wood floor, gave me no purchase. Pam stared in horrified disbelief as I scooted my white-cottoned, lace-edged butt over to the table and hauled myself up. I jerked my skirt back down over my rear end and grabbed Cassie's cape. I didn't wait for the elevator. Instead, I flung the door to the stairwell open and ran down all fifteen flights.

I waited in Bert's car in the parking lot for another hour. When he finally climbed in beside me, I was shivering from the cold. He took one look at the fury in my eyes and didn't say a word. We drove all the way back home in absolute silence.

CHAPTER NINE

Christmas came and went before you could say "Ebenezer Scrooge." I suppose it was pleasant enough, but thinking back, all I can remember were the quiet good times Mother and Cassie and I shared after the guests were gone.

Two days after New Year's Eve, Cassie went back to school and left a big old empty hole in my heart. Aggie and I sulked around the house for the next three weeks like two souls lost in purgatory. One evening after supper, Mother finally commented on my behavior.

"Paisley, for heavens sake! You have to get used to being without your daughter. I did. Believe me, it wasn't easy for me when you moved to South America."

"Well, I'm just not the iron maiden you are, am I? And besides, where is that daughter now, hmmm? Right here, that's where I am, back on the farm. Does that make you happy?"

I stormed off to the library with a huffy little puppy dusting my heels. Aggie was much better at disdain than I. She didn't look like a naughty little child. And she did not feel guilty about acting like a spoiled, middle-aged brat.

We lay down side by side on our stomachs in front of the French doors and looked out at the January night. The first days of the new year had brought warmer winds to melt the snow. With the lovely white blanket stripped away, the land looked stark and dead in the harsh green light of the mercury lamp.

Aggie barked halfheartedly at a dry leaf bouncing across the yard in the wind, then fell asleep. I lay there listening to her soft little doggie snores, wondering why I was so down in the mouth. Mother was right, I should have gotten used to Cassie's being gone by now. After all, she did have a life beyond hearth and home, and soon she would be leaving for good—that I could not deny. How had Mother coped so well, I wondered. The answer was obvious. She had a vast network of friends, not to mention her adoring Horatio. At the drop of the first lonely tear, I'm sure he was at her side with all manner of distractions. I had no one. And that was the problem. I was lonely.

While I was deeply engrossed in writing a book the characters became my friends, or my enemies, depending on how well they got along with Leonard. But those were only paper acquaintances—I needed the flesh and blood kind.

When the phone rang I tried to get up, but my stiff limbs were full of pins and needles. Mother came to the door and peered inside.

"Paisley, dear, the phone is for you."

She held the cordless receiver out towards me and said clearly and distinctly, "It's that charming Bert Atkins you're so fond of, dear."

I managed to raise up on one stiff knee, grabbed the phone, and covered the mouthpiece with my hand.

"For Pete's sake, Mother!"

She winked broadly and closed the door behind her.

I flopped back down and accidentally landed on Aggie's tail. She jumped up and bit the first thing she could reach.

"Ahhhhh, shit!" I screamed as I flung the phone across the room and grabbed my left breast.

"Damn dog!"

I scrambled across the carpet on my hands and knees looking for the telephone.

"I'm coming, Bert," I shouted.

"Please don't hang up," I whispered to myself.

Finally I located the receiver under the upholstered ottoman and put it up to my ear. All I heard was a dial tone. Bert Atkins was gone.

I pulled myself up on the sofa holding the phone against my wounded breast. Tears were starting to fall when he called again.

"Hello," I sniffed. "Bert? Is that you?"

"Yes, Paisley," he answered in a tightly controlled voice. "I can call back later if you have company."

"No, no. It's only Aggie. The dog, that is. Her real name is Agatha Christie, but we call her Aggie. You haven't met her. You would probably hate her. I know I do. I mean, I don't really hate her, but . . . "

I suppose I would have continued making nervously inane remarks, but mercifully, he interrupted.

"Paisley, we need to talk."

"We do?" I squeaked.

"I don't think I should come to your home. I'll explain why when I see you."

Bert calmly instructed me where to meet him in an hour. I would just have enough time if I didn't change clothes. I ran through the house looking for my car keys and jacket.

Mother waved me off with, "Have fun, dear. And put on some lipstick!"

The little "hole in the wall" tavern he'd described was closing when I got there. I had driven faster than the law allowed and actually arrived early, but it looked like I was too late. I cursed my luck once again as I slowly circled the block looking for Bert's old beat-up jeep. When I couldn't see it anywhere, I decided to park across the street on the off chance that he was still inside. I pointed Watson's nose in the direction of the bar and turned off the engine. I watched the door as stragglers came out. I hadn't been waiting long when suddenly Watson's back door opened and a man climbed inside.

"Start the car and head back out of town," he barked.

After my heart came back out of my throat, I recognized Bert's voice and hurried to obey.

"You scared me to death! Did you have to scare me to death? Couldn't you think of another way to shorten my life, like give me the plague, or something? My heart's still pounding."

"I can't hear you, Paisley. I left my hearing aid at home."

"How very convenient. How absolutely and astonishingly handy to have a hearing aid you can put on only when you're ready to participate in a relationship. Meanwhile, I have to swallow your crap because you left your ears at home."

"Turn here," he said quietly. It was obvious he hadn't heard a word of my diatribe.

I took the turn much too fast and was gratified to see him disappear from sight in the rearview mirror while he fought to keep his balance. I yearned for another corner, but he directed me to a narrow driveway on a dark side street. I pulled in and drove slowly all the way to the back. The drive ended in front of a small white bungalow that had seen better days. There was no light inside or outside. Only the pale reflection of the quarter moon kept the night from being pitch black.

I turned around and faced him so he could read my lips in the moonlight. I was still somewhat miffed. After all, I thought, just who did he think he was? I opened my mouth to ask him that, when he cut me off for the second time that night.

"Someone tried to kill me yesterday," he said matter-of-factly.

"Wha . . . what?"

"You heard me, Paisley. There's nothing wrong with your hearing."

"Yes, but . . . "

"But what?" he spat. "You can't believe it? Why not? You set me up. You paid me five thousand dollars to become a target. Now every unbalanced maniac who's read one of your books and wants to go *mano a mano* with Leonard is gunning for me. And thanks to your fancy dressed little buddy, they know what I look like and where I live."

"But Pam wouldn't . . . "

"Oh, yes, she would. She did. Now I'm 'www.leonardmurder.com' and every nutcase online can look me up on the Internet and find a picture of my cabin. Hell, they can even see my poor old dog up close and personal!"

Bert slammed his right fist into the palm of his left hand and cursed loudly and colorfully. I was impressed.

"You must have some seafaring friends," I remarked.

He looked intently at me for a long moment and then burst out laughing. Soon we were both cackling like two old hens. It wasn't long before my laughter turned to tears. I bit on my mittened thumbs and tried to stop. It seemed that all I ever did around this man was cry. He was tired of it, too.

"For heaven's sake, Paisley, quit sniveling. The bullet missed me by a mile. Murphy warned me at the last minute."

He was silent for a moment as he let that sink in. I stopped sniffing and wiped my eyes on my coat sleeve.

"The nutcase didn't fare so well," he added tersely. "I got him right between the eyes."

"Oh," I said in a very small voice. "Who was he?"

"Not much of his face left to identify."

I fought to keep my dinner down while I pondered that information.

"Then how do you know he was a Leonard fan? Don't you have enemies coming out of the woodwork? Death threats for breakfast? Weren't you expecting something like this?"

"Not quite like this. I expected trouble, but from the family of a kid I put away for bank robbery. The one who shot me last year. His drunken dad and four big brothers swore they'd get even. But I suspect that life is so much more pleasant with their little juvenile delinquent behind bars they've forgiven me. Anyway, this guy was a professional. He had no identification in his pockets, no driver's license, no credit cards, and the labels were cut out of all his clothes. He didn't want anybody to be able to trace him."

"Then how do you know he was after Leonard and not you?"

"This was in his jacket."

Bert handed me a dog-eared piece of paper. I turned on the map light and opened it out. It was a page from *Pen and Ink* with a color photograph of Bert looking handsome and sleuthlike in his black turtleneck and tweed jacket.

CHAPTER TEN

Bert offered to buy me a cup of coffee, but I could tell he was only being polite. We both had our reasons for wanting to part company and get home as soon as possible. He was clearly still angry, and I was desperate to talk to Pam. I couldn't believe that she would be so careless as to allow personal information on Leonard's Web page. She had always been very careful about my privacy; why wasn't she that concerned about Bert's?

I drove him back to the outskirts of town where he had left his car. We said a very dry and sterile farewell to each other. He got in his Jeep and drove away without a backward glance.

All the way home I puzzled over our conversation. I had to agree that having your dog splashed all over the information superhighway would be very disturbing. It invited the unhealthy attention of unstable fans or worse. But to be fair, I couldn't remember the article saying anything remotely specific. My memory was that it only referred to his vacation abode being a log cabin on a lake. Anybody who found him from that sparse a description would have to be a better detective than Leonard himself.

Even though it was after midnight when I got home, I called Pam right away.

"Paisley? Wha . . . what in the world? Is Cassie all right?"

"Yes, Cassie is fine," I answered dryly.

"You're not still mad about Helga are you?"

"Helga? Oh, Blondie. No, well, I don't know. It depends. Was she the idiot who put Bert's cabin on the Web page?"

Pam groaned loudly. "I was afraid you would be angry about that. I tried to talk the editor out of it, but he was so gung ho after reading the article, he said he wanted to capitalize on Leonard's interview. Atkins showed that picture to Helga at the hotel. I guess he forgot to get it back when he left. Is Bert really mad?"

"Only because someone went out to his cabin and tried to kill him."

"Oh, my God! He won't sue will he? But, Paisley, what a great lead for a second article!"

"Not on your life. And no, I don't think it would occur to him to sue, but he should. It was a major breach of privacy. I can't believe you let this happen, Pam."

"I'm really sorry, Paisley. All I can say is that I never thought anyone would be able to put enough information together to locate exactly where the man lived. One log cabin looks like another to me, and big red dogs are a dime a dozen. But I'll scratch the Web page tomorrow. And I'll send Bert a personal letter of apology. Anything else I should do?"

I sighed deeply, "No, I guess not."

"Are you still hot for this guy?"

"Pam, I never said I was hot for anyone. As a matter of fact, I'm perfectly happy on my own. I have been quite content to be independent and free of some man telling me what to do, thank you very much. Bert Atkins is way too bossy and obstinate, and on top of that, he's stingy with his hearing aid batteries."

"What? Atkins is deaf?"

"As a door knob."

"Then that must be why he can't hear your little heart going pitter pat every time he comes near."

"Goodnight!" I shouted.

Mother was in the kitchen warming up milk when I stomped in looking for something to eat. She had on her new floor-length red velvet dressing gown, and even though she was ready for bed, she looked like a million dollars. There wasn't a silver-white hair out of place, and the lack of makeup only accentuated her patrician good looks.

She looked at my own disheveled appearance and decided quite wrongly that now was the time for some maternal guidance.

"Paisley, dear, you must control yourself. You have been a veritable hurricane of emotion lately. I'm so glad my parents taught me to keep my feelings to myself. Your sleeve is not the place to wear your heart. Paisley, where are you going?"

"Arrrgh!"

"You sound just like Aggie, dear. That is so amusing."

"'Night, Mother!"

My bedroom was chilly. I slipped into my pajamas as quickly as possible and crawled under the fluffy down comforter on my bed.

I closed my eyes knowing that sleep was a long way off. There were too many things whizzing through my mind. It took longer than usual for my body heat to warm up the little cocoon between me and my duvet. I shivered and found myself wishing for the warmth of the big fireplace in Bert's cabin.

With some effort, I managed to put all thoughts of Bert and the time we'd spent together out of my mind and concentrate on the problem at hand. After about an hour of brain work, I decided that something other than the magazine interview and Web page had directed Bert's would-be killer to the cozy little cabin on the lake. The answer might be somewhere in one of my books, but I really had a hard time accepting that premise. It was far more logical to assume that the dead man really was one of Bert's enemies. After all, he had spent a lifetime making them.

Before I fell asleep, I decided to go about finding the answer the same way Leonard would: eliminate the obvious before you worry about the unknown.

The next morning, I called Danny to ask some questions about the man his stepfather had shot.

"Miz DeLeon, you know I'm not allowed to tell you anything about a case under investigation."

"I didn't ask you who he was, Danny. I asked you if you *knew* who he was."

"Well, okay, that's different," he sighed. "We ran his fingerprints through the national computer data base. We uncovered his identity late yesterday. More than that I really couldn't say."

"Just tell me this much, please," I begged with my fingers crossed. "Where is he from?"

"Sorry, Miz DeLeon."

I hung up the phone thinking that if I were still a possible candidate for mother-in-law, Danny might have been more forthcoming. But that was unfair. He was just doing his job. Then it occurred to me that he might have informed law enforcement agencies in neighboring counties of the incident. The Chief of Police in Rowan Springs was Andy Joiner. We had become good friends since I came back here to live. Maybe he would tell me what Danny had found out.

I always enjoyed driving to town. Each time I circled the courthouse square, I was happy that I had come back home again. Everywhere I looked, I saw a familiar smiling face. Rowan Springs was like the Baby Bear's bowl of porridge, it was just right. It was small enough that you knew almost everyone, but large enough to maintain a semblance of privacy. I loved it.

Andy Joiner had been Chief of Police in Rowan Springs for the last ten years. He was fair and firm and fiercely honest. I trusted him, and his wife liked my books.

Andy's new office was next to the station house of the fire department. Fire trucks were high on my list of favorite things. Rowan Springs had just bought a new one and I hadn't seen it yet. Despite the cold weather, the huge garage door was open. Inside, two firemen in heavy sweaters and boots were waxing the big shiny red truck. I stood and watched admiringly as they polished mirrors and chrome fittings until they sparkled.

"You should see your face! That's the same way Constance looks when we go by Wood's Jewelry Store and she sees that diamond pendant she wants in the window."

I turned and smiled at the tall rangy man in khakis.

"Buy it for her, Andy. I'm surprised you didn't get it for Christmas."

"You're looking at the reason Connie didn't get her pendant."

"The fire truck? Why?"

He gave me a wry smile and tucked his big hands in his pockets.

"Come on in the office. It's cold out here."

Andy held the door open and ushered me inside. The four white walls of his new digs reminded me of the inside of a white plastic ice bucket. A few pieces of cheap chrome office furniture and ugly grey commercial carpet did nothing to warm the place. The run-down office he used to have on the other side of the square had a lot more character.

He sat uncomfortably stiff behind the white Formica table that was his new desk while I sat opposite him in an ugly black vinyl director's chair. He looked at me from underneath bushy salt-and-pepper eyebrows.

"Awful, ain't it?" he acknowledged.

We looked at each other and laughed heartily. I finally wiped my eyes and answered him.

"I take it Constance didn't get to decorate?"

"Something like that," he nodded. "This is the new format for the state. All the new county offices have to follow the same pattern. The powers that be don't want money spent on anything but the basics."

"Give it some time, Andy. You'll warm up the place. And those powers will probably be gone in another three years."

"I just hope I can hold out until then."

"What do you mean? Does that have something to do with the new fire truck, too?"

He got up, walked over to the window, and looked out at his town.

"With the fire truck and the new sewer line at Pumpkin Creek and the replacement pump for the water treatment plant. And probably a half dozen other big ticket items the community needs just as bad."

He leaned back against the window ledge and faced me.

"This is a little town, Paisley, with a small tax base. There's only so much money to go around. For the last couple of years it's been touch and go to make the county payroll each month. I turned down my regular pay raise twice just so I wouldn't have to let one of my men off. I don't know how long I can keep that up. Connie and the kids deserve to have some of the things they want."

I didn't know what to say. The big shiny red fire truck I had so admired lost its luster. I remembered the lean years Cassie and I had spent after Rafe disappeared. It was tough to work hard and still not be able to provide enough for your children.

"Enough of my grousing," he said. "Did you come to town to see that shiny red monster, or me?"

I smiled. "You, definitely, you. I was hoping you could help me with some information."

"Unless it's got something to do with that incident at Bert Atkins's cabin at the lake a couple of day's ago, I'll be glad to help."

My face said it all. He sat back in his flimsy chrome chair and laughed again.

"Come on, Paisley, you know the drill. I can't tell you anything until Chief Hall makes a statement. And from what I hear, that won't be anytime soon. You know Danny Hall. Why don't you ask him?"

"I did. He won't tell me anything. I was hoping you . . . "

"You were hoping I would be unprofessional and spill the beans?"

"Well, yes." I gave him my sweetest and brightest smile. It didn't work.

He scowled at me and shook his head.

"Danny Hall is a good man. A bit disappointed in love, I hear. But he's a good man. And I'm every bit as good as he is. Maybe better, 'cause I'm older and more experienced. I will speculate that the motive was robbery. That's obvious. Ever since Bert came into all that money and went to live in the woods alone, I've been expecting trouble."

"All that money? What money? Bert's rich?"

I was stunned.

Andy seemed surprised that I didn't know.

"Yeah, Bert came into quite a large sum a year or so back. Right after he recovered from the gunshot wound. That's when he announced he was taking early retirement." Andy smiled ruefully. "I don't blame him. I can't say I wasn't envious. Still am. Man, what a stroke of luck. Well, maybe I'll win the lottery, and Connie and I can take the kids and go live in Florida."

"You would hate it, Andy. You're as crazy about this little town as I am. You'll never leave." I stood up and buttoned my jacket. "But I do hope you win the Lotto."

"Say 'hello' to Miz Sterling for me."

"I will. And thanks."

"For nothing?"

"Yeah, for that," I forced a smile as I waved and stepped out into the cold blustery winter afternoon.

CHAPTER ELEVEN

I was mad. Even in the blustery wind my cheeks burned with anger. How dare Bert Atkins be a wealthy man! Somehow it upset the balance of power. I was supposed to be the one with the money—the fancy writer lady—the grand duchess of the literary world. He was the poor lonely soul I might bestow my favors upon if I saw fit. It wasn't fair. Damn and double damn!

I crossed Main Street and plopped down on one of the concrete benches in front of the courthouse. The wind slicked back my short hair and froze my earlobes. I pulled up the hood to my jacket but made no move to seek the comfort of Watson's warm interior—instead, I scooted over on my bench so that I could take advantage of the protection of the Civil War Monument.

My mind wandered to that cold and lonely battlefield for a moment as I stared at the statue of the Confederate soldier frozen in time and space in his ill-fitting uniform. Poor little guy. He and his musket had guarded the courthouse for as long as I could remember. I wondered why the town fathers had made the statue so small instead of life-size. Not enough money, I guessed.

The thought of money brought my mind back to the problem at hand. Okay, I decided, so Bert Atkins was rich. That was a fact. He probably had a great deal more money than I did. Why did that make me so angry?

I didn't like the answer I came up with. I wasn't just being selfish and spiteful, I was angry with Bert because he hadn't been honest with me. He had never said he was poor, but he had acted like he was. Him and his "don't have anything else to wear but jeans," attitude really pissed me off.

Then I had a darker thought. What was the real source of Atkins's surprise windfall? Had he gotten tired of the tough job with the high risk and low pay like so many lawmen before him? Had he felt like Andy was beginning to feel, but been less honest? Had he looked the other way at the right time and collected a bag full of money for doing so? There were plenty of big city drug dealers who were anxious enough to gain a foothold in a sleepy small town by buying off the law. It wouldn't be hard to find one.

The wind was making headway against the fabric of my parka. My nose was frozen and my eyes were tearing up, but it wasn't just from the cold. I hated the thought of Bert's being anything but completely moral and upright. It was at that moment that I finally had to admit to myself that I was a little bit in love with him, or at least the person I thought him to be. He loomed tall and straight as an arrow in my imagination. He was Gary Cooper in *High Noon*, John Wayne in almost anything, and my very own savior in the snow. I didn't mind if he was gruff and angry. And I could care less that he was deaf and had a limp, but I didn't want the star on his chest to be tarnished. My heroes had to be squeaky clean in the virtue department.

Rafe had been my hero as well as my love; but there was something about Rafe I hadn't known—a secret he kept hidden that had eventually taken him from me. Never again would I allow myself to experience that terrible sense of loss and abandonment. I preferred to live and die alone.

I knew then that I had to go back to Jackson Lake. Bert Atkins had confronted me. Now it was his turn for a little confrontation—his turn to answer some questions.

The next morning dawned clear and cold, but there was no snow on the ground and none in the forecast. This time I didn't ask anyone to accompany me. When I told Mother where I was going she asked, "Oh, dear, Paisley, do you really think this is such a good idea? Last time you went out there alone you got into trouble."

"The kind of trouble I got into last time won't happen again, Mother."

"Are you sure, dear?" she winked. "He's still quite attractive."

"For Pete's sake," I protested. "I'm not at all interested in how attractive Mr. Bert Atkins may or may not be."

"That's not what Pam said," she countered.

I stopped buttering my bran muffin and stared at her.

"Pam? When did you talk to Pam?"

"She called yesterday afternoon while you were in town. I'm sorry I forgot to tell you. She said she canceled the webbed page, whatever that is, and sent Mr. Atkins a letter of apology."

"Web page," I responded automatically. "What else did you all talk about?"

"Just things," my mother answered slyly.

"What things?"

"Oh, you know, Cassie's school and . . . "

"Would that 'and' have anything to do with my so-called love life?"

"Maybe," she admitted.

"Well, now hear this. There will be no more speculating on some romantic notion that Bert Atkins and I are an item. We are most emphatically not!"

"The year is young," she laughed as she left the kitchen with the last word.

I followed her to the living room and sat down opposite her on the sunny yellow flowered sofa.

"Okay, Mother, let's discuss this. Do you really want me to fall in love and marry someone who is not Cassie's father? Would you want me to go and live with him instead of here with you on the farm?"

Mother was thoughtful for a moment.

"Paisley, someday when the time is right, Cassandra will leave you for good. She would be happier if she knew you had a friend as loyal to you as Horatio is to me. If that means giving up the status quo, then so be it."

"Well, I'm not ready to give it up. Not for some gimpy deaf man with a smelly old dog. Especially when it appears he has a bull's-eye painted on his forehead. I'd really hate to be in the way if there's a shootout at the O.K. corral."

"The okay what?"

"Old western."

"Oh."

She kissed me goodbye and told me to be home before dark.

"If I'm going to be late, I'll have Bert radio a message to Danny," I promised, adding, "But don't worry if I'm not back and you haven't heard from me. You know it gets dark awfully fast this time of year."

All the way out to Bert's cabin I rehearsed my speech. I had to stay as dispassionate as possible. I didn't want him to get the idea I was out there for any reason other than to find out why he was a target for some murderous nut. If he refused outright to answer my questions, then I might have to accept the fact that he had something to hide. Maybe the man he killed was trying to take back that bag full of payoff money. Maybe . . .

By the time I arrived at the turnoff to the cabin I had a headache from thinking too much. I was seriously considering going back home, but it was too late to turn around. The long twisting driveway was full of deep ruts and mud. It wouldn't do for me to get stuck and have to be pulled out by the wrecker again. I pulled in front of the cabin and decided it would be silly not to get out and say hello after coming all this way.

And then I noticed Bert's Jeep was gone.

"Drat! All this way for nothing."

In my annoyance, I leaned on the horn. The tinny little beeping did nothing to relieve my displeasure, but I kept it up out of shear orneriness. Because of the horn, I didn't hear the first gunshot. I sat in utter shock and surprise as my windshield shattered into a million pieces. I heard the second shot clearly and threw Watson into gear as fast as I could. My right rear tire had obviously been hit, but I managed to get the big Jeep almost all the way to the road before the tire came apart and the metal rim got hopelessly mired in the mud.

I knew that I was a sitting duck in the Jeep, and it didn't take me but a few seconds to decide to get out of the car and run for my life. I grabbed my hat and gloves and beat it for the cover of the brush along the road. I tore my clothes and the skin underneath on thorny bushes as I ran, and twice I stumbled and fell flat on the cold hard ground, but I was able to put some distance between me and Watson.

I had no idea where I was in relation to Bert's cabin. And I had no idea who was shooting at me. It could even be Bert, for all I knew.

My quilted down jacket was dark green. That would have been a good thing any other time of year, but this was the dead of winter. There was nothing green around but me. The brush and the tall grass I was floundering through were bone dry—dead and brown. I stood out like a puffy green bear. I knew if I could get near the edge of the lake the young cedars would be perfect cover. They were still green. I could even climb one and hide in the branches.

I pushed heedlessly though dead sassafras, Indian poke, and blackberry vine. My gloves were leather and withstood the punishment of thorn and stinging nettles, but somewhere I lost my wool cap, and down clusters were puffing out from several rips in the arms of my jacket. That was all I needed.

"Just follow the puffing down, Mr. Shotgun Killer," I panted in disgust.

The ground was getting softer and wetter under my running feet. The lake was dead ahead, and I prayed that I wouldn't get shot in the back before I reached the safety of the evergreens.

I didn't see the arm as it snaked out from behind a tree and grabbed me. The hand that covered my mouth to silence my scream was big, rough, and red from the cold. I struggled as hard as I could to get away, but my flailing, kicking feet dangled helplessly in the air.

"Damn it! Be still woman!" Bert whispered urgently in my ear.

I stopped struggling immediately and my sudden dead weight tripped him up. We both fell to the cold ground just as another bullet whizzed by where his head had been a second ago.

"He's seen us! Crawl over toward those trees as fast as you can. I'm right behind you."

I didn't hesitate for a moment. I followed his instructions to the letter and hugged the base of the biggest cedar I could find. Bert got there a second after me. Flopping down on his belly, he pulled a small pair of binoculars out of his pocket and carefully scanned the path.

"I can't see anybody. Can you hear him?" he asked softly.

I cocked my head and listened intently, but all I heard was the wind in the grass and the wavelets lapping against the shore. I turned so he could read my lips and barely made a sound as I told him.

He got back up on his knees and pulled me roughly against his chest. He buried his face in my hair and whispered urgently.

"You'll have to be my ears. I'll try to be as careful as I can, but if I make too much noise, poke me. And for God's sake, if you hear something, let me know! We need to get back to the cabin. I've got a gun hidden under the privy. You with me?"

I nodded so vigorously I accidentally hit him in the mouth with my forehead. I winced as his lip began to bleed. He looked me straight in the eye and then kissed me fiercely. His lips were unexpectedly soft and warm. The taste of his blood was salty on my tongue. The warmth of his kiss stole through my body and remained even after he let me go.

We twisted and turned through the cedar forest until I was hopelessly lost. The sun had set behind the hills, and it was growing dark. I was tired and shivering from the cold, and when I stumbled and fell, Bert picked me up with an urgent gentleness and held me close for a brief moment.

"We're almost there," he whispered in my ear.

I poked him hard in the back as we came up on the area of tall brittle grass around the cabin. We sounded like bulls in a china shop. He slowed down and we crept cautiously to the back of the cabin and the outhouse.

Bert motioned for me to hunker down while he advanced slowly to the privy and knelt. He reached underneath and pulled out a tightly wrapped plastic parcel. He quickly cut it open with his pocketknife and came up in one swift motion. Bert Atkins was suddenly transformed into Leonard Paisley before my very eyes. In his right hand he held a large menacing revolver, and his left fist was wrapped around the shaft of a wicked-looking hunting knife.

"Close your mouth," he whispered with a soft chuckle. "You look like I guppy I had when I was a kid."

Once again, he motioned for me to sit tight while he advanced toward the open back door of the cabin. I sat as still as a mouse, but my heart had a life of its own—it fluttered wildly in my chest, in my throat, and in the pit of my stomach. When Bert stepped carefully inside the cabin and out of my sight, I almost screamed. Minutes seemed like hours before he came back out.

"Nobody's home, Paisley. I wish it were safe to go inside, but I can't be sure until I take a little trip. You stay here. I'll be right back. Damn," he swore softly, "I wish I knew where Murphy ran off to. I haven't seen him since this thing started."

"When was that?" I whispered.

Bert didn't answer. He couldn't see my lips in the dark. That's when I finally panicked. He couldn't go off in the woods without me. The sniper might be right in front of him and he wouldn't have a clue.

Without Murphy, mine were all the ears he had. I pulled his head down to my mouth and urgently told him so.

"No!" he insisted as he pushed us apart. "I can't take the chance of your getting hurt. Stay here like I told you."

He started back down the path that had brought us to the cabin. I lost sight of him almost immediately, but I could still hear his heavy feet breaking the dry grass. That's when I decided to ignore his orders and follow him.

CHAPTER TWELVE

With the sun down and the moon behind heavy clouds I had trouble keeping sight of Bert's broad shoulders as he snaked his way through the tall grass. I could hear him, but the sound wasn't as loud as I had feared it would be. He was being very careful. I tried to be careful, too, but I paid a price by falling behind. I couldn't keep up without running, and running made too much noise.

It didn't take but a few minutes for his long legs to out distance mine. And the wind had picked up. The bare limbs of the thorn bushes rattled against each other and covered the sound of his footsteps. In the time it took for my heart to skip a beat I was all alone. I was terrified: more afraid of Bert's wrath than of the hidden gunman.

I turned around thinking if I could retrace my steps and go back to the cabin, Bert would never have to know I followed him; but the same wind that had covered his tracks had blown the grass back over mine. I considered sitting down right where I was and waiting until morning, but I knew I would freeze to death. I had to find some kind of shelter for the night. I looked around desperately for a place to hide. The moon came out from behind the clouds and mercifully gave me some light. About one hundred feet off to the right was a thicket. The brush was dry and thin and it wouldn't hide me in the daylight, but it was a place to stay until dawn.

I stumbled though the grass heedless of the sound I was making. Just as I got to the clearing that surrounded the low lying jungle of vines I tripped and fell over something.

The fall knocked the breath out of me. Tiny white shooting stars exploded behind my eyelids as I tried to struggle to my feet. It wasn't until then that I realized just how exhausted and cold I was. I leaned down to help the blood flow back to my head and caught sight of the body I had fallen over.

It was Murphy! The dog's long red hair was matted and filthy with mud and clots of dark blood. His tongue was protruding impossibly long from his mouth, and his eyes were open and full of dirt. The dog's throat was slit from ear to ear. I reached down to touch him—hoping I would feel the pulse of life; but as my hand touched his head it rolled off to the side away from the body

I jerked upright and screamed in horror. Suddenly Bert was there not thirty feet from me with his gun pointing at my head. The sound of the shot was the last thing I heard. It was like a cannon ringing in my ears. I fell to the ground knowing I was dead.

My last thought was of Cassie.

The flashing red lights of the ambulance burned through my eyelids. The acrid smell of something medicinal teased me back to consciousness. Men were speaking in voices that were unpleasantly loud. That made me angry. Had they no respect for the dead? I tried to sit up so I could reprimand them, but I was strapped down. I struggled against the restraints, and for my trouble I got the painful prick of a needle and the sting of something cold going into my vein.

I woke up in my very own bed on Meadowdale Farm. I turned over and looked out the big bay window. The front yard was covered with a new dusting of snow. It looked like confectioners sugar. My stomach grumbled. That's when I realized I wasn't dead.

"Good morning, dear. How are you feeling?"

I turned back around and saw my mother's anxious face hovering over me.

"Fine, I guess."

"Oh, thank the good Lord!"

She sank back in the bedside chair. I looked closely and saw signs of exhaustion and worry in her eyes.

"It wasn't a dream then?" I asked.

"No, dear, it was a nightmare."

"What happened? All I remember is Bert Atkins shooting me. I thought I was dead."

I saw the suspicious glint of tears on her cheeks. She pulled out one of her dainty lace handkerchiefs and dabbed at her nose. Then she laughed and shook her head.

"You're not dead, Paisley. Except for a few bruises, you're not even hurt. But I'd like to get my hands on that Atkins fellow."

I sat up slowly and fluffed two pillows behind me. My arms and hands were covered with scratches. They were sore but nothing else hurt.

"What happened? Did Bert shoot me?"

I peeked under the covers and saw more scratches on my legs and ankles but no bullet holes.

"That crazy man fired at you, but fortunately you fainted and he missed." She shivered involuntarily. "Danny said Bert realized it was you at the last minute and pulled the muzzle up, otherwise he would have gotten you right between the eyes."

"Then how come the ambulance, and the shot they gave me to knock me out?"

"I'm surprised you remember that. Hypothermia," she explained. "You were suffering from exposure. That foolish man had you traipsing around in the cold for hours."

"To be fair, Mother, Burt told me to stay at the cabin. The traipsing was all my idea."

"Humpf! Well, he's no gentleman, that's all I have to say. And I hope you refuse to have anything more to do with him."

She gave me a tired little smile.

"I heard your tummy growling earlier. How about some nice homemade chicken noodle soup?"

"Sounds great," I sighed contentedly.

Mother and I sat in front of the fire in the library and ate our supper. The snow had fallen all day and the ground was covered with a soft white counterpane. Inside where it was cozy and warm I almost forgot the discomfort of my night in the woods.

After my second bowl of soup and a slice of chocolate cake I called Cassie to tell her I was all right. She was blessed, or maybe cursed, with a remarkable sixth sense. She would know something was wrong sooner or later.

"I felt it! I knew you were in trouble. Last night, right? Around seven or eight? Well, that would be eight or nine here in Atlanta. I knew it! Are you really okay, Mom?"

And then she started crying.

"Oh, Cassie, honey, I promise. I'm fit as a fiddle. I have some scratches and my hair looks like hell, but other than that . . ."

After I reassured her for ten more minutes, I said goodnight and handed the phone to Mother. I snuggled back against the soft cushions of the sofa and gazed into the fire. Aggie was sleeping on top of my feet and her little doggie warmth felt good. I winced as I remembered the sight of Murphy's decapitated body.

"Are you in pain, dear?" asked Mother anxiously.

I smiled to reassure her like I had Cassie. There was no point in telling her that part of the story. I had told her almost everything else. No point in telling her I got kissed, either. Especially when she was so mad at Bert. I had even hesitated to ask how he was, but she had finally volunteered that he was staying with Danny.

I dozed off, passing in and out of that wonderful state of total comfort the body feels when it's healing from mental or physical stress. All my cares drifted away and a warm sense of well-being washed over me. I smiled contentedly and shifted my legs slightly to another position. Aggie woke up and bit my big toe with all her might.

"Damn dog!" I shouted.

"Paisley, dear, please watch your language."

"Damn my language!"

"I should think you would be reconsidering your use of foul words after such a miraculous escape."

"And damn that piss ant little dog. What a spoiled rotten brat!"

"That makes two of you, dear."

CHAPTER THIRTEEN

Two dozen roses with my name on them arrived shortly after breakfast the next morning. In her own socially acceptable manner, Mother was telling the delivery boy what he could do with them when I grabbed the long white box out of his hands. It had been a very long time since a man had sent me flowers. I was determined to enjoy them no matter what the circumstances.

I don't know what I was expecting, but the card read simply, "Bert."

Andy Joiner drove up in his cruiser, and while I was putting my roses in water, Aggie welcomed him in her charming little way. Outsiders always marveled at her sweet and cuddly demeanor. Naturally, they liked her. She never bit strangers, just the people who loved and cared for her.

I showed Andy into the kitchen while Mother fussed over a fresh pot of coffee and some of her feather-light cinnamon raisin buns. Aggie finally stopped dancing, curled adoringly at Andy's feet, and rested her fuzzy little head on his boot.

"Connie's been wanting us to get a dog," he confided as he scratched Aggie's ears. I watched with growing apprehension.

"What breed is your puppy?" he asked. "She's really sweet. A cute little dog like this wouldn't be so bad."

"Aggie's a Lhasa Apso," I answered as I watched her carefully for signs of aggression.

Aggie turned quickly.

"Watch out!" I warned.

But the puppy was just rolling over on her back so Andy could rub her stomach. I breathed a sigh of relief when Andy came away with all five fingers and put another spoonful of sugar in my coffee.

"What brings you out here this morning, Andy?" asked Mother. "You never come just to visit. You need to relax more. All work and no play . . . "

"Thank you, Miz Sterling. I appreciate that."

I looked him in the eye and asked, "You came about my little adventure at Jackson Lake, didn't you?"

His long face grew serious. "Yes, Paisley, I did. You really are beginning to concern me."

"Why on earth?" I was astonished. "I haven't done anything."

"You haven't *exactly* done anything, but you can't let well enough alone, either. You knew perfectly well that prior incident at Bert's cabin was still under investigation, and yet you went running out there to poke around on your own. And for your trouble, you almost got yourself killed."

"By the intended victim himself, don't forget."

He looked at me even more seriously. "And what makes you so sure of that?"

"Wha . . . what do you mean?" I stammered.

"I told you. The first incident is still under investigation. We don't know what happened. And we don't really know what happened last night, either, do we?"

"Well, of course we do," I insisted. "Someone broke into Bert's cabin and tried to kill him, then he almost shot me by accident."

"Okay, let's address the first part of that statement." He took a small dog-eared notepad out of his uniform pocket and turned over a few pages until he found what he was looking for. "There were no signs of forced entry to the cabin. The locks on the windows and doors were intact and unforced. Even though the ground was soft and muddy along the drive, the only tire marks we found were from your Jeep Cherokee. And after a thorough search of the woods, the only spent bullet we found was from Atkin's own revolver."

"But that's crazy," I protested. "Somebody shot at me while I was still in Watson. They shattered the windscreen. Isn't that's proof enough? And somebody shot at us while we were trying to hide down by the lake. You didn't look very hard there, or you would have found something," I accused.

Andy shrugged his shoulders and stuck the notebook back in his pocket. He stood up and put on his parka. As he zipped it up he turned back to me.

"All I'm saying is, be careful, Paisley. I've known Bert Atkins a long time; but things change—people change—and sometimes it's not for the best. Just remember that next time you want to go digging around for answers to questions you shouldn't be asking."

I was furious. For a very long time I had managed to get along without a man telling me what to do or how to live my life. I wanted to tell him so in no uncertain terms, but this was Mother's kitchen—the heart of her home. She would never forgive me if I threw Andy down on top of her starched Irish linen tablecloth and strangled him with one of her monogrammed napkins. So, I smiled tightly and thanked him as I opened the door and ushered him quickly outside.

Once he was gone, I slammed the door and plopped back down in my chair.

"What a nerve. Who does he think he is?"

"A friend," answered Mother softly.

"Humfp!"

I stormed out of the kitchen and back to the library. I turned on the gas logs and got a big yellow pad from the desk. I drew two long lines for columns down the sides of the paper and numbered the lines from one to ten. I sat back on the sofa with my pad and pencil to think.

It was hard. Trying to force the truth to fit the pattern of your wishes is always difficult. And there's nothing quite like having a potential lover nearly kill you to cool a growing sense of ardor. When I finally allowed myself to remember the exciting touch of Bert's lips on mine, I was also forced to recall the ugliness of the gun he had pointed at me and fired point blank.

I let the pad and pencil slide off to the floor and hugged my knees. Chin on hand, I stared into the flames and remembered Bert's gentleness when he cared for me. I had so desperately wanted him to be a knight in shining armor. He didn't even have to be *my* knight—I just wanted to know that they still existed. But maybe I was wrong. There weren't many windmills anymore. Dragons had disappeared. Why should knights have fared any better? And if there weren't any knights, what was a poor damsel like me to do?

"Do what you have always done, you silly fool," I answered myself roughly. "Take care of business."

Mother brought me a luncheon tray a couple of hours later. She had to nudge me awake before my food got cold.

"Umm, Mother, this is wonderful. Thanks. I'm sorry I've been acting like such a bitch."

"Language, dear. And I understand. You've been somewhat under the influence."

"Under the influence? I haven't had a thing to drink since New Year's Eve."

"Love, dear, not alcohol."

"Nonsense!" I wiped my mouth with the napkin and responded more truthfully. "Well, maybe for a while there I was somewhat infatuated, but I have my feet back on the ground now. I won't be acting impulsively anymore."

"My," she considered dryly. "That will be a first."

"Whatever do you mean?" I asked wide eyed.

"Paisley, my dear, you have always been a trifle impetuous. And living in South America only made you more so."

"Okay, so Rafe was a bit of a loose cannon, but I've always had a good head on my shoulders. I've never been one to act on impulse. Cassie can vouch for that even if you don't agree," I responded heatedly.

"Umm," she mused as she eyed me over tented fingers. "Which one of my darlings is the kettle and which the pot?"

CHAPTER FOURTEEN

Horatio picked Mother up a little before eight. They were partici-
pating in a bridge tournament at the country club. Aggie and I
remained in front of the fire in the library where she slept and I stared
at the blank yellow pad.

I finally wrote "reasons to kill Bert" in one of my columns, and
"reasons to kill Leonard" in the other. I thought briefly about one
entitled "reasons to kill Paisley," but that was just way too morbid
for my taste. Besides, I couldn't think of a single one. Andy Joiner was
just trying to scare me so I wouldn't muck up his investigation by
getting in the way.

Under the first column I wrote "bank robber, other enemies from
the past," and "source of mysterious income." The Leonard column
was more difficult. After all, Leonard wasn't real. He didn't even
exist on paper until two years ago. How, I wondered, could anyone
hate a fictitious man enough to want to murder him? That was easy.
Maybe someone thought Leonard was real. I shivered slightly. The
idea that I had created a man totally out of my imagination who
could engender that much enmity was frightening.

I got up from the sofa and went to sit on the hearth. Aggie raised
her bushy eyebrows to follow my movements. When she was sure
that I was going nowhere, she closed her eyes and went back to sleep.

The fire soon warmed me and I moved back to the sofa and took up pad and pencil once more.

I remembered the day "Leonard" was born. It was Cassie who had suggested his name. She wanted him to be a tough guy, and that he was. I had created a background of violence and a long history of bloodshed for my *nom de plume.*

Like Bert, Leonard Paisley was an ex-cop. The difference was that Leonard had gotten kicked off the force because he had committed some sort of unforgivable "cop sin." I had never been very specific about what it was, but it had earned him a lot of enemies. Of course, those enemies were not anymore real than he was. I shivered involuntarily again as I realized that somewhere along the line he had acquired a flesh and blood foe.

I wondered briefly if it could be a woman. Leonard had his share of women. I had always enjoyed writing about his "love 'em and leave 'em" romances. He respected women a great deal. He always told them up front he wouldn't stay, that he could never be faithful, and they never seemed to mind, at least on paper. Apparently one night with Leonard was enough of a memory for a lifetime. It was a crock and I knew it, but it sold a lot of books.

Maybe that was it, I thought. Maybe some raging feminist with an estrogen overload was out for Leonard's blood. Perhaps "Super Fem" saw herself as the avenging angel for all slighted women everywhere. But that made no sense, Leonard loved women. He left them, but he always left them smiling.

Perhaps Leonard had angered some other cross-section of humanity. I had never singled out any particular lot for ridicule except maybe pimps and drug dealers, but perhaps, unknowingly, I had incensed some other group with a hit man on their payroll.

I thought carefully through my plots for each of the three books and the villains I had created. The first was based on something that had actually happened. I had disguised the antiheroes but apparently not enough. They sued me. I won because they were guilty. Now one villain was dead and the other was serving a life term.

The second book was based on something I read in a medical journal. The villains in that story had suffered similar consequences. That left only *Virtual Violence.*

My last book had been in print about three months. As I had told Bert on the way to Nashville, it had an unusual provenance. Cassie's gift to me of a used laptop computer had proven to be a treasure trove that sparked my imagination. The story I wove around the letters and notes left on the hard drive was full of excitement and violence. Leonard had barely escaped with his life. He'd fought with a drug dealer on a precipice overlooking Niagara Falls for sixteen pages before the evil villain fell to a watery death.

I had saved all of the information I found on the laptop hard drive to a disc. I still had it somewhere. I stood and stretched. Maybe, I thought, it wouldn't hurt to look at it once more. I would have to be thorough with my investigation in order to go back to Bert and tell him it was not Leonard's enemy who was after him, but one of his own. And that was exactly what I hoped to be able to do.

Before I put the disc in the computer and turned it on, I went to the kitchen and fixed a midnight snack for Aggie and me: two dog biscuits and a people biscuit with blackberry jam.

The computer disc hadn't magically created any new information since the last time I looked at it. I scanned quickly down the file, pausing only to read the really awful poem addressed "To Ronda, with love." It hadn't gotten any better either.

Besides the poem, the self-pitying narrative that I had used for my story line, and some financial statements, the file contained several letters. They were addressed to companies that sold such things as commercial linens, kitchen equipment, and heavy duty cleaners and disinfectants. In each case, the company was asked to submit a bid for a contract. In the same file with the query letter was another letter telling the unfortunate company they had been underbid and had therefore lost the sale.

I hadn't paid much attention before because there was nothing very romantic or exciting about a bunch of business letters, but this time I noticed the rejection letters all had the same letterhead. They came from the army base outside of Morgantown. The office of the Quartermaster at Fort Morgan had asked for bids from at least forty different companies, only to reject each and every one.

Mother and Horatio arrived home at midnight. I had absolutely no knowledge of the military or business, but Horatio was well acquainted with both institutions.

"Odd, don't you think?" I asked while Mother went to fix us some hot cocoa.

"Mmmn, perhaps, my dear Paisley."

Horatio smiled gently. He was sitting under one of the soft recessed ceiling lights and the light reflected off his white hair and small Van Dyke beard, making him appear almost saintly. I knew that was far from the truth. Horatio Raleigh was shrewd and cautious, and even though he was almost seventy, some still thought him dangerous. I was certain he would gladly lay down his life for my mother and Cassie, and quite possibly for me.

"Why would this person, let's call him "Bob" just for convenience, why would he have letters from the Quartermaster's office on his own personal laptop? Looks to me like that would be illegal," I mused.

"Perhaps Bob was a secretary. Maybe he simply took some of his work home," suggested Mother as she set down the coffee tray.

"Can they do that, Horatio?"

"Paisley, my dear, in the dark ages when I was in the army, we were at war. Everything that came across my desk was sensitive. I was not allowed to even speak about it, much less carry it about with me. That is tantamount to what has happened here. This is a portable computer, is it not?"

"Yes, of course."

"Then he has transported it out of the office. I would have been shot for doing that."

"Are all the letters the same?" asked Mother.

I scanned quickly through the file and found one that appeared slightly different from the rest. This one had no letterhead. It appeared to be a form letter requesting payment for a shipment.

Mother and Horatio looked over my shoulder at the information in the files.

"Maybe our 'Bob' is a spy. Did you consider that possibility, dear?"

"I don't know, Mother. Somehow I think a spy who's after secrets concerning pots and pans and pillowcases is not one who would stalk Bert Atkins and try to kill Leonard."

"Perhaps you're right, Paisley," agreed Mother.

"What about that love poem?" suggested Horatio. *"Cherché la femme."*

"Ronda? Why do you think she would want to kill Leonard? I only used one line out of the poem in the book. I can't see why that would set anyone off on a murderous rage."

"Ask your young policeman friend, Andy Joiner. Most deadly crimes are crimes of passion," he countered.

"How would I go about finding Ronda?"

"Ask Leonard, dear."

"Very funny, Mother. Really, Horatio, how in the blue-eyed world would I find this mysterious woman?"

"Well, let's go with obvious. You said Cassandra bought this computer in a pawn shop in Morgantown. See if the pawn broker will part with the name of the gentleman who left the laptop."

"Or lady," I suggested.

"Or lady. It could even be our delightful Ronda. You have a description of her, don't forget."

"I do?"

"The poem."

"Oh, you're right, Horatio! Let me pull it up on the screen."

Mother looked over my shoulder again.

"Oh my, Bob is no secretary. He makes too many errors. Unless that's meant to be 'Ta Ronda With Love'."

"No, I'm sure it's supposed to be 'To Ronda'."

"It's rather poisonous isn't it?" she said.

"I thought so when I read it the first time," I agreed. "I certainly wouldn't want this on a valentine."

"'Blood red lips and heart as black as coal.' And look, Paisley dear, he says her hair is dark with a 'tortured forest of curls.'"

"'And eyes that 'are burned dead black with passion's thunder.' Talk about your mixed metaphors. But, Horatio, you were right. We have a description. The lady has curly dark hair and black eyes. Now where is she?"

"Perhaps you should start looking in the Quartermaster's office at Fort Morgan."

CHAPTER FIFTEEN

I mulled over the problem of finding "Ronda" for at least two hours after I went to bed. When I finally dozed off, it was to a fitful and uneasy slumber. Several times during the night I disturbed Aggie with my tossing and turning. She snarled and attacked my toes but refused to leave the warmth of my bed. Someday, I mumbled to myself, I'll have to remind her that this really is my room.

To add insult to injury, she woke me up at seven in the morning with her loud and insistent barking. I reluctantly left my cozy nest and stumbled to the library door to let her out. A chilly wind lifted the hem of my nightshirt and brought out goose bumps on my legs. I shivered and begged silently for Aggie to hurry. I knew if I called to her she would ignore me and take her time just out of spite.

The sun was shining meekly from behind several large intimidating grey clouds. We hadn't had snow since right before Christmas, and we were due a big one. I wondered if this would be the day for it.

Aggie came running back inside and hopped up on my bed to eat a souvenir leaf. I looked at her for a moment trying to decide if this was the time for a showdown. She stopped chewing and stared at me, her beady little eyes intent underneath those deceptively innocent and fluffy white brows.

"Okay, dog. You win one more round. But one of these days, pow! Right in the kisser."

I grabbed my clothes and headed to the bathroom for a shower. Aggie finished consuming her leaf, crawled up on my expensive down pillow, and went back to sleep.

Mother was in a delightful mood. Her Sunday School class was going on a trip. She always looked forward to these outings with such gusto. It made me wonder if I would ever enjoy piling on a tour bus with forty elderly and possibly seriously incontinent women. I wished her "Bon Voyage," and set off for Morgantown.

The sun peeked in and out of the clouds as I drove. The wind was cold and raw, at times pushing hard against Watson's square silhouette. I was glad for the cozy comfort of the big Jeep heater.

Morgantown had been a small country town like Rowan Springs until World War II. When Fort Morgan was built, the town grew and grew. The incoming troops and their families tripled the population. The old folks complained and fussed about the necessity of building schools and roads to accommodate the newcomers, but the merchants and businessmen saw dollar signs popping up all over town for many years to come. They were right. Morgantown was still thriving. My friend Bubba owned a car dealership in town that had made him a small fortune.

On the north side of Morgantown away from the military base there were avenues of lovely old homes. I always enjoyed driving through the quiet streets under the big oak trees that arched overhead. The houses were from another time and place when servants cleaned and washed and cooked, and all you had to do all day was sit on your veranda and sip lemonade. Of course, I thought, I would have been so bored from all that sittin' and sippin', I would have been putting something else in my lemonade.

As I passed through town to the south side, the neighborhoods got seedier and the homes more rundown. You could still see some lovely little "Arts and Crafts" bungalows, but they had been chopped up into duplexes and quadriplexes. Their yards were devoid of grass and instead were littered with cans and bottles and the eternally indestructible pieces of brightly colored plastic toys.

The streets got cleaner as I approached Fort Morgan. Soldiers dressed in work khakis were policing the grounds. The entrance was surrounded by two huge WWII tanks, one on each side of the guardhouse. Two little boys were posing on one tank while their father took photographs. A guard watched them carefully. From time to time he directed the man's camera away from a view of the inside of the fort. It made me conscious of the fact that this really was a military installation. These were real soldiers carrying real guns with real live bullets. Maybe "Bob" was a spy, after all.

As I approached the gate, a tall young military policeman signaled for me to stop.

"Help you, Ma'am?"

"The Quartermaster's office, please," I asked pleasantly.

"Yes, Ma'am! And who will you be seeing, Ma'am?

I thought for a second before I spoke, "Eh, Ronda."

"Check in at the visitor's center. It's on the right as you enter the gate, Ma'am," he clipped briskly. "Get your badge and proceed from there, Ma'am."

"Thank you very much. I . . . "

"Move right along, please, Ma'am," he ordered as he saluted smartly.

I drove quickly inside the gate and then proceeded at the proscribed speed limit of five miles an hour until I reached the visitor's center. There were signs everywhere telling me how to drive, how to park, how long to stay, and where to go. I shuddered. I could never be in the army. I hadn't been here five minutes, and I was chafing under the silent dictatorship of paint on metal.

I parked Watson in the proper space and headed in the direction of another sign, one that told me where I could get my temporary pass for the day.

Soldiers were policing the grounds on all sides of the road. Every candy wrapper and cigarette butt in sight was dutifully picked up and put in a big black plastic bag. I smiled at one of the young men, but he grimly went on about his job of collecting the debris of a messy and uncaring public without acknowledging me.

The line inside the visitor's center stretched all the way to the door. Actually, there were two lines. One was for relatives of men who were lived on the base, and the other was for people who had business there. I decided that I fit into the latter category and sidled over to join the company of about twenty salesmen who had come to ply their wares.

After a few minutes I realized that the fates had smiled upon me. From listening to their conversations I was able to glean enough information to sound like I knew what I was doing even if I didn't look like it in my jeans and barn jacket. By the time I reached the cheerless young woman in fatigues and shiny black work boots who was the clerk, I was ready. I simply parroted the phrases of the soft drink salesman who had been in front of me and got a badge which proclaimed "Day Visitor, Vendor" to one and all.

I gratefully climbed back in Watson and warmed up the heater as fast as I could. The walk across the parking lot chilled me to the bone. The temperature had dropped about ten degrees since I started my journey. I hugged my jacket around me and only relaxed when the interior of the car was warm and comfortable again.

While I was waiting for the car to heat up I looked around at Fort Morgan. A playing field with grass that was still green and healthy was just to the left of the entrance. Two soccer goals were pulled off to the sides. They were freshly painted and in good repair, but the field itself looked too perfect and untouched to have been used frequently.

Off in the distance I could see the olive green rooftops of barracks where the unmarried enlisted men lived. Between them and the visitor's center were rows and rows of low white buildings that appeared to be offices and classrooms. In the other direction were the modest one-story duplexes for married men and their families. Spaced at intervals of about every tenth house were playgrounds. They were outfitted very sparsely with a basketball hoop and a swing set. I didn't see any children or even very many soldiers outside. Only the men on litter detail were out and about in the cold.

The roads that traversed the grounds were black with new asphalt. Whitewashed rocks lined the shoulders. Everything was spic and span, and reminded me of my father's favorite parental refrain, "A place for everything and everything in it's place.'"

I wondered where the business of soldiering took place. If the guard at the gate wanted to prevent people from taking photographs, there must be something to see. I started up Watson's engine and went to look for it.

I didn't get very far. At almost every turn in the road was a barricade that prohibited further travel. At some points there were also two military policemen with rifles who politely turned me back. In less than an hour I had turned around so many times, I was dizzy. I astutely decided that the sightseeing was over. It was time to look for Ronda.

By now I was so confused I had to stop and ask for directions. A very polite but reserved young soldier pointed out the Quartermaster's office after I had passed him twice in my aimless search.

I parked in front of a cavernous warehouse that appeared to be the largest building on the base. Rows and rows of wooden palettes stretched down the length of the building. Most of them were piled high with boxes and cartons, some almost reaching the ceiling. On one side of the warehouse was a long narrow enclosure divided into separate offices by partitions. As I walked around looking for someone who could help me I realized I had come at a bad time. It was exactly twelve o'clock.

"Damn! Everyone is probably in the wha'cha-ma-call-it having lunch," I swore to myself, then jumped half a foot when a woman's voice responded from somewhere behind me.

"Mess hall," she laughed. "It's called a mess hall. Didn't you ever watch *M.A.S.H.?*"

I turned and saw a very attractive young African-American soldier. She was dressed in a smartly pressed khaki blouse and skirt. Her uniform gave her an air of authority, but she couldn't have been much older than Cassie. Her smile was the first one I had seen that day. I told her so.

"Everybody's on pins and needles waiting for our Commander in Chief," she explained.

"The President?" I gasped. "He's coming here?"

She laughed again. "No, but he's going to decide some time this week whether or not this base stays open. Almost everyone has put down roots here. They don't want to move their families. And they don't want to lose their jobs."

"What about you? You don't seem to be too upset about it?" I blurted out.

"Not me! Number one, I'm overdue for a change. Number two, I just might like another job. Number three, I definitely might like relocating. And," she added with a wry little smile, "last but not least, khaki is too close to the color of my complexion to be flattering."

We chuckled for a moment, then she asked politely,

"Can I help you with something? Captain Burke is in charge of procurement, but he's at lunch. I'll be glad to . . . "

"I'm not really selling anything," I interrupted. "I'm looking for someone named Ronda."

She looked at me a little suspiciously for a moment, then answered slowly as though she were thinking it over.

"Ronda. We don't have anyone here with that name. As a matter of fact, I can't remember anyone on the base with that name. Why do you ask?"

I had thought only briefly about what my answer would be if anyone asked me this question.

"I have something she may be interested in," I answered cryptically.

The girl looked at me intently and then crooked her finger for me to follow her. We walked past several office doors, our footsteps echoing hollowly in the cavernous building, until we reached her office. Before she opened the door to let me inside, she paused for a moment with her hand on the door knob, as if making a decision. As I brushed past her to enter, I saw the lettering she was trying to cover with her body. The name stenciled in black on the glass was Lieutenant Ta'Ronda Yancey.

CHAPTER SIXTEEN

Right then and there I should have run like a bunny for the exit. But I was stupid. And I had led a more or less charmed life. With the possible exception of losing my husband in the jungle and escaping a revolution, I had never really known many moments of terror or anxiety. I could have saved myself a bunch of trouble if I had left well enough alone and departed company with Ta'Ronda at that very moment. Instead, I calmly sat down in the wooden chair in front of her desk and crossed my legs.

"Looks like I'm in the right place," I said cocking my head at her name on the closed door.

Ta'Ronda crossed over to the long narrow window that looked out onto the parking lot. She opened the sagging grey aluminum blinds and peered out before she turned back to me.

"Who are you?" she asked abruptly. "And who sent you?"

When I didn't answer right away, she plopped her slim figure down in the swivel chair behind her desk and inspected me contemptuously.

"You don't look smart enough to have come here on your own. Who are you working for?"

I bristled at the intended slight.

"Leonard Paisley," I blurted out. "And I don't work for him. We're partners."

Her dark eyes widened with fear. The sardonic smile that had lifted the pretty curve of her cheek disappeared. In its place was a grim line that showed the pointed ends of her bicuspids. She looks like a cat, I thought, or better still, a panther. But cats have a quickness, a springy life in them that was suddenly absent in Ta'Ronda Yancey. This young woman looked defeated and frightened. Her shoulders slumped forward and her chin sagged. She looked ten years older than she had ten minutes ago. I wondered what in the world Leonard Paisley or I represented to her that had wrought such a change.

She wiped the brow under her shaggy black curls with a trembling hand and asked in a shaky voice, "Okay, what do you want from me?"

I didn't know what to say. This whole thing had taken on a life of its own. I was completely at a loss. Again my silence had a cathartic effect on her. She spat out in a somewhat stronger voice, "There's not much left of me. Take your best shot!"

I marveled at the anger in her young face. It was frightening. I shifted uneasily in the hard wooden chair and stifled my desire to jump up and run for my life. My curiosity was stronger than my fear.

"Leonard wants to see you," I finally said, taking a shot in the dark.

"Why?" she asked in a sad little voice. "I can't tell him anymore than he already knows. Besides, if they found out I had talked to him I'd be dead before the sun set."

Ta'Ronda's anger had vanished as fast as it appeared. A small tear escaped from the corner of her right eye, slid down her cheek, and fell on the breast pocket of her khaki blouse. I stared at the little dark spot as I tried to figure out what in the hell I had stumbled onto.

Her dark eyes opened and she saw me staring at her breast. A tremulous smile lifted her full lips.

"Do you want me, too?" she asked hopefully. "Is that what all this is about? That's no problem at all. You didn't have to come here and scare me half to death. All you had to do was ask."

Her hope gathered momentum with my silence. She got up from her chair and walked slowly around the desk. I tried desperately to think of something to say as she moistened her lips with the point of her tongue and leaned back against the desk in front of me. She pulled back her shoulders and forced the fabric tight against her chest. The frightened and angry little girl had become a seductress.

Sweat popped out on my face and around the corduroy collar of my jacket. Even the bottoms of my feet were perspiring in my hiking boots. What in the hell was I going to do now?

"I should have known when I saw you what you wanted," Ta'Ronda crooned. "You could have saved us a lot of trouble if you had just spoken up."

She reached over and stroked my cheek as I tried to pull away.

"There's no reason to be shy," she whispered.

Her fingernails were long and well manicured: painted blood red with white tips. One of those white tips traveled down my chin and neck and was about to disappear inside the collar of my red flannel shirt when I finally found the strength to jump to my feet.

"I . . . I gotta go!" I stammered.

Ta'Ronda laughed delightedly. The cat was back and she was practically purring. "But you'll call me, won't you," she said.

It was a statement instead of a question.

"Yeah, sure thing," I promised in a hoarse voice.

"Wait!" she commanded.

I paused with my sweaty hand on the metal doorknob. My inner eye was seeing myself as she perceived me: a middle-aged woman in men's clothing with short unruly hair and no makeup. She had jumped to a conclusion that anyone who did not know me could have made. I promised myself right then and there to go directly to the nearest Lancôme counter and buy them out. It was definitely high time to quit taking shortcuts with my appearance.

Ta'Ronda scribbled hastily on a scrap of paper and tucked it in my jacket pocket. I steeled myself while she gave me a provocative pat, then bolted out the door. I heard her calling as I practically ran for the exit.

"Don't forget to phone, girlfriend!"

I almost got a ticket as I raced toward the gate at ten miles over the speed limit. After being waved down twice by M.P.'s, I pulled over to the side of the road and tried to gather my wits. Being propositioned by another woman was a definite first for me. I was still shaking.

I shrugged out of my jacket and mopped my sweaty face with my scarf. A burly blonde soldier with a military police band around his upper arm saw me illegally parked and started towards me. I didn't wait for another reprimand. I swung back out on the road and headed for the exit. I couldn't get out of Fort Morgan fast enough.

As soon as I got out on the main road I increased my speed. The ratty streets of the south side of town soon gave way to the grace and beauty of the north, but it gave me no comfort. The wide arching limbs of the big oaks seemed to lean down and try to prevent me from fleeing. Leaves brushed against the top of the Jeep like clutching fingers. I didn't feel free until I was out of town and on the highway to Rowan Springs.

When my heart slowed to a steady pace and my sweat cooled, I began to feel the chill again. The big grey clouds that had hung in the sky earlier were gone. In their place was a low white cover which looked for all the world like a dirty chenille bedspread. I knew what clouds like that meant. More snow was on the way.

I tried not to think about what had happened back at the base. Before I considered what had taken place, I wanted to be at home, preferably in the library in front of the fire with my nasty little dog asleep on my lap. I was scared, really scared. I had a feeling that I had come very close to something very evil, and I wanted my mommy.

CHAPTER SEVENTEEN

Aggie was outside with Mother when I pulled up in the driveway. The puppy was busy chasing dry leaves as the brisk wind tumbled them across the backyard. Mother turned and waved and walked on behind Aggie. I watched them for a moment and thought how lucky I was to have this safe haven and a warm loving family. Mother looked so smart in her red woolen coat and brightly colored Versace silk scarf. From this distance you could never tell that Aggie was a nasty tempered little bitch. The two of them resembled a cover photo for one of those silly magazines of Mother's—the ones with articles about the socially elite and intellectually deprived. I smiled as she reached down and patted Aggie without getting nipped even once.

I was home safe and sound, and I was starving. I shrugged back into my jacket but still had to race to the back door to keep from freezing. Tiny little snowflakes were beginning to fall and the side-walk was already slippery.

Aggie came running back to the house with Mother in laughing pursuit. The puppy scampered inside as I held the door. I gave Mother a quick peck on the cheek and followed her into the kitchen.

"My, that didn't take long!" she smiled as she took off her scarf and coat. "I thought you would be gone all day. I asked Horatio to join me for tea. I hope you don't mind?"

"Since when have I ever minded Horatio's presence? And what good would it do if I did?"

I hung my jacket in the hall closet and took her red coat to her bedroom. I smiled as I heard her prattling on as though I was still at her elbow.

"I can't hear you, Mother," I called.

She couldn't hear me either. I caught the tail end of her sentence as I walked back in the kitchen.

" . . . so he left without a by your leave. Connie Joiner says it's very unlike him. She said Andy is beginning to suspect something."

"Who are we discussing?" I asked as I sneaked a hot cornbread stick from the iron baking pan that had been my Grandmother Sterling's.

"Why, I thought you heard me, dear. Bert Atkins, that's who. He's gone. Even Danny doesn't know where he went."

The hot bread sizzled in my mouth and burned my tongue as I stared at her in astonishment. How dare he leave, I thought, as my heart sank. I'm not finished with him!

"When? Mummf, when did he go?" I asked with my mouth full.

"Don't speak with your mouth full, dear."

"Dammit, Mother! This is important!"

"So are good manners, dear."

"I don't have time . . . "

"One should always make time for . . . "

"Damn!"

"And cursing is the last resort of the uneducated," she added.

I stormed out of the kitchen, my appetite and my warm familial feelings forgotten.

Bert Atkins had left and not even said goodbye. I was furious. I threw myself down on my bed, unaware that Aggie had followed. I landed on her long fluffy white tail when we both hit the bed at the same time. I'm sure I didn't hurt her, but she was startled. She lunged and bit my hand before I could pull it out of the way.

"Damn dog!"

I jumped back up and tried to push her off my bed. She nipped at me again and growled viciously. She backed up until her fuzzy little canine behind was pressed against my down pillow. That did it! I advanced on her with every intention of doing some doggie damage. She knew it, too. She snarled and barked and bared her teeth like a badger. I grabbed my satin house slipper and held it out menacingly. She snagged the toe with her front teeth and tore it out of my hands, shaking it madly as if trying to break its back.

I gave up. She had me beat. The whole world had me beat. I sank down on the floor with my back up against the bed. I took a deep breath and let it out with a loud despondent sigh. Aggie crawled up behind me and licked my ear.

"You're insane, dog," I told her. "Don't you know you're supposed to be my best friend? All you ever do is cause me grief."

Aggie finished licking my ear and cocked her head attentively. I heard it, too. It was the expensive hum of Horatio's Bentley coming up the drive. Aggie hopped off of my bed and skittered around the corner and down the hall, her little toenails clicking on the wooden floor until she reached the carpet in the library. She barked and barked at the French door as Horatio parked his car. I knew she would bark incessantly until I got up and let him in, so I cut short my pity party.

Horatio looked handsome and dapper in his black Chesterfield coat with the black velvet collar. His white hair was as thick as whipped cream and his goatee was neatly trimmed. He stood tall and slim outside the French doors as I unlocked them and let him inside.

"Hello, my dear," he greeted me. "Are you under the weather? You look somewhat glum on this beautiful winter day. Usually you're the first to welcome the snow. What is the reason my lovely Paisley is not smiling?"

I had to smile at that. I took his coat. I was folding his cashmere scarf when I burst into tears.

"Oh, ho! I thought so!"

He took the scarf from my hands and led me over to the sofa. He sat me down and turned on the gas logs. I cried dispiritedly for a few moments while he fussed with the fire screen. He turned to regard my performance.

"Not very convincing, am I?" I snuffled.

"On a scale from one to ten, I would give you a three," he smiled.

I wiped my tears away and smiled back. "I'm just so damned, so damned . . . " I searched my mind for a word to express my feelings.

"Frustrated?" he offered.

"Yes, that and more. I'm at a loss to understand how I do feel."

"You do look a little frazzled," he observed.

"Is that what you think when you look at me? Is that all you see? Is that what I have become since I moved back here?" I started sniffling again.

Horatio moved over to the sofa and sat beside me again. He lifted his hands and cupped my face. He looked at me closely and grunted. I had to laugh. I had never heard him make such an undignified sound, and I told him so.

"To quote a famous Broadway musical—you're a 'puzzlement,' my child. At the best of times you seem happy beyond belief. And yet, on occasion, this being one, you appear to be quite inexplicably anxious."

He patted my cheek, and went to sit on the other sofa.

"Do you mind?" he gestured with his pipe. "The new tobacco I ordered from London came in today and I'm quite excited about trying it."

"Go ahead," I sighed. "I love the smell of your pipe."

He busied himself with the process of filling his pipe and lighting it. I blew my nose on a tissue and got up to throw it away. I crossed over to make sure I had locked the door and sat back down. I looked up and saw that he had watched my every move with enormous interest.

"I think I have had an 'ah ha' experience," he ventured and went on to explain. "A friend from my bad old days in the er, service, used to work on coded messages that frequently passed our way. He was quite the absent-minded professor in his daily life, but an absolute genius at breaking encryptions. For days he would exist only on coffee and cigarettes while he worked away, and then suddenly you would hear him shouting, 'Ah ha!' That was my signal to order a fortifying meal and a cot. He had broken the code. It was time to eat and sleep."

I laughed at Horatio's story. I knew he had a million of them, and there were only a few he could relate even after all these years.

"And what 'ah ha' experience have you had about me? I can't believe you've discovered something new about me. You've known me for over forty years. How could I possibly do anything to surprise you?"

"You're a woman, my dear. And even as a girl child, you were constantly a surprise. Haven't you realized that while Velvet is fairly predictable, you are ever the chimera?"

"Velvet predictable?" I laughed. "Not likely! I would have never have guessed that she would be a divorcee three times over, a widow once, and a wife to her fifth husband before her fortieth birthday."

"Really? Think back. Imagine her in your little sandbox under the maple tree in the backyard. I can see her now," he mused. "You would play for hours with the same little shovel and bucket, while our lovely Velvet would lose interest at a moment's notice. She would run from sandbox to swing, to wading pool, and back again, a dozen times over. Don't you remember her capricious behavior as a child? How is that different from her actions as an adult?"

I pulled my legs up under me and snuggled back in the corner of the big sofa.

"I've never thought about it that way, but I guess you're right. If you knew her so well, how come you don't know everything about me?"

"Like I said before, you are quite different. You enjoy taking risks. You like the unknown. That brings an element of unpredictability into your life."

"So what's the 'ah ha'?"

"You're terrified," he said quietly.

The smoke from his pipe was deliciously aromatic. I watched as it wafted above his head like a fragrant cloud. It was on the tip of my tongue to say he was crazy, but I knew he was absolutely correct. If I protested, I would reveal even more of myself than I already had. And I wasn't sure I was ready to do so.

Mother, bless her heart, saved the day. I could hear the wheels of the tea cart in the hallway. I jumped up to open the door and let her in the library. A dozen lovely smells entered the room along with her.

"Yum! I am famished, Mother. I hope this is high tea and not some skimpy little cucumber sandwich thing."

She ignored me completely and went over to greet her friend.

"Horatio, dear. Your new tobacco arrived!"

CHAPTER EIGHTEEN

The snow fell throughout the rest of the afternoon and into the night. Mother and Horatio sat in the library, laughing and talking for hours. They were so cozy and companionable, I felt even more isolated and alone. I finally excused myself and went to my room. I tried to call Cassie, but her roommate said she was out on a date. I hung up the phone with a self-pitying sigh and decided to take a long hot bath.

When the water was hot and sudsy with bubble bath and fragrance, I undressed. I was just climbing into the tub when the phone rang. Naked and shivering, I ran back to the bedroom to answer it. Mother had already picked up in the library. I started to hang up but I caught the menacing sound of the voice on the other end. I sat on the edge of the bed, my bare skin covered with goose bumps, and eavesdropped. My heart chilled as I heard:

" . . . stone cold dead if she doesn't mind her own business!"

"Who is this?" demanded Mother. "How dare you call my home and threaten my daughter!"

The dial tone was the only answer she got.

With shaking hands, I threw on my pajamas and housecoat. Mother would need some calming down, and Horatio would want some answers.

Mother and I met head-on at the library door. Her face was almost as white as her hair, and her lips were trembling. I took her cold hands in mine and led her back in front of the fire.

"It would seem you have a good reason for being afraid, Paisley," observed Horatio, calmly. "Perhaps now you'd care to tell us all about it."

His voice was tightly controlled, but I knew he would allow no more evasive maneuvers on my part. No matter how much he might care for me, his first priority was Anna Howard Sterling, and she had just had the fright of her life.

"Oh, Paisley, darling, what in the world?" she cried.

"I'm sorry, Mother," I sighed, putting my arms around her. "I honestly don't know who that was, or how they got this number. I really don't even know what's going on."

I hugged her and pulled her down beside me on the sofa. I turned and faced Horatio. "You were right when you said I was terrified. But the crazy thing is that I haven't a clue as to why."

I shook my head and bit my lip to keep it from trembling before I continued.

"People are shooting at one another and talking about getting killed, and now they're threatening me. I just don't get it."

My voice ended on a quavering note as I sat back in the cushions and held Mother's hands in mine. No one spoke for a long moment. The flames of the gas logs flickered and warmed the room with a rosy glow. The gilded letters on the spines of my father's books twinkled in the firelight. The polished walnut paneling, lovely oriental rugs, and red chintz flowered sofas made this room a welcome refuge from the world. I tried to draw comfort from the pictures of family and friends, and other beloved objects placed on tabletop and mantle. It was a room designed with love. It was a paean to generations of a family. And my family would see me through anything, I was positive of that. I told Mother and Horatio everything that had happened.

When I had finished my narrative, Horatio asked if we could fix "a small repast" to "fortify his ancient brain." The tea cart had indeed been just a cucumber sandwich sort of thing. Mother and I hastened to the kitchen. She cut paper thin slices from a Broadbent country ham while I buttered biscuits and slipped the ham inside. I warmed up some apple cider and cut thick wedges of mince pie. She filled one large bowl with potato salad, and a smaller one with piccalilli.

"There," she said with satisfaction. "That should keep us awake for hours! The heartburn alone should be enough to fuel our imaginations. We'll figure this out, don't you worry, dear. Horatio is on the case!"

I had to smile as I followed her back to the library with our midnight supper on a large tray. Mother was the eternal optimist, and like any true Southern lady, she had enormous faith in her men. But then she had reason for that faith. Her men had never let her down. I wasn't so lucky. But I was willing to give Horatio a chance. After all, I had nothing to lose but my life.

He was speaking quietly into the telephone when we entered, and it occurred to me then that he had requested the food in order to get rid of us while he made his call. I put the heavy tray down on the table between the sofas and ran back to the kitchen for the cider. I didn't want to miss anything else.

It wasn't a ruse after all. When I returned, Horatio was eating as though he expected a famine. I poured his cider and watched in amazement as he served himself two more biscuits and heaped on the piccalilli. My stomach was too nervous for more than a cup of cider, so I filled Mother's cup and sat back to wait. I knew Horatio would take the floor when he had fortified himself sufficiently.

After another biscuit and a small wedge of mince pie, Horatio cleared his throat and sat back in the big leather wing chair to the right of the fireplace. Mother and I, each perched on a sofa in front of him, watched and waited for what he had to say.

"Paisley," he began. "I took the liberty of making a few phone calls while you and your Mother were in the kitchen. I have alerted a network of my former, ah, colleagues to the possibility that we might be in need of their assistance. By this time tomorrow night, we should have their considerable resources at our command. One member of this august group has already provided me with vital information. He convinced someone in the local communications network to trace the unpleasant phone call my Anna received.

"Wow! Horatio, who was it?" I marveled.

"Unfortunately, we cannot answer that question as of yet because the call was placed from a public telephone. But we do know the location. It was in a shopping mall on the interstate exit outside of Morgantown."

"The Beaver Dam Outlet Mall. I know where that is. And it's not far from Fort Morgan. That call must have had something to do with my little visit to Ta'Ronda."

"Precisely what I was thinking, my dear," he winked.

"But why, Horatio? How could anything my daughter have done cause someone such distress. I'll be the first one to admit that she can be trying at times, but to threaten her life?"

Horatio and I grinned at each other in spite of the circumstances.

"I don't believe it was Paisley who caused the distress, my dear."

"Then who?" she demanded.

"Leonard!" Horatio and I answered together.

"Why, of course, Horatio!" I exclaimed. "At the time I didn't realize it, but it was Leonard's name that wigged Ta'Ronda out! Somehow my paper detective, Leonard Paisley, has created real live enemies."

"Precisely, my dear," agreed Horatio. "Somewhere down the line, Leonard has stepped on some very tender toes."

"It can't have been too long ago, Paisley," offered Mother. "Or they would have come after you before now."

"You've made two very good points, Anna," observed Horatio.

"Why two?" I asked.

"Paisley, you've been writing Leonard's books for almost two years. The first two did not engender this sort of interest. The last one, the one Anna gave me when I was ill—*Virtual Violence*—is our catalyst."

"Okay for point number one. What's point number two?" I insisted.

"They came after you, Paisley, instead of Leonard. Today a new ingredient was added to *le bonne soupe.*"

"Me? You mean when I put my own self in harm's way?"

"Isn't that what you do best, my little unpredictable one?" he smiled knowingly.

Horatio insisted on spending the night, or what was left of it. We talked between yawns until almost three in the morning. Twice he received phone calls that he preferred to take in the hall and out of our hearing. Mother never once mentioned how tasteless it was to place a telephone call after nine in the evening. She sat without speaking until Horatio returned and looked at him expectantly as if he were going to announce that all was well and we could go to bed. After the last call, when he said no such thing, she began to realize we were in for the long haul and should make the best of things. She said as much and then began to make plans.

"Horatio, you might as well take the summer suite. It's been closed since August, but it won't take much to air it out and warm it up. You'll have plenty of room there with the two bedrooms and sitting room in between. I'll have the separate telephone line activated tomorrow and you can have complete privacy for your, ah, business. I'll fill the bar fridge with you favorite beer and . . . "

"Whoa, Mother, what in the hell are you planning for, a siege? I hardly think this is that serious. It's not, is it Horatio?"

"Hard to tell yet, my dear. Could be, and again, maybe not. Better to be safe than sorry."

"Well, that's a cryptic answer," I complained crossly.

I was getting really sleepy. I never was able to stay up very late, and it was way past my bedtime.

"I have to go to bed. Please excuse me, but I have some things to do in town tomorrow and I have to get some . . . "

"Ahmmm," interrupted Horatio. "Please don't plan on going anywhere alone until this thing is resolved, Paisley."

"WHAT? Don't what?"

"Horatio is quite correct, dear. We must take precautions."

"I don't believe this! I'm perfectly capable of taking care of myself, I'll have you both know!"

"Yes," responded Horatio with a dry laugh. "We've seen the results tonight."

"Hummpf," I grunted childishly. "Come, Agatha, let's go to bed."

I don't know which one of us looked sillier. Me grumping off to bed like a spoiled child, or the dog grinning like a fool with the knowledge that she had been invited back up on the bed with my down pillow.

CHAPTER NINETEEN

I tried to sneak out of the house before breakfast the next morning, but snow had drifted against the screen door in the back, and the library door was iced shut. The fruitless banging and cursing alerted Mother to my plans.

"Remember what Horatio said about going out alone, dear. I'll get dressed in a moment and come with you."

"Oh, great," I snorted. "My mother, the bodyguard. And what are you going to do if I'm accosted? Get out your hair spray? Or maybe beat the buggers to death with the September issue of *Vogue*?"

"No need to be cheeky," she sniffed, and turned to go back to her room.

I felt instantly contrite and stopped laughing. "I'm sorry, Mother. I'm an unfeeling cad. I know this must be upsetting for you. But you know me, the court jester. I have to make fun of everything."

Slender shoulders shook underneath her white satin dressing gown as she cried silently.

"Oh, Mommy, I'm sorry!" I begged. "Please forgive me?"

I held her in my arms. Mother was always so vivacious, so on the move. It wasn't until moments like this when she was still and standing close to me that I realized how slender and small she really was. But fragile she wasn't, and I told her so.

"You'll be fine," I promised. "And so will I. Horatio and his old fogey brigade will see to that. And our vicious little watchdog will destroy all intruders."

She laughed and wiped away the tears with one of the little lace-trimmed hankies she always has tucked into whatever she happens to be wearing.

"I know, dear. You must forgive me. It's been a long time since I've had to worry about anything. I've just lost the hang of it."

I smiled and hugged her tightly. "That speaks well for our life, doesn't it?"

"Yes, darling. We've been very blessed," she agreed.

"I'll start the coffee and scramble some eggs. You get dressed and we'll go to town together. You can help me pick out some girlie makeup."

"Oh!" she exclaimed clapping her hands. "Why didn't you say so? How absolutely delightful. And maybe Gennie can even up your hair a bit."

"Don't push it!" I warned.

She smiled brightly, full of anticipation and hope for my improvement, and hurried off to get dressed.

"Old fogey brigade, is it?" spoke Horatio from the shadows in the hallway.

I jumped half a foot straight up.

"Oh, my God! Horatio! You scared me half to death!"

"Quite! And I'm just an old . . . "

"Oh, for Pete's sake! Not you, too. Just accept my apology and get the eggs out of the refrigerator."

"That's how it could happen, my dear. You must become more aware of your surroundings. The very air in any given space holds clues to . . . "

"Horatio, I'm starving. Can we at least wait until I've had my first cup of Earl Grey before we have our little class in Cloak-and-Dagger 101?"

He smiled and tightened the belt on his burgundy velvet smoking jacket.

"I'll fetch the eggs."

We had a very nice breakfast. Mother was in high spirits anticipating my makeover, and Horatio announced that he had done a bit of ruminating after we had gone to bed.

"Yes, I think I've settled on quite a few things we need to do. Anna, my pet, do you mind if I arrange some minor security measures?"

"Why, of course not. On the contrary, anything you can think of to protect Paisley will make me more than happy."

"Very well, then. That's settled. You two go on to town and have fun. I don't think we need worry too much about anything during the daylight hours. Just keep an eye open, Paisley. Remember, be aware of your . . . "

"Yeah, yeah, I know—the very air around me."

Rowan Springs wasn't exactly a shopping mecca. Aside from a very nice antiques mall, a craft shop full of wonderful handmade furniture, and a spiffy sporting goods store, there wasn't much to choose from. The "five and dime" had closed long ago, and the only cosmetics the feed store had were tins of Bag Balm. That was great stuff for winter hands, but I needed something more. I turned my nose up at the offerings in the big discount store on the edge of town. As I told Mother, it's not worth doing if you can't do it right. And as far as I was concerned, doing it right meant spending way too much money on something totally overpriced in lovely little containers with charmingly decorated boxes. For that, we had to drive to Wieuca City, which was almost fifty miles away.

"I'm not sure Horatio would approve of our traveling so far out of town, Paisley."

"Relax, Mother. What Horatio doesn't know won't hurt him. Besides, nobody is stupid enough to attack us in Lord & Taylor's."

"I have to admit, I am having fun. It's been a while since we went shopping together. Maybe we can even have lunch at that delightful . . . "

The truck hit us hard from behind, then sped up and went barreling past as we slid helplessly into a wild and uncontrolled spin down the center of the highway. We careened off the guardrail on the left and went sliding across the road to the one on the right as I tried desperately to control the skid. The car finally came to a shuddering halt on the shoulder after scraping the paint off the passenger side of the Lincoln.

The engine had cut itself off and the ensuing silence actually hurt my ears. I tasted blood in my mouth and glanced up in the rearview mirror. I had bitten into the tip of my tongue, but I was grateful to see Mother was sitting ashen-faced but unhurt next to me.

"My goodness," she gasped. "What an interesting experience."

"You do have a talent for understatement, Mother."

"That truck . . . "

"Did you get a good look at it? I was too busy trying to stop the car."

"It was olive green, that's all I remember."

"My God, they had the *cojones* to come after us in a military truck!"

"I don't know what that means, but it sounded quite nasty, Paisley. You should be saying a little prayer of thanks instead of fouling your mouth . . . "

"Say one for me. I've got to get us out of here before they come back to finish the job."

"Finish? You really believe they meant to . . . ?"

"I think so. Otherwise they wouldn't have dared use a truck that is so easily identifiable. Without witnesses . . . "

"Someone's coming, dear," she said urgently. "Is that the truck?"

"Yes! Quick, Mother," I shouted. "Open the door and run as fast as you can."

"I can't! The door is jammed against the guardrail! Get out, Paisley," she screamed. "Please, jump. Never mind me!"

I grabbed her tightly and held her face against my chest as the big green truck came speeding down the highway. The driver crossed the median and headed straight for us. I could hear the mumbled words of Mother's prayers and feel her warm breath against my collarbone. The thunderous blast of an air horn drowned out her voice as a big eighteen wheeler came rushing up from behind us. At the very last minute the army truck veered away, and the huge eighteen wheeler loaded with cattle went by close enough to rock the Continental from side to side.

I dropped my head against Mother's and said a prayer of my own. My arms were trembling so much I had a difficult time turning the key in the ignition. But I knew we had to get far away as quickly as possible.

"Do you think they'll come back again, dear?"

"I'm not waiting around to find out. Let's vamoose!"

The car miraculously started on the first try. We pulled away from the guardrail with the sound of scraping and tearing metal, but neither of us gave it a second thought.

"Mother, you know this area like the back of your hand. Can't we get off the main highway and take some little cow path back home?"

She closed her eyes tightly and tried to remember.

"Yes!" she answered after a few moments. "Your grandfather Howard used to go fishing around here somewhere. Don't wait until the next exit. Make a U-turn and go back the other way. The original road runs parallel to this highway for about a half a mile. If the bank is not too steep we can drive down to it. Then we can go east and double back to Rowan Springs."

"Terrific! If we manage to do it before the truck comes back, he'll think we're still going north. He'll go all the way to Wieuca City before he realizes we're not in front of him. Way to go, Mommy!"

I increased our speed and watched for the silhouette of the truck in the distance. Mother sat in the edge of her seat looking for signs of the old highway below and to the right of us.

"There! Up there," she shouted. "Do you see it?"

I slowed down and looked over the snowdrifts and taller dry grass on the shoulder. The embankment was too steep. Her car was so low—I was afraid it would never make it down without flipping over, and I told her so.

"Never mind the flipping car!"

"Mother! Language, please!"

I laughed even though it sounded hollow.

"And never mind your silly jokes! This is serious business, dear. My car can be replaced—you and I cannot. If you slow down, I think you'll see a place up a little farther where you can get off safely."

And she was right. I headed the big car down the steep embankment as fast as I dared. The snow and mud underneath the wheels finished the job for me. I tried to brake but it was impossible. We went skidding and bumping down the hill at an alarming rate. Before Mother could say another prayer we bounced out onto the old road and came to a sudden stop as we knocked over a mailbox on the shoulder.

"Wow!"

"My sentiments exactly, dear."

I turned around and looked at out tracks. The gouges in the hillside were raw and deep, exposing the red earth below. Anyone who bothered to look would know immediately where we had gone. I hoped Mother was right—that the murderous little turd driving the army truck would assume we were still headed north and keep going in that direction.

I started the faithful car again. We drove parallel to the highway for five hundred yards or so and then turned left into an old tunnel that doubled back under the highway. The road was rough and full of potholes, but it was our road to salvation. I followed Mother's directions past the farm where my grandfather used to fish for crappie and then on a few miles farther until we reached the outskirts of town.

"Don't you think we should go see Andy Joiner and report this?"

"Let's wait. We need to talk to Horatio first. We can always call Andy later."

"Very well. But do stop at the Quickie Mart, dear. We need some milk."

"You're some piece of work, Mother. I love the way you keep your priorities straight."

CHAPTER TWENTY

Horatio was in the library when he saw us drive up. He opened the French doors and came out to greet us. The blood left his face when he got a good look at Mother's car. I must admit, I felt like an old friend had died when I climbed out and saw the havoc our little adventure had wrought. Mother's beautiful Lincoln Continental, her pride and joy, was a wreck. She couldn't have cared less.

"You should have seen us, Horatio!" she laughed excitedly. "We outsmarted the devils. They tried to kill us but we escaped using our wits and Paisley's driving skills. It was thrilling. You should . . . oh, I don't feel very well."

"Mother? Are you all right?" I asked in alarm.

Horatio got to her side before I did. He was the lucky one she threw up on. I will hate myself forever, but I couldn't help it. I lay across the damaged hood and laughed until tears came to my eyes at the sight of my elegant Mother barfing on Horatio's patent leather toes.

"Paisley," he shouted gruffly. "Stop that! Help me get your Mother inside. You're both suffering from shock."

I hiccoughed and stumbled my way over to Mother and helped Horatio walk her into the library. We got her down on one sofa and he insisted I lie down on the other. Horatio started the fire and covered us both with blankets. I didn't realize until that moment how cold and shaky I was.

I closed my eyes for a moment and went spinning off into a tunnel of darkness. When I opened them again, Horatio was at my elbow.

"Drink this soup, Paisley, love. You'll feel much better."

"Mother?" I asked, as I tried to raise up on one elbow.

"She's fine. She had some soup and a little brandy. When she wakes up again she'll be fit as a fiddle. It's you I'm worried about."

"Me? I'm fine. Don't worry about . . . "

"Someone wants to shut you up, Paisley. And they're not afraid to commit murder."

"Maybe they were just trying to warn me. You know, like the phone call."

He shook his white head vigorously. "One bump from behind with a twenty ton truck is a warning. When it turns around and comes back to smash you head-on at sixty miles an hour—that's attempted murder."

"Oh," I responded in a very small voice. "Oh."

"Oh, indeed."

Horatio made me finish my soup. When I was done, he handed me a cup of hot tea laced with brandy. While I drank, he told me what he had been up to.

"I drove your mother's car down the lane and back over in the field where I parked it under some cedar trees. If it weren't so big and white, the overhanging boughs would have been enough cover, but I had to cut off a few extra limbs to drape over the top just to make sure it couldn't be seen from the air."

"From the air?" I asked in astonishment.

"Paisley, until we know exactly what we're up against, we must take every precaution," he explained. "With the car hidden, there's a good chance they may think you've gone to ground somewhere else. But we can't take any chances. We'll have to close the shutters and draperies tonight. We must keep the lighting to a bare minimum if we don't want any unwelcome visitors."

He patted me gently on the cheek and smiled over at Mother.

"I'll hold down the fort until dark," he said. "You get as much sleep as you can now and take over for me until midnight."

"You mean we have to keep watch all night tonight?"

"Tonight, and every night from now until we solve this mystery."

He took the empty cup out of my hand and pulled the blanket up under my chin. I closed my eyes and was glad to see nothing spinning. I tried to stay awake. I needed to think—to try and make some sense of this whole idiotic situation—but my eyelids were too heavy.

My hunger woke me up a little after five in the evening. Mother was snoring softly on the other sofa with Aggie curled up at her feet. Her doggie snores were just slightly softer than Mother's.

I sat up and rubbed my eyes as the day's events came rushing back to me. This whole thing was insane. I felt like Alice in Wonderland. Horatio was the White Rabbit and Mother was the Queen of Hearts. What did that make Bert, I wondered. The Mad Hatter? He certainly was no Dormouse. I could sure use him right about now. Horatio probably wouldn't turn down his help either. I wasted a few moments wondering where he was, then got up quietly and tiptoed into the kitchen.

Horatio was sitting at the table drinking coffee. He smiled when he saw me.

"Feeling better?" he asked.

"Much! And I'm starving."

"I took the liberty of preparing an *omelet des fines herbs* for myself. Shall I make one for you as well?"

"No, thanks. A simple all-American pimento cheese sandwich will do for me."

While I ate, Horatio outlined our situation.

"Unfortunately I wasn't able to set up my security perimeter. The friend who was going to help me had a doctor's appointment." He smiled ruefully, "You were more correct than I cared to admit when you called us old fogies, my dear."

"Oh, Horatio, I told you I was sorry. And, honestly, I think I'm very lucky to have your friends on my side. Where else could a girl find such a wealth of expertise?"

"In a nursing home in Nashville," he said with a wry grin.

"You're kidding?"

"Only two of them. But they both have computers online so it doesn't matter where they are, or how infirm. One's a language expert, and the other is a financial whiz. Henry's blind in one eye and a stroke left him partially paralyzed two years ago, but he can access practically any bank account in the world."

I couldn't help laughing. I was beginning to feel much better.

"Like I was saying," Horatio continued. "I didn't get to arrange for our security, so we'll have to be especially vigilant tonight. And we have no fire power to speak of, only the handgun I carry under the seat of my car and your father's shotgun."

"What are we going to do if they come after us?"

"Call 911 like any other citizen in trouble."

"Are you sure that's such a good idea?"

"Don't you trust our stalwart Chief of Police?"

That was a question I had been tossing around in my own mind lately. Bert and Andy were very good friends. If Bert was involved in something unpleasant there was a good chance Andy either knew about it, or was involved himself. I took a bite out of my sandwich and washed it down with a swig of cold sweet tea before I answered.

"I have no concrete reason not to trust him. But what if the police take a little longer than usual getting here? What if both squad cars have flat tires? What if . . . "

"Very well, then we must make alternate plans. Do you have any suggestions?"

I finished my sandwich and chug-a-lugged the rest of my tea while

I thought. Foremost in my mind was the belief that Horatio was exaggerating the situation just a tad. Being attacked by weirdoes on a nearly deserted highway was one thing, but this was our home. Meadowdale Farm was one mile as the crow flies from the town square. We might live on the edge of one hundred acres of rolling farmland, but our house sat on a hill just inside the city limits. I could not bring myself to believe that anyone would try to storm my mother's castle. That thought gave me an idea.

"How 'bout hiding in the dungeon?" I proposed with a wink.

Horatio's expression told me he had no time for jokes.

"Perhaps you would care to elaborate on that suggestion," he said in a stern voice.

I hastened to appease him. "Mother knows more about it than I do, but there are tunnels all underneath the house."

"Do go on, my dear," he urged. "This is fascinating."

"Fifty years ago, when my grandfather decided that four fireplaces couldn't provide enough heat in the wintertime, he had a floor furnace placed in every room. This was originally a log house and there was no basement. The tunnels were dug so the units could be serviced. Over the years, as he and my father built new additions with new furnaces, more tunnels had to be created. There's room down there for an army. Oops," I grinned. "I keep forgetting they're the bad guys."

"That has yet to be proven, my child," he replied gruffly. "And if it is true, I'm sure it's only a few mavericks. I'm a firm believer in the gallantry and honor of our men at arms."

Nighttime arrived as we talked. The kitchen grew dark and unfamiliar without the warmth of the oven or glow of the lights. Horatio had unscrewed the bulbs to make sure no one forgot and turned anything on. When I went to put the tea and the pimento cheese away I found that he had even remembered the light inside the refrigerator.

"Gee, you're good, Horatio. I would have forgotten that one. And I guess you took out the light in the microwave, too."

Horatio took his cup and saucer to the sink and looked out the window without answering me. I sat back down and watched him as he scanned the backyard with his binoculars. I started to tease him, but I didn't want to hurt his feelings. It had been a long time since he had played spy vs. spy. Might as well let him enjoy it.

"Do you want to see where the tunnel entrance is now?" I asked. "I mean, just in case we need to hide down there?"

"Yes, and now might be the best time, my dear. It's early, yet. Too many witnesses still up and about."

Oh, my God, I thought, that's just a smidge melodramatic. But I cheerfully led him to the closet in the front hallway and explained how to get down to the tunnel below.

"There's a hole in the floorboard. You lift the floor up. The opening is about two and a half feet square."

Horatio opened the closet door and shone his hooded flashlight inside. He shook his head when he saw the jumble of old shoes and empty fruit jars on the floor.

"How very unlike Anna to have such a messy closet," he observed. "Help me clear away this junk, if you please, dear."

He bent down on one knee and tried to lift an old boot. When it wouldn't come up, he tugged hard and fell back on the floor as it slipped out of his hands.

"I should have warned you," I chuckled. "Velvet and I glued and nailed that mess on the trapdoor one day when we decided we needed a secret hiding place. We thought it made a great disguise. Mother wanted us to clean it up, but Dad thought it was funny. It's been there for thirty years. It really looks good now with all that dust, doesn't it?"

"I should say so! It certainly fooled me. Show me how it opens."

Together we lifted up the cover to the tunnel. The musty smell of dirt and mildew floated up from below and made me sneeze.

"Mustn't do that if we have to hide down here later. Take an anti-histamine or something," he said as he shone his flashlight down the dark hole.

I shuddered at the thought of going down underneath the house. Although as a child I was fairly adventurous, I had never dared go into the tunnels. I was terrified of two things: spiders and enclosed spaces. The tunnels under my Mother's house were sure to have plenty of both.

CHAPTER TWENTY-ONE

Horatio insisted that we let Mother sleep as long as she could. The night was bound to be an anxious one, he said, and it was best to let her gather her strength. I was glad she woke up sooner than he planned. She had some very practical suggestions that I had not considered.

"You've already had one computer stolen, dear. Don't you think it would be prudent to hide your new one? And," she added, "I must make sure my jewelry is out of sight."

Hiding my computer would do no good unless I could hide the fact that I had one altogether. If these people ever did break into the house and saw a printer and heavy cables they would probably do some damage looking for a missing PC. It took me twenty minutes of huffing and puffing before I managed to unplug everything and tote it all to the hall closet. Horatio, bless his heart, climbed down in the tunnel for me. I wrapped the printer in a plastic bag with all the cables and handed it down to him. Mother passed down three shoeboxes of trinkets and some photograph albums. She would have hidden more, but Horatio called it quits.

"Perhaps if I might make a suggestion, Anna, my sweet?" he asked in his most diplomatic manner. "Tomorrow we can investigate the length and breadth of these subterranean passages at our leisure. I will locate a safe place for your valuables then."

"Very well," she agreed. "But don't you think we should have a cooler down there with some drinks and a bite to eat?"

"Way to go, Mother! I wonder what James Beard would have suggested for a underground picnic?"

Horatio sighed deeply before he responded. "I suppose making light of things does ease the tension somewhat. But do try to keep it to a bare minimum, Paisley, if you please."

With both of us now at his disposal, Horatio was able to map out a plan to keep the areas he considered important under surveillance.

"I don't think we need worry about the front of the house—the entrance is protected by solid oak doors and the wrought iron grill-work. All the windows facing the street are protected by wooden shutters, which I have closed and locked. Also, these villains want to do their dirty work unseen, and there is always the chance they could be spotted from the road."

"What about the orchard, Horatio? Couldn't they park some-where by the side of the road and sneak up through the trees?"

That had happened once before, as I remembered very well.

"I know what you're thinking, Paisley, but we are not dealing with amateurs. If these men do indeed have a military background, they will act with stealth. No commando worth his salt would double park his vehicle on a main road. No," he said shaking his head. "I suspect they will either walk across the fields from the highway on the other side of the farm, or drive out on the landing strip of the county airport and hide their vehicle in the woods. Either way, they will have to come up from behind the house," he concluded. "And that's where we will be watching."

He turned and scrutinized us with the protected bulb from his flashlight. Mother's face looked pale and worried in the reddish glare. I was sure I looked equally bad, but Horatio nodded with approval.

"You're both wearing dark clothes. That's perfect. Anna, dear, please take off your earrings and necklace. They are lovely," he added tactfully, "but much too shiny."

Horatio placed us strategically in the back of the house. Mother's post was in the kitchen, Horatio would stay in the library where he could keep an eye on the carriage house, the lane, and just in case, the orchard. I was to maintain a roving surveillance from the bedroom windows in the newest wing of the house. Horatio knew I had a hard time staying awake late at night. I'm sure he thought if I had to walk back and forth between all four bedrooms and the adjoining hall, I would be more alert.

"I thought you were going to sleep until midnight, Horatio?" I teased.

"Would you rather I did, Paisley?" he asked seriously.

"Nope!"

He grinned and looked thirty years younger. He was having a fine old time. I knew he wouldn't miss this for the world.

We kept up our fruitless watch until dawn. I don't know whether Horatio was relieved or disappointed when he announced that we could relax our vigilance. I didn't wait to find out. I went to my room and tumbled into bed, heedless of the fact that Aggie had once again been sleeping on my pillow. I smiled when I felt the warm place her little doggie body had made and fell fast asleep.

I wasn't so happy when she woke me up a mere three hours later with her barking.

"What the hell, you crazy little dog?" I mumbled sleepily. I jumped up when I remembered our fears of the night before and ran to the French doors in the library. Andy Joiner was coming up the driveway in his police cruiser.

I pulled on my jeans and sweatshirt and splashed some cold water on my face. I hadn't discussed my concerns about Andy or Bert to Horatio as yet, and I wanted to be in on whatever conversation they had.

Mother had just opened the kitchen door to let our Chief of Police inside when I burst into the kitchen. Mother and Horatio turned and stared at me, but Andy was standing open-mouthed at the sight of Horatio and Mother dressed in house robes having breakfast together.

Horatio Raleigh had been a dear friend of my father's, but he had never hidden the fact that it was my mother he had adored since they were in grammar school over sixty years ago. For the first few years of my parent's marriage, Horatio had lived in Europe. But as time passed and emotions mellowed he returned to Rowan Springs and forgave my father for stealing away the love of his life. The three became great friends, but even so, Horatio always maintained a respectful distance. When Dad died ten years ago, Horatio, after a decent period of mourning, took up his position as suitor once again. Many people in Rowan Springs expected them to marry. Andy Joiner was probably thinking he had the latest tidbit of gossip to tell his wife when Horatio spoke up and burst his bubble.

"My ladies had an accident yesterday," he explained. "I remained overnight in the guest suite in order to be of any possible assistance."

His firm smile and formal demeanor left no room for doubt or speculation. Andy's chance to do his wife one better in the area of tattling was quashed.

"Andy, would you care for some breakfast? I'm not as good a cook as either Mother or Horatio but I've had more sleep. Let me fix you something."

"Just some coffee, please. And thank you, Paisley," he smiled.

Andy sat down with Mother and Horatio at the kitchen table. In spite of his firm voice, Horatio looked tired and drawn. Mother didn't look much better, and I had a pretty good idea of the less-than-pretty picture I made.

Andy shucked off his leather jacket and let it fall over the back of his chair.

"I'm glad Mrs. Sterling has such a loyal friend, Mr. Raleigh. But don't you think you should have advised her to call me after the accident?"

"Unfortunately, neither she nor Paisley could identify the car that hit them. It was a hit and run, you know." Horatio held the young man's gaze and continued, "You knew about the accident before I told you. How did you find out?"

Andy dropped his eyes from Horatio's and pulled out his battered little notebook.

"A dry goods salesman traveling south on Highway 63 at approximately ten in the morning, saw a large truck lose control and hit a white Lincoln Continental from behind."

"I don't remember seeing another car," interjected Mother. "And why on earth didn't the gentleman stop to see if we needed aid?"

"Apparently he was not where he was supposed to be yesterday. He didn't wish to get involved for fear his boss would find out. He only called my office early this morning. Guilty conscience, he explained. He wanted to make a statement in case you had a problem with your insurance."

"A very helpful gentleman, indeed," said Horatio, thoughtfully. "And quite timely," he added.

Andy ignored Horatio and went on to say, "I didn't see your car when I drove up, Miz Sterling. Is it already at the repair shop? If it's not, I'd like to see it. You never know what kind of evidence we might find—paint samples, things like that."

"I'm afraid you're too late, young man," said Horatio. "A friend of mine from Nashville came and fetched the car yesterday. He promised it would be ready this afternoon; therefore, I must assume the repairs have already been made. I'm sorry if we've inadvertently destroyed any evidence."

Horatio's smile was deceptively innocent. Anyone who did not know him well would see a tired old man who had acted too quickly and without thinking. But Andy wasn't just anyone. I wasn't sure he was going to buy it.

"I hear you have quite a few friends, Mr. Raleigh. Some of them have very interesting backgrounds. Would this gentleman in Nashville be one of them?" Andy asked pointedly.

Horatio's eyes narrowed. His smile turned dangerous. I jumped in to avoid a confrontation.

"More coffee, Andy?" I said, and went on to ask, "What have you heard from Bert Atkins?"

"Why, eh, nothing," he answered, turning a bright embarrassed red from his Adam's apple to his ears. "I, eh, better be getting back to town."

He pushed back his chair and stood up. His leather uniform jacket slid off and landed with a thump on the kitchen floor. I leaned down to pick it up, but Andy grabbed it first. We almost bumped heads. I laughed. He smiled and turned even redder.

"Thanks for the coffee, Paisley. See you all later," he said as he wheeled toward the back door.

I let him out and watched as he walked to his car. I waited until he drove down the driveway before I turned back to Mother and Horatio.

"How very odd," remarked that wise old soul.

"I couldn't agree with you more, Horatio," I nodded.

"What? Did I miss something?" asked Mother in a tired and dispirited voice. "I tried to pay attention. But my mind kept drifting. What happened, Paisley, dear?"

"Never mind what happened, Anna. What did you pick out of his pocket?" asked Horatio.

"Paisley, you didn't!"

"I'm afraid I did, Mother," I laughed. "I wondered if you would notice, Horatio," I said as I sat down at the table. "Do you think Andy saw me?"

"Absolutely not. If he did he would have said something. He was flustered, but not about that. It's quite obvious that he's hiding something."

"I couldn't agree more. And I think it has to do with my old friend Bert."

E. JOAN SIMS

"Right you are, my dear!" Horatio exclaimed. "Now share your find with us. And by the way, you did that with the finesse of an expert."

"Thank you," I chuckled as he bowed from the waist.

"What is going on?" asked Mother crossly. "If you've stolen something from Andy Joiner, you must call him and return it this instant. I simply cannot have this kind of behavior in my house."

"Relax, my dear," said Horatio. "I've no doubt our Paisley will return young Joiner's notebook, as soon as we've examined it, that is. Right, Paisley?"

"How did you know what it was?" I laughed.

"I watched him put it in his coat pocket. When the coat fell you simply took advantage of gravity and purloined . . . "

"Paisley, I cannot believe you did such a thing!"

"Mother, hold on just a moment. Let's see what Andy writes down in these little notebooks. Ever since I've known him he has one stuck in some pocket or other."

I leafed quickly through the pages looking for a specific notation.

"Well, that is interesting," I observed. "There's not a single note about our accident. All that crap about a traveling salesmen came right off the top of his head!"

"Well, I'll be damned!" exclaimed Horatio. "I have to hand it to the young man. I didn't think he was that fine a prevaricator."

"This is too much for me," sighed Mother. "I'm going to bed. Call me if you need me."

She got up and left the kitchen without even a word from Horatio. His eyes were dancing with excitement.

"Do you mind sitting next to me, my dear? I have a most intense desire to view the notebook for myself."

I scooted my chair around the table and turned on the lamp. For good measure, I grabbed Mother's magnifying glass from the kitchen drawer and handed it to Horatio. The two of us sat there

131

looking for all the world like Holmes and Watson as we leafed through Andy's notebook.

The first few pages had notes on what appeared to be a shoplifting incident at the Quickie Mart a month ago. Next, there was a page with tag numbers and the notation, "stolen cars," then two pages of complaints from the local citizenry about the need for a speed bump near the high school. Traffic citations and court dates filled a good part of the first half of the notebook. The back pages had several grocery items, all scratched through except for anchovy paste. We almost missed a page in the blank middle of the book with the initials, "B. A." and directions to "m. camp," and a phone number.

"What do you think, Horatio?"

"Of course, 'B. A.' could mean anything, but my best guess is, Bert Atkins. 'M. camp' is most likely a person, since there is a phone number. And I would think that the directions are to that someone's house. Perhaps that's where Bert has gone. If so, Joiner knows where he is, and why he's there. And if that is the correct conclusion, then they're both in on whatever, as the young people say nowadays, 'is going down'."

Horatio stood and stretched. He seemed frail and tired in the morning light. I wondered if he had slept at all, but I decided against suggesting that he get some rest. He knew his limits better than I.

"Do you have a map?" he asked. "A state map won't have enough detail. A map of Rowan Springs, and maybe the surrounding counties, will do nicely.

I spent the next half hour looking for the stupid map. When I finally found it, and returned to the kitchen, Horatio was speaking quietly into the telephone. When he hung up he looked at me intently.

"This line is now compromised, my dear."

"In English, if you please, Horatio."

"Your telephone is bugged."

CHAPTER TWENTY-TWO

"Now I'm really mad! Trying to kill me is one thing, but invading my privacy is quite . . . !"

"Relax, Paisley, dear. The line is under scrutiny by my own operative. If you receive anymore threatening calls, Hollis will be able to record and trace them immediately. By finding the map coordinates, we can better locate the relative source of your mysterious attacker."

"I thought we knew already? Fort Morgan is . . . "

"Not necessarily," he said with a wink.

Horatio took the map and unfolded it on the kitchen table. With the magnifying glass in hand, he examined the map intently for a full two minutes before he spoke again.

"I never realized before how much virgin forest there is in Lakeland County."

He pushed the map toward me and used the tip of his Mont Blanc pen to point out the area he was talking about.

"Here is the edge of the state park. The marina and the resort are over here. And all this is uncharted woods."

He unfolded the map once again to show more of it. "I remember at one time," he continued, "the federal government had an option to buy all of the area that backs up on the park. I cannot for the life of me remember what ultimately happened. Perhaps a phone call to the right person . . . " he mused.

"Why are you so interested in an area way out there on the other side of the county?" I asked. "Morgantown and Fort Morgan are in the opposite direction."

"Because, my dear Paisley, if we were to follow the directions in Chief Joiner's battered little notebook, we would discover that our Mr. or Ms. Camp lives just about here."

He took his pen and made an "X" on the map. I pulled it closer to me so I could see. Horatio's mark was almost in the middle of the county. It was in a heavily wooded area about ten miles from the edge of the state park. It was also just northeast of the spot where Sandlick Road came to an abrupt end on the shores of Jackson Lake.

"Oh, damn, Horatio! It's just a hop, skip and a jump from Bert's cabin."

He looked at me sadly. "I know my dear. I am sorry, but it would appear that your friend may quite possibly be in this thing up to his ears."

"Yeah," I answered despondently. "Whatever 'this thing' is."

About an hour after lunch, an unmarked van with tinted windows pulled up behind the carriage house. Four young men dressed in dark blue overalls got out and worked swiftly for the rest of the daylight hours. It was hard to tell exactly what they were doing. They worked like beavers, rarely speaking to each other, and not taking a break of any kind. When they were finished, one of them came and spoke briefly to Horatio, then they all piled back in the van and left.

Horatio took the little black plastic box they left with him and called us in to see his new toy.

"If you tell me that cute little thing is a computer, Horatio, dear, I'll be truly impressed with your old fogey brigands."

"Brigade, Anna, my sweet, brigade—if you must used Paisley's terminology."

"Is it a computer?" I asked impatiently as I examined the plastic case. It measured a mere ten inches across and weighed less than a pound. "If it is, then I'm with Mother on this one."

Horatio smiled like the proud father of a gifted child. "I mustn't mislead you. It cannot perform all of the functions of a computer but in certain areas it is quite astonishing. Watch!"

He opened the case and placed it on the kitchen table. A small screen in the top half, and a keyboard in the bottom made it resemble a smaller version of my laptop. Horatio pushed a button on the side and a grid flashed up on the screen. Horatio typed in a command and a bright green outline of our house and the outbuildings appeared.

"Paisley, open the door and let Aggie outside, if you please," he said.

Mother and I looked at him in amazement. It was hard to believe that Horatio had been around us so much and was still ignorant of our haughty little dog's personality. I decided a picture might well be worth a thousand words and put my finger to my lips when Mother started to explain.

As usual, Aggie was asleep on my pillow and ignored me when I called her. When I picked up her ball and threw it, she raised her head and stared at me. Obviously annoyed, she turned around and scratched a bit to fluff up the expensive down, then lay back down facing the other way. I knew better than to try and pick her up. I had the scars to prove it. I returned to the kitchen empty-handed.

"Sorry, Horatio," I told him. "Aggie, ah . . . she was asleep."

"Hummpf," he grunted as he headed for my bedroom. He remembered his manners and turned around. "With your permission, my dear?" he asked.

"Be my guest," I grinned.

My grin disappeared as Horatio came back immediately with Aggie prancing smartly in front of him. Horatio opened the back door and stood to one side.

"Out you go, my girl," he directed. "And don't stray far."

Aggie barked as if to say, "Aye, aye, Sir!" and ran outside. Horatio hurried back to the table and looked expectantly at his new toy.

"Ah, ha!"

We hovered next to him and stared as the little green blip that was Aggie moved around the screen. She ran to her favorite corner and accomplished her task, then the green dot headed back for the house. Suddenly, another green dot appeared and Aggie took off after it. I could hear her barking at the cat as they both ran by the kitchen window.

"Wow! Horatio, I don't know whether I'm more impressed by this gizmo, or the way you handled our resident beast."

I sat down and studied the screen carefully. Mother asked the question I was considering.

"Why does it stop at the back fence? That's only two hundred feet away. I would imagine we could use more advanced warning if anyone is coming from the direction of the field." She shuddered and rubbed her upper arms briskly. Her face looked worried in the waning light of late afternoon.

Horatio was filling the coffee maker with fresh water. He finished what he was doing before he answered.

"Unfortunately, my friend has only a limited supply of the material required for our surveillance. I won't go into details that you may or may not understand, but as you might imagine, these things are not sold on the open market. And not just anyone can purchase them. Doing so can send up too many little red flags, so to speak."

I gave him a sly smile.

"So!" I said. "Your friend is a clandestine operative who doesn't want his cover blown."

Horatio looked at me very calmly and answered. "None of us are eager to have our cover blown. Are we, Paisley, dear?"

I let Horatio have the last word since I couldn't think of a clever enough retort. I put on my denim barn jacket and went to fetch Aggie.

The afternoon was blustery and grey. A pale, exhausted sun was rapidly seeking a resting place behind the wooded hills in the distance, its feeble attempts to warm the winter day at an end. The temperature dropped noticeably as the last light vanished behind the distant cedars.

I heard a "click" and then a "hum" as the green light from the mercury lamp on the carriage house blinked on. For a moment I was startled, forgetting that Horatio had said that since the light turned on automatically at dusk it would appear odd if it didn't come on every night.

Aggie always refused to come if I called her, but I knew she would find me if I stayed outside long enough. The chill wind found every little gap between my jacket and me. I shivered and decided some exercise might help to keep me warm while I waited for the dog.

The ground was cold and hard and my toes grew numb as I walked, but I was restless, and it felt good to stretch the muscles of my legs. The path took me down through the orchard and back to the lane. I smiled as I imagined myself on Horatio's screen: a large green dot advancing slowly toward the carriage house and the edge of the perimeter. My smile vanished as I remembered that beyond the screen's limits we were blind and unprotected. I stopped and squinted through the dark at the jagged outline of trees and bushes at the edge of the field. I saw nothing moving, but there could be a silent army of men waiting and watching unseen in the tall grass.

Aggie appeared out of nowhere to nip at my heels as I ran back to the house.

"Stupid dog! You want me to break my neck?"

The last turn she took between my ankles tripped me up. I fell hard and flat right at the edge of the patio. I lay there for a full minute trying to catch my breath. Something small and shiny fluttered across the concrete and caught my eye. I reached out and picked it up. It was a band from a cigar, the kind of cigar Bert Atkins liked to smoke. I slipped it over my ring finger and stared at the gold and red paper circle while I tried to decide if I should show it to Horatio.

Aggie came back and stuck her cold little black nose in my ear. It was her favorite way of waking me up in the morning.

"I'm not asleep, dumb dog. And thanks to you, I've stumbled across something I must keep from an old friend who is trying his best to save my sorry hide."

I had made my decision.

CHAPTER TWENTY-THREE

After a light supper of soup and sandwiches we had a heated discussion about what to do next. Mother wanted to call Andy Joiner back so I could confess all and return his notebook. Horatio and I voted her down. Horatio wanted all of us to stay awake once again and play spy. Mother and I wearily voted against it on the grounds that what seemed like fun and games for him was exhausting for us. I wanted to go to bed and get a good night's sleep and wake up for a breakfast of ham and eggs before I made anymore decisions. Mother and Horatio were afraid we wouldn't wake up at all if no one kept watch. They voted me down. I protested.

"What's the use of your handy dandy little spy spotter if we can't feel reasonably secure? I mean—that's a lot of trouble for your friend's grandsons to go to if we can't really count on their surveillance system."

"Paisley does have a point, Horatio, dear. And it is so delightfully James Bondish."

"Very well," he conceded. "I suppose one of us could keep watch at a time. But the others must sleep close by. As you so astutely surmised, Anna dear, two hundred feet is not so far away. We won't have much time when the enemy approaches."

"Lovely! I'll make up the chaise in my dressing room for you,

Horatio. Paisley and I can take turns sleeping in my bed, and we'll all be within whispering distance of one another in case of an emergency. I had a nice long nap this afternoon so I'll keep the first watch. That way I can get up early in the morning and fix Paisley's ham and eggs."

I grinned and Horatio grumped, but we all agreed. I decided not to say aloud what I was thinking: Mother would make a terrific general.

As tired as I thought I was, I could not sleep. I tossed and turned and listened to Horatio's muffled snores through the bedroom door until I could stand it no longer.

Mother was in the kitchen perched on the edge of her seat with her eyes dutifully fixed on the little screen. I pulled up a chair next to her and poured myself a cup of coffee from the carafe.

"Mmmm, is this one of your special concoctions, or something from Celestine's?"

"It's from the coffee shop. Truffle cinnamon praline, I think she calls it," sighed Mother rubbing her eyes. "I'm not sure there's much caffeine in it. If there is," she yawned, "I'm immune."

"Go to bed, Mother. I'll take over. I'm wide awake."

"But it's not your turn," she protested. "Besides, I cannot possibly let Horatio down. He's depending on me to do my bit."

I smiled in the dark, secure in the knowledge that she wouldn't see me and think I was making fun of her.

"Your bit, as you call it, is to get up tomorrow morning and make me a full-scale, no-holds-barred, fat-gram-laden breakfast. I want as many calories and as much cholesterol as one china plate can hold. No more bran muffins and yogurt for this little secret agent. Now, go on!"

"Very well," she agreed. "But let's keep it to ourselves, about my quitting early, I mean. I don't want Horatio to think I'm a," she paused to think of the word, "a wuss."

After another cup of coffee, I was wide awake and raring to go. I actually found myself wishing for something to happen. Long ago I had learned that forced inactivity is more stressful than anything—and not knowing when something expected is going to occur is the most stressful thing of all.

Aggie wandered morosely around the house. She was unsettled by the break in her routine. I could almost hear her thinking what was the fun of sleeping on someone else's pillow if that someone no longer cares? She finally settled down under the table with her head resting on my feet. Her woeful little doggie sigh made me smile.

By the time Horatio came to relieve me, the level of truffle fantastico had fallen to the bottom of the coffee carafe and I was wired for sound.

"There's no way I'll ever sleep, Horatio. Want me to keep you company? I'll make more coffee."

He lowered his voice and whispered, "Just, please, I beg of you, none of that sissy coffee. Good old fashioned Kenya mountain roast is fine with me."

Whatever happened to Maxwell House, I wondered with a smile.

The smell of fresh coffee filled the darkened kitchen. The only sound to be heard was the occasional burp of the machine as it perked away. Horatio and I sat companionably side by side and kept our vigil. After an hour or two, my back began to hurt and my eyes started to itch. I wondered how many more nights we were going to have to repeat this little performance. I asked Horatio.

"The very thing I was considering, my dear. It would seem that all our efforts are for naught. Perhaps we are expending our energy in defense when we should go on the offense."

"Offense? Where? Against whom? With what?" I sputtered.

"Whoa, hold on. One question at a time, please," he laughed.

"Okay, first question. Do we even know what it is we are up against?"

"Yes, and no," he answered vaguely.

I grumbled and filled our cups with more coffee. My stomach was beginning to feel the sour effects of so much caffeine. I got up and opened the refrigerator in search of a munchie. While fumbling around inside the darkened interior, I heard a "splat" and felt something cold and wet on the top of my foot.

"Rats!"

I cleaned the broken egg mess from the floor and tried to put the grumbling of my stomach out of my mind. My irritation focused on Horatio and his enigmatic answer to my perfectly legitimate question.

"I've given this thing some thought, I'll have you know," I complained. "I'm not some silly, empty-headed woman. Some people consider me to be quite bright."

"Relax, Paisley, my love. And do us both a favor. Cut back on the coffee."

He stiffened suddenly and we both gave our full attention to the screen as a small green blip traversed from one corner of the yard to the other. Aggie raised her head and growled sleepily.

"The cat came back," he grinned.

"I wish something would happen," I blurted impatiently. "I hate all this waiting."

Horatio patted me on the shoulder and exhaled deeply.

"You have no idea, my dear, how lucky we have been. I am actually beginning to think we are out of the woods, in a manner of speaking. Though," he added carefully, "it is still much too soon to be sure we are really safe."

I started sputtering again. "Safe? Safe from what? I just don't get it. What is going on? Do you have any idea, or are you keeping something from me?"

"Please, my child, the thought of keeping something hidden from one another should never cross any of our minds!"

The little cigar band I found on the patio earlier was burning a hole in my jeans pocket, but I forced a smile.

"I'm sorry, Horatio. I didn't mean to . . . "

"Insinuate that I would try to protect you just because you're a member of the fair sex?" he asked.

I didn't answer as I watched the first rays of the sun peek tentatively over the horizon.

"I wonder if the sun is ever hesitant to start a new day knowing that some people will die before it sets?" I asked in a gloomy voice.

Horatio stood and stretched with some difficulty after so many hours bent over the small screen. I heard an ancient joint or two pop, but he managed to straighten to his slender height and square his elegant shoulders.

"Too much coffee, and too much imagination," he remarked. "A bad combination, my dear. Best to seek your warm bed and try to sleep it off."

He held up a hand as I protested. "I promise we'll have a war council when you awaken. I'll give you the questionable benefit of my meager thoughts on the matter then."

Arguing was useless, of that I was certain. In all my years, I had never won an argument with Horatio. Aggie and I went off to bed without even trying to change his mind.

In spite of all of the coffee in my system, I slept deeply for six hours. I awoke feeling refreshed and happy. I was me, Paisley, once again.

Mother had my breakfast waiting. She never said one word about middle-aged women having heart attacks from eating too many eggs, or stroke victims arriving at the emergency room with bacon bits between their teeth. I enjoyed myself thoroughly until the last mouthful when she remarked, "Celestine called from the coffee shop. She just got in a new shipment and wants to know if we want more truffle cinnamon praline, or perhaps try her new chocolate hazelnut caramel surprise."

I started to tell her that I preferred something a little less exotic, but my mouth was still full. It was at that moment that my darling and beloved mother took the opportunity to zoom in for the kill.

"Poor thing, she'd been crying all morning. Tommy's great-grandmother died last night. She had catfish and hush puppies for dinner. They're positive all that fat clogged her arteries and killed her."

"Don't be ridiculous, Mother," I sputtered.

She gave a large heartfelt sigh and picked up my empty plate. She stared at the yellow smear of egg yolk and wrinkled her nose at the greasy residue.

"Just the same, dear, I do wish you would be more prudent in your diet. We can all live longer if . . . "

"For goodness sake!" I burst in, "Tommy's great-grandmother had to have been ninety-eight if she was a day! Probably ate fried catfish and hush puppies three times a week all of her life."

"And she could have lived another twenty years if she had made wiser choices," observed Mother with a knowing smile.

"I give up!" I said, throwing up my arms. "Thanks for the breakfast, Mother. And remember, you're an accessory after the fact. If I die of a fat embolism, I'll come back to haunt you with nightmares of butter and cheesecake."

"Fat melts faster in heat, Paisley," she said with a sly little smile. "You may not make it back up from down below with the butter."

CHAPTER TWENTY-FOUR

Horatio shepherded us into the library after his breakfast of yogurt with honey, dry toast, and a banana. Mother smiled approvingly as she took her seat on one of the sofas next to him. I plopped carelessly down on the other one, sulking like the black sheep she perceived me to be. It was amazing how Mother had the power to send me back to childhood in disgrace with a mere sentence or two.

"So, Horatio, now that you've had the soothing benefit of a few hours sleep and the more than adequate nourishment of a simple breakfast, tell us what we are to do next.

And remember," she admonished, wagging her finger, "I still vote to call Andy Joiner and return his notebook."

Horatio looked at me helplessly as he cleared his throat. I knew he hated to refuse his beloved Anna anything, but I didn't mind at all. I was still mad at her. I decided to get him off the hook.

"Forget it, Mother," I snorted. "Horatio knows as well as I do that Andy Joiner and Bert Atkins are somehow involved in whatever is going on. Until we're sure they're wearing white hats instead of black ones we can't call either of them. Even if we knew where Bert was," I added.

"White hats, black hats?" she asked with a perplexed frown on her face.

"Old westerns," Horatio and I laughed together.

"By the way, Horatio," I demanded, "you promised to tell us what is going on here. Spill it now, if you please."

"I very distinctly remember that I told you I would give you the benefit of my 'meager thoughts'. I'm afraid we'll need to do some more surveillance before I can come to any real conclusions."

"Oh, dear, not another sleepless night!" groaned Mother in alarm.

"Not you, Anna, my sweet. I propose that we spirit you out of town to a motel somewhere away from Rowan Springs. Or perhaps," he mused, "to one of the resort hotels near the lake. Yes! That's quite the most perfect idea. That way Paisley and I will have a base of operations nearby."

"Nearby what?" I asked suspiciously. "Where are you and I going to be?"

"*Au bois, mon cherie,*" he sang out. "To the woods!"

While Horatio outlined his audacious plan, Mother and I watched him with open mouths. I felt like some prankish little boy's mother listening to her son propose a trip to the pond to find a frog for his teacher's desk drawer. Only this little boy wanted our whole-hearted approval.

"I simply cannot believe it, Horatio. You are usually the most level-headed of men!"

"I gotta agree with Mother. This is really a pretty hare-brained idea."

Horatio managed to look offended and perplexed at the same time.

"My goodness," he said smiling sheepishly. "I somehow expected a warmer reception to my proposal. Especially from you, Paisley. 'Once more into the fray . . .' and all that, I mean."

"The 'fray' wasn't so much fun last time I looked. I almost got myself killed, just in case you forgot. Looking before you leap is highly underrated as an outdoor sport. Maybe we'd better try to think of . . . "

"What other way is there, my dear?" interrupted Horatio. He stood in front of the fire—warming his hands before the flames. "We cannot go to the authorities. We both agree on that point. You know I'm a very cautious man as a rule, but this calls for taking some small risk."

"You call hiking ten miles into the woods in the dead of winter to sneak up on a stranger's house a small risk?"

"Yes, Horatio, my dear, you're acting quite like a vigilante. There must be someone in authority we can turn to," insisted Mother.

"You tell me who, Mother. Horatio is right about that. The local cops, even Danny Hall, are off limits. And I've already thought about going back to the army base but I'm not sure who I could trust there." I made a sour face as I added, "Ta'Ronda is definitely out."

Horatio sat down in the leather wing chair by the fireplace and took some time to light his pipe. The fragrant smoke rose slowly to the ceiling as we all sat in thoughtful silence. Finally Horatio cleared his throat and spoke.

"I don't mean to alarm either of you, but I must tell you some of my friends have given me to believe that Paisley may have stumbled into something of a very distressing nature."

He paused for a moment and watched us both carefully. When neither of us flinched, he smiled and continued. "If we do nothing, there is a fair chance we will be left alone to pursue our lives as we always have, in peace and contentment. I have come to this conclusion because no one has approached us for the last few days."

I did my best to keep my feelings from showing. I was torn with the question of whether or not to tell Horatio about the cigar band I had found on the patio. It had to have been dropped there before the electronic surveillance system was put in place three days ago. Bert Atkins had been here. I was sure of it.

"However," he went on in a very somber tone of voice, "there is the distinct possibility that at some time in the future, when we least expect it, something quite dreadful could happen to either of you.

And that, my dear ones, is something an old man like me can hardly allow himself to contemplate."

He cleared his throat again and wiped a suspicious glint from his eye, then squared his shoulders and spoke in a firmer voice. "No. We must take care of business ourselves. We have no one else to count on except my old friends, the fogeys, as Paisley calls them. Their knowledge and experience is something we may come to appreciate above all else in the next few days."

He regarded us as we sat still and quiet. Mother's face was hidden in shadow, and I wished that mine was. I was still fighting with my conscience. Ultimately, Mother was the one to speak.

"I, for one, do not wish to have to look over my shoulder for rest of my life. Freedom is very important to me. I cannot have my freedom if I have to live in fear. I'm with you Horatio. I'll do whatever you ask."

She stood up and went to his side to hold his hands in hers. It was one of the very few gestures of intimacy I had ever seen her make toward him.

"I think we could all use something to drink," she said, smiling at me. "Paisley's had enough coffee to last her a lifetime, so I think I'll make us some hot apple cider."

"That sounds lovely, my dear. And thank you for your vote of confidence. Perhaps while you're in the kitchen I'll be able to persuade Paisley to jump on our little bandwagon."

By three o'clock that afternoon we were the new and temporary residents of one of Jackson Lake Resorts luxury cabins. Horatio had studied the brochure carefully before he chose our spot. It sat high on the hillside overlooking the lake. There were no other cabins close by, so we also had a private dock. Each of us had a bedroom with a bath and a private balcony on the second floor. The downstairs was one large open area with a terrific kitchen and large living area with big comfortable sofas and armchairs scattered in front of a huge stone fireplace.

The view was fantastic. It was the kind of place that convinces vacationing people of means that they must own a cabin on the lake. Business cards of real estate companies were discretely tucked around the kitchen, ready to take advantage of in case anyone might fall under the spell of the lush beauty of the natural surroundings.

Horatio chose the only bedroom that faced away from the lake and toward the road. Mother and I decided to occupy the largest bedroom and leave the other one vacant so that Horatio could set up his telescope out on a balcony with a lakeside view. Aggie would sleep with Mother and me. She seemed a little disconcerted until she saw me unpack the down pillow and place it on one of the double beds. After her little ritual of turning and scratching, she settled down for her usual nap.

Mother and I set up housekeeping in the kitchen. Since this was a "luxury" cabin, it was even furnished with an espresso machine and a food processor. With a happy smile on her face, Mother put away the mountain of groceries we had purchased. I think she quite liked getting away for a while. We all felt a little safer now that we were in an anonymous place. Even Horatio was whistling a happy tune until he fell head over heels down the steps and broke his ankle.

CHAPTER TWENTY-FIVE

The hotel doctor insisted that we take Horatio to his office in town for an x-ray. Horatio fumed and fussed, but after an hour of arguing back and forth I could tell the pain had an upper hand. Horatio's face had taken on an unhealthy pallor.

I sat down beside him and handed him a damp washcloth so he could wipe the perspiration from his forehead. Mother and the doctor were in the kitchen quietly talking over treatment options. I was fairly certain they couldn't hear us.

"Horatio, you must go for an x-ray. You're looking a little ragged around the gills. Please do what the doctor advises, if not for your sake then for Mother's."

"Paisley," he whispered in a tight voice, "if this thing really is broken, they will put me in a cast and I'll be *hors de combat* for weeks. Instead of being a functioning soldier I'll be a silly old man who lost his balance carrying your mother's make-up case up a flight of stairs and fell on his bum. What will my friends think?"

"You mean the ones in the nursing home, or the one in the wheelchair who's paralyzed from the waist down?"

He smiled ruefully then grimaced in pain.

"Point well taken, my dear," he sighed. "Very well, I'll go like a lamb to the slaughter. But you must promise me one thing!"

"Whatever it is, I promise," I assured him.

"Don't let them put me under anesthesia, and don't let them keep me in the hospital. Even if I'm in a cast, I can still protect you and Anna."

The doctor and I were able to help Horatio hobble out to the hotel van. The ride into the little town of Jackson Lake took about three minutes. The x-ray took ten. Horatio was lucky. Only one small bone in his foot was broken. The swelling and bruising were in response to a severely twisted ankle. Nonetheless, he would have to be in a cast for at least three weeks. The doctor also recommended bed rest for a couple of days until the swelling went down.

Horatio put up quite a fuss about the bed rest, but I could tell he was vastly relieved that he wasn't injured more seriously. After the cast was applied, he grudgingly accepted a small amount of pain medication and listened carefully to the doctor's instructions. I agreed to fill a prescription for some mild pain killers and a sleeping pill, and the doctor lent Horatio a pair of adjustable crutches. When Horatio was ready, the nurse took us back to our cabin in the van.

After we settled our patient on one of the sofas, I worked on a fire while Mother fixed our dinner. By the time our meal was ready, Horatio had dozed off. He was resting so peacefully we decided not to awaken him. Mother and I sat at the breakfast bar and ate by the firelight as we watched the moon come up over the lake.

"How beautiful," sighed Mother. "You forget how really lovely the moon is until you see it reflected in the water."

"It's a full moon," I observed absently. "That should make things easier."

"Paisley! Don't you get any crazy ideas about going off on your own tonight. I simply won't allow it!"

"Shhh, you might wake up Horatio," I cautioned as I looked warily in his direction.

"I will wake him up if I need his help in preventing you from doing something foolish."

"All right," I lied, "I won't go anywhere. I'll stay right here, I promise."

I got up and poked restlessly at the glowing embers.

"Do you want some ice cream for dessert, dear?"

"No thanks. I'll bring in another log and then get a blanket for Horatio. Let him sleep downstairs tonight."

I stretched theatrically. "I think I'll turn in early," I offered, faking a yawn. "It's been an exhausting day."

I turned to look at Mother. She looked as tired as I was pretending to be. I continued with my charade. "If you don't mind, I think I'll move my things back to the other front bedroom since Horatio won't be needing it for an observation point tonight. Maybe we'll both sleep better that way."

She sighed and looked at me suspiciously. "I truly hope you're not planning to take advantage of the situation, dear."

"Mother, relax. You need to save your worrying for Horatio. He's going to drive you up a tree for the next few days. After he quits complaining about being a burden, he's going to start asking for things. 'Anna, my sweet, I really hate to be a bother,'" I mimicked, "'but as long as you're fetching my pipe and slippers, could you please bring me just the tiniest bit of that chateaubriand with béarnaise sauce? Oh, and perhaps, if you don't mind, some of that divine pear clafoutis for dessert.'"

Mother smiled gently in her old friend's direction.

"Of course, you're right," she admitted. "He will be hard to contain. And I am tired, I must admit. After all, you are right, it has been quite a day."

She patted me on the shoulder and kissed my cheek. "Good night, dear. Do you mind turning off the lights and seeing to the kitchen?"

"Not a bit," I assured her with a hug.

I smiled as she checked on Horatio and gently tucked the blanket under his chin. She climbed the stairs slowly. By the sound of her footsteps I could tell she paused at the top to watch me for a moment.

When she was sure I wasn't going to make a run for it, she went into her bedroom and closed the door. That's when I got up and crossed quickly to the balcony. My hand was on the knob of the door when I heard Horatio's voice.

"Going somewhere?"

I spun around and glared angrily at our patient.

"Drat! Do you make some kind of habit out of sneaking up on people?"

Horatio gestured at his cast. "As you can see, my child, I'm hardly able to sneak up on anyone."

"Yeah, but you were supposed to sleep through the night."

He smiled slyly and produced a pink and blue pill from his smoking jacket pocket.

"I probably would have if I had not tucked this little gem inside my cheek instead of swallowing it as you intended, my dear."

I sat on the coffee table in front of him.

"Not me, Horatio. The doctor intended for you to sleep well tonight. You must be in pain."

He pulled himself up to a sitting position against the arm of the big sofa. He tried to hide it, but I saw him wince when he moved his leg.

"Not so much pain as you might expect," he lied.

We were both getting to be too good at this prevarication thing. I decided to put an end to it.

"Okay. I'm sneaking out tonight and you know it. You can't go with me, and you can't stop me, so let's not even start that pointless argument."

He raised his elegant eyebrows and looked at me sternly. I had bordered on disrespect, but he was accepting my position.

"So," I continued, "you might as well tell me what to do, and how to do it. Knowledge is the best protection you can offer me. You're the clandestine spy expert. Make me a Mata Hari for the night."

"I wish it were as simple as that, Paisley. I would gladly transform you instantly into James Bond if I could. But even that excellent gentleman, who was modeled after one of my friends by the way, might not be able to save himself from those I suspect to be our enemies."

Horatio's skin had taken on a greyish hue even in the ruddy light of the fire. His chin sagged and his eyelids drooped. He looked older than I had ever seen him. I felt instantly contrite.

"What in the hell am I thinking about?" I slapped myself hard on a blue denimed knee. "I should be worrying about you and your injured ankle, not planning some stupid midnight prowl. I am so sorry, Horatio. Forgive me? And don't tell Mother," I hastened to add. "Can I get you something? Soup maybe? There's some left over from our supper."

Horatio sagged back against the sofa pillow and closed his eyes for a moment.

"A large brandy," he announced. "A large brandy and some chicken noodle soup."

I swallowed back a sour burp. "Yuck! Are you really sure about that?"

"Absolutely! Also I require a large yellow legal pad and a sharp pencil," he added firmly.

CHAPTER TWENTY-SIX

I busied myself in the kitchen trying to warm up Horatio's soup without making any noise. I didn't want Mother to come bustling downstairs to see what was going on. According to what I had told her I should have been in bed at least a half-hour ago.

When everything Horatio had requested was ready, I loaded up a tray and carried it over to the coffee table. While he was eating, I brought in three more logs and poked at the fire until it was burning merrily. I sat on the hearth and warmed my backside until my jeans felt like they were on fire, then settled in a big chair and waited for Horatio to finish.

"Ahh," he sighed with contentment. "Chicken noodle soup from a can is still my favorite meal." He winked broadly at me and went on to say, "While we are swearing each other to secrecy, please promise you will never tell your lovely mother that. She would be forever injured. She thinks I love her bouillabaisse more than life itself."

"Cross my heart and hope to die," I laughed as I made the childish sign over my sweater.

Horatio's smile disappeared. He looked old and distressed once more.

"Please take your pill now," I urged. "What you have to say can wait until tomorrow."

He shook his head slowly and swallowed another mouthful of brandy.

"'Fraid not, my dear. I've been fretting since we had to go to that damn fool medicine man. I registered under an assumed name here at the hotel to preserve our privacy. I even paid cash in advance so there would be no reason to use a check or credit cards that could be traced. But the doctor's office was a different matter. Before I could warn her, your sweet, naïve mother unwittingly gave the nurse my real name and address. It will be a simple matter now to trace my whereabouts. And it won't take a genius to put two and two together and figure out you all are with me as well."

I stared at him in amazement. "You make it sound like we're up against the KGB or something!"

"This is not just an old man's paranoia speaking, Paisley. Have you ever heard of the Underground Special Forces?"

"Good grief, no!" I laughed. "It sounds like something out of a comic book."

"Well, it's definitely not. And you can be assured there's nothing comical about it. Several years ago the Pentagon discovered a covert paramilitary operation in North Carolina. This clandestine group existed for the express purpose of training civilian personnel to take over control of the federal government."

"The United States government? Come on! You're pulling my leg."

He smiled grimly. "I wish I were. But unfortunately I'm telling you the absolute truth. Several officers and scores of enlisted men were involved. The purpose of the exercise was to prepare men who could then fan out into the hinterlands and train others like themselves. When the time was right, these various individual paramilitary units would be in position to seize control of the local, state, then federal government in their area."

"And what time was that? When would it be right, I mean?"

"Who knows? I've read a great deal of hate literature from these rascals, but they never really say anything concrete. They talk in vitriolic circles about 'white supremacy' and hatred of other races. Some are violently opposed to immigration, and even to women having voting rights. Most have a great deal in common with fascist movements, past and present. They use arguments about fearing gun control to gain members and intimidation and veiled threats to keep them. I have to tell you frankly, my child, I am really very afraid of men like these. They are fanatics who believe in their God-given right to protect themselves from the rest of us with every means at their command. Their credo is: Take no prisoners and show no mercy. I believe you have stumbled upon another cell of such a group."

I felt my upper lip quiver just a bit as I asked hopefully, "Aren't you exaggerating just a smidgen?"

"Not a bit of it, my dear. Not a bit of it," he responded with grim force.

An unnatural coldness settled at the base of my spine. I shivered and got up to warm myself in front of the fire again. The light of the flames threw shadows on the wall. At home in the library, the shadows always seemed friendly and comforting. Here they appeared menacing and strangely sinister.

After pondering for a moment, I asked a question that had been in the back of my mind for weeks. It had hovered as a nameless foreboding, but now I knew what to call it and what to ask.

"Do you think Bert Atkins and Andy Joiner are mixed up in this covert operation somehow?"

Horatio looked at me sadly and shook his head. I could tell he hated to give me an answer.

"Let's pray they are not," he answered reluctantly.

I decided not to let him off the hook.

"But you think there's a pretty good chance they are, just as I do. Isn't that so?" I insisted.

"It would appear that way, my child," he finally agreed. "I know you have some feelings for Atkins. I'm sorry if they have been misplaced. You, of all people, deserve the attentions of a fine man."

"Ha! A fine man," I snorted. "Like there is such a thing! Anymore, I mean," I hastened to add.

"Never mind, my dear. I realize I'm a dinosaur. Young people nowadays have very little in the way of honor and heroism in their makeup. I think they believe it's something you only see in the cinema, and therefore you need not be a hero yourself. Too bad," he mused. "I loved Tom Mix, but I knew I had to stand tall in my own life."

I fixed us a fresh pot of coffee while Horatio busied himself with his yellow legal pad. By now, my frugal supper was a dim memory, so I heaped a plate with cookies and added that to the coffee tray.

Horatio studied me carefully while I poured our coffee and added cream and sugar. Finally, I became uncomfortable enough under his scrutiny to ask why.

"What's the matter? Do I have crumbs on my face? I only sneaked one cookie in the kitchen."

"No, dear, nothing like that. I was simply wondering how tough you are."

"Come on, now," I smiled as I tried to lighten the conversation. "You're beginning to scare me again. Anyway, just how tough do I have to be? All I plan to do is hike cross country a few miles and do a little peeking on a farm house until Mr. Camp decides to come outside and let me see what he looks like. If Andy or Bert is there, then so be it. Nobody will ever spot me, and if they do, so what? They'll hardly try to run me over with a tank! Don't worry."

"I have to worry. That's how I've stayed alive so long. And now I have to keep you and your Mother alive as well. Damn this cast! If only I could go with you as I planned. There are so many things I haven't told you that you need to know. These men are . . ."

"Really, really scary, I know."

"No, you don't, Paisley. You really haven't the faintest notion."

"Maybe it's better that I don't."

"You said it yourself," he counseled. "Knowledge is your best weapon. Listen to me for awhile, and let me arm you as best as I can."

CHAPTER TWENTY-SEVEN

In my uneasy sleep, I dreamed of flapping wings and pounding hoofs. I was left with the vague memory that I had spent the night riding with Alfred Noyes' highwayman when I awoke before dawn, my cotton gown wet with perspiration. Stumbling into the bathroom, I stood under the reviving spray of a hot shower until I felt the water wash away the half-remembered dread.

I dressed carefully in layers like Horatio had advised. Under my jeans I wore a pair of ankle-length silk long johns which I tucked into two pairs of socks, one thin and one thick and wooly. I slipped on two turtleneck shirts; again, the first was a silk undershirt and the second a cotton shirt I wore under a heavy woolen cable-knit sweater. I felt myself beginning to perspire again as I tied on my hiking boots. I opened the door to the balcony just a tad and felt instant relief from a rush of cold early morning air. A thin, waterproof anorak with lots of pockets and a hood completed my outfit.

I buckled on the fanny pack I had filled the night before under Horatio's direction, then pulled on my gloves and a stocking cap. On impulse, I grabbed my sunglasses and tucked a tube of lip balm and a packet of Kleenex into one of my pockets. I was as ready as I would ever be.

Before I closed the door, I stepped out on the balcony and surveyed the winter landscape below. The surface of the lake was black and shiny. The waves moved slowly and heavily towards the narrow shore like liquid mercury. The sun rose over the hills on the eastern horizon, but dark clouds soon obscured its pale winter light.

It's definitely a dark and stormy morning, I thought morosely, and briefly considered backing out. My previous air of bravado had disappeared some time between last night and that very moment. Horatio would forgive me, I was sure about that. And Mother was still oblivious of my intentions. I could shuck off all my outdoor paraphernalia and tuck myself back in my warm cozy bed, and no one would ever say a thing.

As I closed the balcony door, Aggie looked at me contemptuously through bushy eyebrows, then snuggled back in the comfort of my pillow. That settled it.

"Okay, you selfish little bitch," I told her. "You win. I'll go save the world. You stay here and keep your hairy little butt warm and dry."

Horatio had fallen asleep shortly after he helped me plan my trek. He was still snoring peacefully as I tiptoed awkwardly past him in my heavy-soled hiking boots. Mother's bedroom door was closed, and I had already bade farewell to the dog. I opened the front door and left without any more fanfare.

At first the frigid morning air was invigorating, but as I trudged along the road I felt it burn my throat and lungs just as Horatio warned me it would. I pulled my scarf over my mouth and let the wool warm the air as I breathed in and out. It made a big difference. I hoped the rest of his advice would come in just as handy.

The dark skies overhead made it seem like twilight instead of shortly after dawn. Even so, I was glad Horatio had convinced me to wait until daylight. It was a bit warmer and definitely less scary.

I had about eight miles to walk in this nasty weather. I wasn't an Olympic athlete, but I was in fair shape. My boots were old and comfortable, and I had on just the right clothing for these conditions.

If all things remained the same and I had no mishaps, I would arrive at my destination well before noon.

At first I watched my surroundings with interest. I could see the tracks of rabbit and deer and other small animals in the mud on the side of the dirt road. Each time I heard a noise in the woods I watched expectantly for an animal to break out of the dry brush and run across in front of me as the buck had on my first trip to Bert's cabin. But after an hour of walking with nothing happening, I grew tried of the same dead, leafless winter scenery and plodded on in bored apathy.

The road ended quite suddenly. I stopped short just before I tumbled over a row of small boulders placed to warn motorists. I sat down on one of the larger rocks and opened my fanny pack. From now on I was going to have to depend on Horatio's instructions. I dug around inside and found the compass he had given me. Once I located the direction I needed to take, I rewarded myself with a mouthful of trail mix and a swig of water from my canteen.

When I served time as Cassie's Girl Scout troop leader I had often joked about being totally at sea in the woods. Of course, in San Romero, the woods had been a tropical rain forest and very different from the ones in the scout manual. Somehow I had managed to teach the little girls how to build a fire and avoid all manner of creatures that would like to have made a meal of them. They all earned their outdoor skills badge, and I was lucky enough to hang on to all my fingers and toes. I only set fire to the jungle once, and none of us ever had to be rescued by the National Guard.

Nevertheless, I had never felt quite at ease with the raw elements of nature. I hated being too cold or too hot. I intensely disliked peeing in the bushes, and I missed taking a warm sudsy bath before bed. Meals cooked over a fire never tasted quite done to me, and sleeping bags seemed too prone to harbor creepy crawlers. In short, I would rather have stayed at home.

Mother was probably waking up right about now. Horatio would have to do some fast talking to keep her from sending the forest rangers out looking for me. We had discussed that possibility last night and Horatio assured me that he would be able to keep her from worrying herself to distraction. I still had my doubts, but that hadn't kept me from leaving.

The path through the woods, which had looked so sterile and bleak when I was walking along the open road unhampered by thorns and briars, was much harder going than I imagined. The ground was uneven, and I kept tripping over hillocks of dried leaves and twigs. Even though most of the trees were bare, they were so close together I could not see very far ahead of me. The tall pines reached above the others and their branches closed off the sky. What little sunshine there was didn't have much of a chance of reaching the forest floor. I mentally added an extra hour or two to my estimated time of arrival and promised myself a meal at noon, which was now two hours away.

The compass was my guide. I constantly referred to its white face with the little dancing arrow. Occasionally, I would have to veer to the right or left of my course when I came upon a fallen tree or a gully too deep to cross, but my silent little companion always brought me back to the proper direction.

The woods were strangely quiet. It had been a long time since I had heard the sound of a bird or the scamper of little varmint feet through the dry leaves. Of course, it was the dead of winter and most little creatures were hibernating. I pictured them as I imagined them when I wrote my children's books—baby squirrels and chipmunks all nestled comfortably in tiny beds made of twigs with blankets woven from the silk of spider webs. It was nonsense and I knew it, but I preferred it that way.

Walking had become automatic, and I didn't realize how tired I was until I failed to lift my foot high enough and tumbled over a fallen tree. I fell into a soft pile of leaves so I wasn't hurt, but I lay there for a moment to catch my breath. The thought occurred to me that it would be so easy to stay there in my own little nest and sleep, if not for the winter, at least for an hour or two. I closed my eyes and imagined how it would be to sleep in the woods like a little animal, all curled up in the leaves snug and cozy. That's when I heard the voices of the approaching men.

My heart slammed against my ribs. I was terrified. I told myself I really had no reason to be frightened. I could get up, sit on the log, wait for their arrival, and have a chat. Why was I hiding, and why was I so afraid? I didn't take time to ask myself any more questions. The log I had fallen over was rotten and partially hollow. I pulled up as close as I could to its length and dug down into the leaves to toss them over my exposed legs and shoulders.

My anorak was a dusty beige. I pulled the hood up over my bright green knit cap and auburn hair. The only thing I could do after that was hold my breath and pray. I did both as I heard their voices grow louder.

" . . . the hell were you and Ben thinkin' of goin' down there in the dead of night and stirrin' up trouble? You know the man wants up to keep a low profile until the shipment comes and goes."

"You ain't my keeper, and neither is Mr. High and Mighty!" answered a surly and petulant voice. "I do as I please. Ain't that what this whole thang is supposed to be about—bein' free to do what you want?"

"No! You idiot! Why can't I get it through your stupid head. Money! That's what we're goin' for here. Dinero, pure and simple."

"Well, not me! No sirree! I got me some principles," protested the surly man.

"But if you get a nice little piece of pocket change, it won't hurt, right?"

"Maybe, but another thang. I don't take kindly to bein' called stupid. You gotta take that . . . "

The voices faded in the distance. I lay very still as my heart slowed its pace and my breathing returned to normal. After what seemed like an eternity I felt the terror ebb, leaving me weak and exhausted. My legs were stiff and cold, and my muscles protested as I tried to straighten them and sit up. I grabbed hold of the rough bark of the log and pulled myself with great difficulty to my knees. I was trying to stand up when I felt the cold steel of the rifle muzzle against the bare skin on the back of my neck.

"Stay right there, you son of a bitch! I wanna see yore legs spread out behind you, and keep yore hands where I can see 'em."

These instructions were accompanied by a vicious kick from a heavy-booted foot. I screamed involuntarily. The tall, lean man with the rifle grabbed my shoulder and turned me around.

"Damn! It's a female! What the hell are you doin' out here, girl?"

Unable to answer because of the intense pain in my thigh, I groaned and fought back the quick tears that threatened to spill down my cheeks.

"I betch'a she's one of them reporters, Henry," said his companion. He was shorter than Henry and bearded, with a square body and a belly that spilled out over his belted jeans. Both men wore heavy flannel shirts and down vests. They had dark knit caps not unlike mine on their heads, and they wore heavy paratrooper boots laced midway up their calves.

"For Christ's sake, ya dummy! If she is a reporter, the last thing we wanna do is tell her our names!"

Henry pulled my knit cap off and slapped my face hard. The tears I had been holding back burst forth like water over a broken dam. I cried like a baby.

"Well, whatever she is, she ain't much to worry about, that's for sure," spat Henry in disgust. "Woman! Stop yore caterwaulin'!"

I sniffed loudly and wiped my runny nose on my scarf.

"Oh, Jeez, Hen . . . , I mean, don't you have a handkerchief or somethin'? You really hurt the pore little thang. She's kind'a cute with that red hair and all."

"The bitch ain't supposed to be here, it's that simple. She's a spy or she wouldn't be way out here. Whoever she is, she's in for a real bad time when the captain finds out. And forget cute! You're just horny. She ain't that good lookin'."

That made me mad. I pulled off my gloves and wiped the ice cold tears off my face. I went to stick my hand in the pocket where my Kleenex was only to have my hand knocked painfully away by the barrel of Henry's rifle.

"Easy does it!" He ordered. "Check out her pockets, Dummy. And don't forget that sissy bag around her waist."

"I betch'a she a reporter, Henry, eh . . . , man. She's got one of them little bitty recorders here and a notebook and pencil."

"Goddamn it, you stupid shithead! Now I'm gonna have to kill her just 'cause you keep tellin' her my name!"

He slapped the other man hard on the shoulder and punched him in the belly with a gloved fist.

"And," he spat, "I'm gonna have to kill you 'cause yore just too damn stupid to live!"

Henry stood over the other man as he fell to his knees gasping and wheezing from the blow to his midsection. Clouds of white vapor puffed from his mouth as he coughed.

"Aw, Henry, you know I didn't mean . . . "

The rifle bullet slammed into the man's head, splattering blood and bits of bone on my face and chest. I looked in stunned horror at the bloody pink shreds of flesh on my hands and fell forward into the darkness and safety of not knowing.

CHAPTER TWENTY-EIGHT

A hard metal button pressed painfully into my cheek. I opened my eyes and saw nothing but the blue and white stripes of cheap mattress ticking. I was cold, and my leg throbbed with a deep and unrelenting pain. I decided being awake wasn't so much fun, and closed my eyes again. I hoped to fall back down in a comforting cocoon of darkness, but nothing doing.

I tried to move, and discovered that my hands were tied behind me. The button on the mattress scratched my face as I struggled to turn and look around at my surroundings. The iron cot I was lying on had metal springs, that much I could hear. The walls of the small room looked like waffled aluminum siding. And they were curved at the top. I was in a Quonset hut! The Girl Scouts in San Romero had been given one as a camp headquarters by the National Guard. I remembered that the roof leaked when it rained, and spiders found the baffling particularly appealing for laying huge egg sacs.

I shuddered from the cold and the thought of eight-legged critters. The sooner I could get up and back on my feet, the better I would feel. The rope on my wrists was not tied very tightly. I twisted and squirmed as I struggled to get free. One final tug on my right arm released me and almost threw me off the cot. The springs protested loudly. I lay very still until they quit bouncing. I had no idea how closely I was being watched. Announcing that I was awake and untied probably wouldn't be a very good thing.

My shoulders ached from being in one position too long. I shrugged them up and down to ease the pain while I surveyed my prison. The cot, an aluminum folding chair, and a metal table were the only pieces of furniture in the little room. I didn't count the small camp stove as furniture since it looked like it was attached to the wall. I looked around for some matches but didn't see any. There was, however, a dark olive-green, woolen blanket folded at the bottom of the cot.

When I got to my feet, my right leg almost gave away underneath me. The throbbing pain in my thigh increased with every step I took. I limped over to the wooden door and listened. I heard nothing on the other side, but I could feel cold air seeping through the cracks. It was an outside door. That meant this room was at the end of the larger structure. The wall behind me probably sealed off the larger portion of the building.

The floor was concrete and stained in places with heavy machine oil like the surface of some garages. If it hadn't been so cold, it probably would have smelled like the place I took Watson to have the oil changed.

The Quonset hut in San Romero had fold-out windows all along the sides so you could see out, but still be protected from the rain. This building had no windows, at least not in my room. Even if I had any matches it probably would be a very bad idea to light the camp stove without ventilation. I wouldn't want to die of carbon monoxide poisoning.

That thought made me wonder if I was going to die of something else like Henry's friend. My head started spinning again, and I sat down heavily on the cot. I tried not to remember the blood and gore splattering on my face. I wiped my cheek and looked at my hand. It was relatively clean. Either the blood on my face had dried, or someone had wiped it off. I couldn't imagine that kind of thoughtfulness in a murderer so I decided I was still wearing bits and pieces of the man in the forest. The thought made me cry. I started out with small silent sniffles, but before long I was sobbing loudly.

I had never seen a man killed before. Leonard wrote about violent death all the time. He described with infinite detail the jagged, broken edges of splintered bone and the red, glistening maw of bleeding muscle. He delighted in the sounds of his dying enemies—the groans and screams and escaping of gases as sphincters released. He was a whiz at bullet wounds and knife wounds and never gagged or vomited at the sight of the exposed innards of his fellow human beings. But Leonard was an insensitive, unfeeling pig, not to mention the fact that he was only a figment of my imagination.

The dead man lying on the forest floor whose bright red blood was the only touch of color in the dry and desolate landscape had breathed and loved and appreciated life. That life had been taken from him by a casual and impulsive pull on a trigger. I cried for him, and I cried for me.

When I was exhausted, I pulled the blanket tightly around me and found escape from my fears in the sleep that had eluded me before.

I woke up feeling much better. My nap could have lasted fifteen minutes or fifteen hours. I would never know. My beloved and ancient Rolex as well as my wedding band and my diamond earrings were missing. I didn't mind parting with the earrings. I had bought Mother and Cassie ones just like them with the proceeds of my first book. They could be replaced, but the Rolex was a first anniversary present from Rafe, and since we only shared a few, it was special to me. The wedding band I would have to get back, even if I begged for it on bended knee as my dying wish. It was a simple gold band, but Rafe had placed our initials inside with the date and the tiny letters, *"te quiero mucho."* I would always know he loved me, but the ring had to be buried on my cold dead finger!

I stretched experimentally and felt the pulling tenderness in my thigh, but the rest of my body was rested and more comfortable. My nose was no longer cold and my breath was not going out in little white puffs. It was almost warm in the little room. Someone had come in while I was asleep and turned on the camp stove.

For a moment I held my breath in alarm. But when I sat up and inspected it more closely I saw the heater was vented through a hole in the wall. I also saw a tray of metal dishes on the table. Whoever was keeping me prisoner wanted me to be warm and well-fed. Sounded like the wicked witch in Hansel and Gretel to me. But I didn't care. I was starving.

I lifted off the aluminum covers and sniffed the heavenly aroma of a thick and hearty stew. Chunks of meat and vegetables swam in a golden sauce around an island hunk of coarse dark bread. I had never seen or tasted anything so heavenly. I ate every bite. Since no one was around to see me, I wiped the empty bowl with my finger and licked until there was nothing left.

The tin cup of cold water was all I had to drink, but the stew was a bit salty so I downed it in three gulps, which was much too fast to taste the bitter residue of the drug before it was too late. Even on top of a full stomach, the chemical hit my blood stream almost immediately. I didn't even have time to get fully alarmed before I passed out on the cot.

Sometime during the night, a cup was pressed to my parched lips. I drank deeply. Soft words from a soothing voice comforted me back to sleep, and when I awoke the next time I felt refreshed and full of energy and determination. I was going to escape some time that day, although how I knew that I could only guess. It must have come to me in a dream.

I waited impatiently throughout the morning for a repeat of last night's meal. Just thinking about that dinner made me salivate. But the time passed without a glimpse of anyone through the little crack in the door.

I had discovered the crack early in the morning when I awoke with a full bladder. The single naked bulb overhead was off for the first time since I arrived and I could see the grey light of the dawn through the narrow strip between door and jamb. The thoughtful stranger who had brought me a drink during the night had also left a large white ceramic potty. It was just like one my Grandmother Howard used to have. I recognized its purpose immediately and made hasty use of it.

With enormous effort, I pulled and pushed and tugged the heavy metal bed across the room so I could sit on the edge while I peered outside through the tiny opening. After several hours, I noticed that down toward the bottom of the door the gap was wider and I could see more of the world on the other side. But more of nothing was just as boring, and after another couple of hours I was cross-eyed and disappointed. Where in the world, I wondered, did I ever get the idea someone was coming to help me escape?

I pulled the iron cot back across the room, heedless of the screeching noise it made. The springs protested angrily as I plopped down in disgust. Since the heater had been turned on, the little room was warm enough even for me. I had taken off my anorak and heavy sweater earlier. Now I folded them up to use as a pillow. I lay back down and puzzled over my predicament.

Someone had come in here last night to give me a drink of water and a wellspring of hope. I had no idea who my guardian angel was, or why I believed he would make good on his promise to set me free. But since the bad old days in San Romero, when Rafe had disappeared and I had no one to depend on to save me and Cassie but myself, I never put all my hopes in one basket. So now, just in case my angel had gotten his wings clipped, I'd better start trying to find a way out on my own.

CHAPTER TWENTY-NINE

By my own reckoning and the angle of the sunlight as seen through the crack in the door, I guessed that it was late afternoon. The grumbles from my empty stomach agreed. I had gotten used to my mother's kitchen since I came back to Meadowdale Farm. There, I never had to wonder what was for dinner. Something delicious was always on the stove or in the oven. I don't think I had been this hungry since my last quarter in college when I spent all my food allowance on a new prom dress.

I looked around the room and took mental stock of the articles I had at my disposal. My anorak and sweater would provide whatever warmth I needed once I escaped. They would also protect my hands if I had to climb over barbed wire. I knew that much from the movies. My fanny pack, with all the goodies Horatio had packed for me, was gone. I was sorry about that, especially since I no longer had my little compass. Unlike my daughter, who knew every constellation in the western hemisphere, I was ignorant of the night sky. I would have to wait until daylight to travel, but once the sun came up in the east I'd be home free.

In novels, prisoners usually dismantled iron cots like the one I was sleeping on, but I would be hopeless at that sort of thing. I immediately gave up the fine idea of using one of the legs as a weapon. The ceramic slop jar, on the other hand, would be a handy dandy tool for knocking out anyone who came through the door, if I heard him coming first, that is.

The aluminum chair could be used to whack an unwanted visitor as well. I got up right away, folded up the chair, and put it by the side of the cot in readiness. The potty was something else. Its contents were already giving the air in my quarters a pungent odor. I didn't want it any closer to my bed than it already was.

The only thing left was the camp stove, but I was as ignorant about that as I was about the crab nebulae. It did, however, have something that interested me: another view to the outside world. If I didn't mind doing without heat for the rest of my stay in this delightful place, I could turn it off and disengage the vent. The hole in the wall was no larger than a dinner plate, but what I could see on the other side might give me some more clues about where I was being held. It was a toss up between comfort and knowledge. Of course, I had to recognize that comfort was relative. Being dead was not my idea of comfortable. I voted for knowledge.

I got down on my hands and knees to inspect the stove more closely. I don't know why I hadn't realized it before, but the stove ran on kerosene. By the hollow sound it made as I tapped on the reservoir, I could tell it was nearly empty. I turned the only knob I could see and watched the flames flicker and die. The heater was off, but it was still hot to the touch. So was the vent. I would have to wait for it to cool down before I removed it.

Now I was impatient and wished I had made my decision earlier. The afternoon that had seemed endless was passing rapidly. I was afraid the sun would set and leave me with nothing to see but the darkness of what promised to be a very cold night.

I played several mental games of solitaire and cheated madly. Twice I burned my hand as I impatiently tested the hot metal of the vent pipe. I lay back on the cot and sucked my hurt fingers like a sulky little child.

173

The overhead bulb had been off all day, and the only light in the room was that which filtered in through cracks in the eaves and around the door facing. It was gloomy in my little cell. It finally struck me that I had been forgotten. No light, no meals, no water, and now I was looking forward to no heat. But unless someone had come to refill the dwindling level of fuel in the reservoir, that would have been gone soon anyway.

I wondered what was going on. Had my captors really forgotten my existence? Had something happened to Henry? Maybe he dumped me here and went back to bury the other man's body. Maybe someone else got mad at Henry for killing what's-his-name and executed him. Maybe, maybe, maybe. I tried to force all these questions out of my mind. I knew I would go nuts if I didn't stop mulling over the infinite possibilities. My only recourse was to take each step at a time and then improvise as fast as I could.

I knelt back down on the floor and licked my fingers to touch the stove. It was still hot but not uncomfortably so. The air coming through the vent from the outside had helped cool it down. I tugged at the base of the stove and saw the vent pull out a little way from the wall. I pulled harder and the vent pipe came loose and fell with a loud clanking sound to the floor. I ignored the noise and impatiently shoved the rest of the stove to one side.

The vent had been held in place by a metal plate. It was attached to the wall by four screws, one in each corner. I dug down in my pocket and came up with a dime that had been missed when I was searched. After a few frustrating minutes I undid all four screws and set aside the cover plate. The hole was about ten inches in diameter. I was thrilled!

I plopped down on my stomach and stuck my face up against the wall to peer outside. The sun was just about to pass behind the tree line. The day outside had not been the gloomy one I had taken it for in here. The sky above the trees was clear and still—a lovely shade of blue. Directly in front of me was a parade ground of sorts, or perhaps just a large, bare central meeting place surrounded by five other Quonset huts.

There was not a soul in sight. As a matter of fact, there was not a sign of life to be seen anywhere. There was not a squirrel, not an opossum, not even a mouse. I had indeed been forgotten, because there was no one here to remember me.

I dropped my chin on my folded arms and pondered that sobering thought. What the hell was I going to do? One thing I didn't have to worry about was being afraid somebody would hear me trying to escape. I could bang around all I wanted to, and that was just what I had in mind.

The cot was difficult enough to move without any added weight so I pushed the mattress to one side before I pushed and pulled and tugged to stand it on one end. During my morning watch through the crack in the door, I had noticed that the lock was reinforced by a padlock, so there was no use in trying to get out that way. I had to find a weaker spot.

I squinted in the growing darkness as I examined the four corners of my prison. After a lot of climbing up and down on the folding chair, and judging the amount of rust on the screws that held together the sides of the aluminum walls, I decided the front left corner was the weakest. I turned the iron cot on its end, aimed, and kicked it as hard as I could. The resulting noise was deafening in the enclosed space, but I was rewarded with a narrow gap in the bottom corner of the structure.

I pulled the cot upright again and repeated the exercise. The gap widened. I was elated.

"Take that you piece of crap!" I screamed. "Lock me up in miserable little room with no food or water. I'll show you!"

At least thirty minutes and as many attempts to break the wall down passed without any further widening of the opening. Thoroughly discouraged and sweating like a pig, I slumped down on the hard concrete floor in exhausted tears. This wasn't working. I had to find a weaker spot.

By now it was almost completely dark in the hut, and beyond the vent hole the sunlight had all but vanished. I shuddered as I considered the thought of a night in the small confined space without heat or light.

"I'd rather die now of heart attack," I murmured, and got back to work.

I hefted the bed back up on its end and turned it around to face the right hand corner. But I was tired and the bed fell backwards—crashing into the back wall and knocking it down into the other side of the enclosure.

When the deafening noise stopped, I stood there in total shock. I had never considered the fact that of necessity the temporary partition would be weaker than the outside walls.

Finally it dawned on me that I was free. I grabbed my sweater and jacket and climbed gingerly over the fallen wall until I was in the other side of the building.

I felt my way cautiously toward the faint outline of light that had to be the door. Fortunately for me, the center of the building was clear of the boxes and crates I could feel on either side as I crept along.

When I reached the end of the building, I leaned gratefully against the door and offered up a small hopeful prayer that it wasn't locked. I felt around for the handle and turned. My heart sank. I was still a prisoner.

I was tired and hungry and thirsty. And I was more than convinced by now that I had been left for dead. It would be the perfect crime. No one, not even me, much less Horatio and Mother, knew where I was. They could comb the woods for days but no one would ever find me.

"Poor little me! Poor pitiful little me," I laughed hysterically. "Let's have a pity party! All the mice and rats and spiders, and . . . "

Chills ran up my spine as I heard something in the distance.

" . . . and wolves are invited," I ended bravely.

CHAPTER THIRTY

I had two choices. I could stay where I was, or I could go back to where I had been. I decided to stay where I was and feel around in the dark for anything I might eat or use to escape. Who knows, I reasoned, I might be in the food storage building. For all I knew, this could be a huge pantry filled with Godiva chocolates, or Scottish smoked salmon, or even cans of Mighty Dog, which didn't sound too bad to me right about now.

I pulled my sweater back on and hung my coat on the doorknob. I considered putting on my gloves in case I ran into a spider or two but decided against it. I would be able to tell so much more by touching things with my bare fingertips.

For what seemed like hours, I felt my way in the darkness up and down the center aisle of the warehouse. I pried and pulled at the tops of every crate and box I could reach but nothing opened up.

The big room had a pervasive smell. After a while, I decided it was some kind of machine oil. Then I remembered the stains on the floor of my cell. Maybe I was in some kind of car or truck storage space, and if that were true, I might as well stop looking. I couldn't eat a tire, although I was almost that hungry.

I crept back up to the front and felt around the door for my jacket. I was tired, and a nap seemed the only thing left I could enjoy. My jacket had slipped off the knob to the floor and as I reached around to find it, my hand knocked over a large metal cylinder. It rolled around on the concrete and, I had a devil of a time grabbing it.

Heedless of spiders and desperate to find whatever it was, I finally got down on my hands and knees and crawled back over the entire area in front of the door. My right hand finally closed over the long tube just at the switch. I pushed and the flashlight turned on blinding me with its glorious light.

"Wow!" I said. "Wow!"

I sat on the cold floor and marveled at the light as it played over the mountains of boxes and crates piled high in each corner of the room. The flashlight was a big one and the light it gave off was bright. I could see as far back as the wall I had knocked down to escape. After the novelty wore off, I got up and returned to my search in earnest. Some of the boxes had labels. I had felt them in the dark. Now that I had a light, maybe I would be able to tell what was inside at least some of the crates.

I was astounded. Most of the larger crates were full of guns and ammunition. The odor I had thought was machine oil was the grease used to pack the rifles. I knew moving any of the heavy boxes was out of the question, so I climbed up over the nearest ones to inspect those higher up. I found boxes of blankets, which I mentally marked for possible later use, and cookware, which would come in handy if I could find any food.

Exhausted and weak, my lips dry and parched from lack of water, I crawled back down from my crate mountain to the door and my jacket. The temperature had fallen and I was cold again. I set the flashlight on the nearest crate and shrugged into my coat, then plopped next to the light and stared at the door that refused me exit.

It was a few moments before my brain registered what my eyes were seeing. Next to the door, hanging on a nail, was a large silver key ring. I got up carefully and reached my hand out as if I were afraid it was a mirage—like a beautiful green oasis seen by a dying desert traveler. My fingers closed over the metal ring. With shaking hands, I tried each key until I heard the beautiful sound of the tumblers falling into place. I turned the knob, and the door opened out into the frigid winter night.

High above, the stars twinkled in a clear black sky. The night had dressed in black velvet and put on diamonds to celebrate my freedom.

"Thank you!" I whispered. "Thank you."

I sighed deeply and looked around. For some reason, I felt a nervous sense of urgency. Even though there was no one in sight, I had a feeling someone could possibly appear at any moment. I tried to figure out why I felt that way. It finally occurred to me as I walked across the big clearing. This place wasn't abandoned or deserted. It was temporarily unoccupied. The inhabitants could return at any moment.

The doors of all the huts were closed, but when I opened them and looked inside I saw cots like mine made up military style with army blankets and no-nonsense looking pillows. Clothes hung from nails or pegs on the walls, and boots were stored neatly under beds. This was a camp, a military camp, probably some kind of outpost. Then it struck me. I had found the underground paramilitary training camp. Or rather, the camp had found me.

"M. Camp," I whispered, then shouted. "M. camp, military camp! Of course, Horatio, don't you see? This is what Andy meant in his silly little notebook. Now you know where to start looking for me!"

That knowledge filled me with renewed energy. I practically ran to the last building and flung open the door. All military camps had a mess hall. Ta'Ronda had told me so.

The door opened onto a large room filled with rows of wooden tables and benches. In the back was a kitchen with empty steam tables and polished stainless steel counters. And best of all, there was a large two-door refrigerator next to a pantry with open shelves.

Boxes of food lined the walls. Oatmeal and graham crackers, sardines and Crisco—I had found paradise.

First, I opened the fridge hoping to find something to drink. Big jugs of milk and orange juice filled the first shelf. I grabbed a quart of orange juice and drank straight from the carton. That was something I had always wanted to do.

"Here's to you, Mother," I chuckled. "And Dad was right, it does taste better this way."

I found a plate of biscuits and some ham and cheese. I made a hasty sandwich while stuffing my mouth with chunks of cheddar. It was delicious. After three biscuits and a half a pound of cheese and ham, I was stuffed. I finished the quart of orange juice and poured some milk into a mug from one of the cabinets.

I briefly considered making coffee, but decided it would take too much time. Instead, I found some plastic bags and packed a make-shift picnic with the rest of the biscuits and a good portion of the cheese. I had eaten all the ham. There was no use trying to hide my attack on the refrigerator, so I looked around for anything else I could use. A couple of apples and a pear in the bottom drawer added to my picnic, along with two tins of sardines and a plastic liter bottle of Coke from the pantry. I found some plastic bags under the sink, dumped my goodies inside, and I was ready to go.

When I got back outside, the freezing wind struck my face with the cold force of reality. I needed a lot more than a Coke and some biscuits if I was going to survive a night like this in the woods.

I hurried back to one of the huts and grabbed two woolen blankets. A knapsack on one bunk gave me an idea. I dumped its contents out on the cot and filled the empty knapsack with my picnic. Before I left, I rummaged through the articles I had emptied out and found a knife, some matches, and a smaller flashlight to add to my loot.

"Way to go, Paisley!" I congratulated myself as I slipped the knapsack on.

I folded a blanket over each shoulder and pulled on my knit cap and gloves as I stepped outside into the cold. I was as ready as I would ever be. I had to get as far away from here as possible. I needed a relatively safe haven where I could spend the long winter night.

I swung the light around the clearing trying to decide which direction to take. The stars I had thought so beautiful an hour ago were now mocking me from the sky above. I cursed myself for not remembering all the information in the scouting manual about celestial guideposts. If Cassie were with me she would know immediately which way to go.

Thinking of my daughter brought a lump to my throat. That's when I began to realize just how tired and vulnerable I was. With some difficulty, I put thoughts of hearth and home out of my mind. I simply could not afford that luxury.

I tried to think of the fun I would have telling Pam that I had outwitted the bad guys all by myself. She would be tremendously impressed. So would Cassie. My heart swelled again with tearful yearnings, and again, I shut off that avenue of thought as quickly as I could.

My feet decided on a direction of their own when my mind avoided the decision. They took the path of least resistance around briars and thorny underbrush that pulled and tore at my clothes. Occasionally I stumbled over a rock or fallen branch and had a hard time recovering, but I struggled on through the night.

The wind picked up when I left the camp. It whistled and moaned through the trees and blew dead leaves up in my face. Every so often, I felt a tiny drop if icy moisture touch my cheek, and I prayed that it wouldn't snow until I had found my way back to civilization.

I thought longingly of the library back on the farm. I imagined myself sitting in front of a big roaring fire with a cup of hot cider in my hand and a bite of Mother's caramel cake in my mouth. I couldn't believe I had ever taken that bounty of warmth and good fortune for granted. I vowed that I never would again.

I didn't realize I was walking down a dirt road until I tripped over a dried, muddy tire track and almost fell. Stumbling forward to keep the weight in the knapsack from pulling me back seemed the best option. If it hadn't been for the tree it might have worked. Instead, I slammed into the trunk on my third stumbling lurch and fell to my hands and knees. Somewhere between the first and second lurch I dropped my flashlight. Suddenly I was once again at the mercy of the darkness.

As dazed and exhausted as I was, I knew getting up right away was very important. It was just somehow a very difficult thing to do. I leaned back against the tree and looked up at the skeletal branches swaying in the wind. It would be so easy to fall asleep, even with the sound of the bare limbs clacking against each other.

I thought dreamily about a lullaby Mother used to sing to me about a rock-a-bye baby in the treetops. That cradle fell, I remembered, and the baby came tumbling down. That didn't bode well for the baby.

With a deep and weary sigh, I pushed up to my knees and used the tree trunk to pull myself up the rest of the way. I was looking around on the ground for the flashlight when I heard the sound of the four wheeler coming through the woods.

At first, like the silly, naïve, nitwit that I was, I was elated. Maybe my worries were over, I thought. A fire and a nice warm bed might be only a few minutes away. And then I came back to my senses and a great cold rush of fear hit my stomach.

I fell back against the tree gasping. Only someone who had anything to do with the camp I had just left would be out here on a night like this. I had to hide.

The first thing I had to do was ditch my bulky knapsack. I ran back off the road as far as I could and dumped the blankets and knapsack in a hollow tree trunk next to a large boulder. Even in the dark I would be able to recognize the spot later—if I had a chance, that is.

I tried to climb up on the boulder but my feet kept slipping on the lichen-covered rock. I knew if I could evade them now, they would come looking for me later when they discovered I had escaped. Logic told me that my goose was pretty much cooked either way.

The sound of the approaching four wheeler was loud and annoying in the crisp winter night. It was almost as loud as a snow mobile. The neighbors won't like it, I thought distractedly. I hunkered down next to the rock and hoped that whatever light the vehicle had wouldn't shine this far off the road. I was afraid to lose sight of my knapsack. If I had to run, I would, but I knew I wouldn't last long without the blankets and food.

The ATV engine sounded like a giant, angry wasp. I covered my ears and closed my eyes as it neared the spot where I had stumbled in the road. Suddenly the machine slowed and whined into neutral. I opened my eyes and squinted fearfully through the darkness as a tall figure got off the seat and walked around in front of the headlights. I was so exhausted it was hard to focus, but there was something so familiar about the way the man held his head and walked with his shoulders bent over.

It was Bert!

A great feeling of joy and thanksgiving swelled up from my chest choking off any outcry I might have made. Instead I struggled to my feet and ran toward the headlights. Tears filled my eyes as I ran out on the road and flung myself against Bert's broad chest.

He took a step backwards to keep us both from falling and then held me away from his body as he looked at my face in the light.

"Paisley! Oh, my God, what have you done?" he whispered hoarsely. "They're right behind me."

I looked up in despair at the sound of his words, but I didn't have the strength left to ask what he meant.

"Remember this!" he said urgently. "You don't know me!"

And he hit me squarely on the chin with his hard bony fist. A blackness darker than the night closed over my mind as I fell to the frozen ground.

CHAPTER THIRTY-ONE

"You don't know me! You don't know me!"

The words echoed in my mind as I fell down a long spiral tunnel. At times, various people I knew stuck their heads out of windows in the tunnel walls. Mother was there and so was Cassie.

"You don't know him," they sang in unison. "You never knew him!"

My head and neck ached. I tried to change positions in the hope that the pain would go away.

"She's coming around," said a strange voice from the top of the tunnel. "Don't you want to put your mask on?"

"It won't matter," came the answer. "She'll never have the chance to tell."

I was sad, very sad. My heart was broken, and I didn't fully understand why. Tears coursed down my cheeks, and my chest rose and fell with sobs. I opened my eyes and took a huge gulp of air as I tried to sit up.

"Wha . . . where . . . ?"

"Better yet, who?" laughed the man sitting at a bare wooden table in front of me.

I tried to rub the film from my eyes, but once again my hands were tied behind my back. I gave an experimental tug, but this time the rope was tight, very secure, and very painful. I squinted through tears as I tried to focus on the rough, bearded face of my captor. It wasn't Bert, that much I could see. And I was glad, because somehow Bert was responsible for the pain in my lower jaw.

"Please, can you untie my hands?" I begged. "Surely I'm not a threat to you."

"Hah!" the man laughed. "You got that right."

He turned to another man on his left and gestured toward me with a nod of his head. The other man crossed quickly behind me and pulled me roughly to my feet. My head swam and pain shot through my neck and jaw as he yanked my arms and cut the rope. I groaned involuntarily. My face hurt more than my wrists. I gently comforted my swollen cheek with a free hand.

"Sorry about that. Ernie's a good man, but he's not very fond of the ladies. He's on the lam for killin' his old woman. Sluggin' you was right up his alley."

The other man leered and added with a suggestive wink, "I'm surprised he didn't have his self some more fun while you were out cold."

Eager to change the subject I asked the question that was foremost in my mind,

"Who are you?"

The bearded man at the table looked genuinely startled for a moment. He threw back his head and laughed.

"You're somethin' else, lady. You really got cojones."

He nodded again to the man who had untied me. The man went through the door to another room and came back pushing Ta'Ronda Yancey in front of him. I couldn't hold back a startled gasp as I saw her bruised and bloody face. It looked as though Ernie had had a busy night. I took a step toward her, but the man with a beard held up a stiff palm.

"Enough!" he growled. "I'm gettin' downright annoyed with this little game."

He turned to the young woman I had met at Fort Morgan.

"Ta' Ronda, is this the gal you told me about?"

The girl looked at me sadly and nodded her head. The man who held her pulled back on her thick black hair and forced her face closer to mine.

"Take a good look, girly," he spat. "The militia don't want no mistakes."

"My, my, my," said the bearded man shaking his head again. "I am truly surrounded by idiots."

He stood up, his figure towering over the rest of us in the small room. His forced his thin lips into a grin and pointed a long accusing finger at the other man.

"Get your sorry stupid, ass out of my sight!" he yelled. "I think I can handle these little women better all by myself."

"But . . . " said the man in disgrace.

"Out!"

The man left the room glaring angrily at me as though it were all my fault.

"Now, let's see if I can make you two ladies talk."

Ta'Ronda sighed deeply. It was obvious she was in pain as she sank down on a wooden chair in the corner. The man gave her an angry look.

"Bitch! Who told you to sit down?"

She raised her battered face and smiled weakly. One of her front teeth was missing and her lips were cut and bleeding.

"What are you gonna do? Beat me up? Kill me? Go ahead," she sighed again. "I don't really care anymore."

"She needs medical help," I snapped. "Has she seen a doctor?"

He opened his eyes in a comical parody of surprise.

"Cojones from hell, little lady. Anybody ever tell you that before? Bet you ain't' got no boyfriend. A man wouldn't put up with that mouth for long."

He got up and walked around the desk. For the first time, I got a really good look at him. He was tall, almost as tall as Bert. His back was straight and his shoulders were held at attention. He was wearing jeans and a dark navy sweater, but he might as well have been wearing a uniform. His attitude and posture gave him away.

I stretched my neck and shoulders instead of answering. My head ached. I just wanted to go to bed and sleep for a week. I was too tired to be as afraid as I should have been, but when he walked around behind me and put his hands on my neck, my heart fluttered with terror.

"Here let me rub that neck for you. I learned how to do this from a lovely little lady I once knew in Cambodia."

He kneaded the muscles at the back of my neck with big rough hands. His fingers smelled of onions and tobacco.

"Relax! I ain't gonna hurt you now, maybe not ever, if you tell me what I wanna know."

"It might help if you ask me something," I protested as I tried to squirm away. "I don't have a clue what you want of me."

"Hey, you're right! And here I am thinkin' you can read my mind."

He gave my shoulders a pat hard enough to make me bite my tongue, then pulled another wooden chair up close to mine. He got a crumpled pack of cigarettes out of his pocket and lit one.

"Smoke?"

"No, thanks. And please don't blow it in my face," I asked.

"You're not making me laugh anymore, bitch. I'm gettin' a bit tired of your high and mighty attitude."

He looked over at Ta'Ronda, who was leaning against the wall.

"Hey, girlfriend! This bitch really has 'tude, what say?"

"Yeah, I guess she does," the girl responded in a tired voice.

"Okay, bitch, let's have your name, rank, and serial number so I won't have to call you bitch anymore, unless you ask for it, that it."

"Paisley, I'm Paisley Sterling DeLeon."

"Okay, so far so good. Now, what's this Leonard Paisley to you?"

"Leonard? Leonard is my meal ticket. I write mystery novels pretending to be him. There really is no Leonard Paisley."

"Then that guy in the magazine was a fake?"

"Yes, precisely. A fake."

"An actor?"

I thought quickly and decided it was best to leave it at that. After all, according to Bert himself, we were strangers. I went with Mother's idea.

"Yes, an actor from New York."

"And the picture of the cabin on the Internet?"

"Just a cabin in the woods. I don't even know the person who lives there."

"Damn! If you're tellin' the truth, we killed somebody's poor old dog for nothin'," he spat disgustedly as though in his world dogs had more of a reason to live than humans.

His grin was wicked now as he brought his face close to mine. I coughed when he blew smoke in my eyes. I tried to pull my head away, but he grabbed my chin and held me close.

"Then you're the person we were lookin' for all along. You bought that fancy little computer from the pawnshop, didn't you? The guy with you must have been just along for the ride."

"How did you know?" I asked. I was terrified he might have a description and not really believe it was me. I couldn't let him go after Cassie.

"Pawnbroker. He told us a man and a woman came in and bought the gizmo the same day the little creep hocked it. Didn't have time to do a police check on it. Tried to hide it from me at first, but he learned that it's much more honorable to tell the truth. That's somethin' you'd better keep in mind, if you know what I mean."

He tightened his grip on my injured chin. The pain was almost unbearable. When he let go, I sighed with relief and thanked him without thinking.

"Why, you're quite welcome, ma'am," he laughed.

"Wh . . . why is the computer so important?"

"I'm the one asking questions here," he snarled. "But I will tell you this. At least three people have died over that little machine. Don't you force me to make it four."

"Of course not. I'll be more than happy to tell you anything. But I'm so tired. Do you think I could take just a little nap? Then . . . "

"QUIET!"

Ta'Ronda must have dozed off, because she jerked upright and almost fell off her chair when he shouted.

"Can I have some water?" she begged. "I don't feel so . . . "

"Goddamn females! Always askin' for somethin'!" he yelled.

He jumped up and grabbed Ta'Ronda by the arm and threw her in the corner. When she raised up once to protest, he kicked her hard in the belly and again in the face. She fell back down with a muffled groan and was quiet.

I shook uncontrollably. I prayed for the strength and the wisdom to keep him from losing his temper again.

He came back to the chair and sat down, rubbing his palms on his jeans. "Now, let's get down to business. Where is the computer?"

"I . . . I don't know," I stammered. I couldn't let him go to the farm. Mother and Horatio might have gone home. I had to protect them.

"It . . . it got stolen," I lied.

The blow was swift and came out of nowhere. I lay on the floor in a daze. I couldn't really tell where he had hit me. I hurt all over. He grabbed me by the neck and hauled me back up onto the chair. He wiped the tears off my face with an exaggerated gentleness.

Now, now," he whispered softly. "We don't want that to happen again, do we? Let's start all over, but how about you tell the truth this time?"

"It's true," I cried. "Someone broke into the house and stole the computer and . . . "

This time he raised his fist in front of my face so I could see what was going to happen.

The door opened and Bert, the man I wasn't supposed to know, sauntered into the room.

"Ernie! Dammit! What the hell? I told you guys to stay out there."

CHAPTER THIRTY-TWO

"Beating defenseless women is my bag, not yours, Sergeant. Give it a rest. It'll be easy enough to find out if she's telling the truth," Bert said as he leaned back against the door. He lit a cigarette and blew the smoke insolently in my direction before he went on. "If she's the person she says she is, then people may be looking for her. When her body's found, it's got to look like it was an accident. Think about it, man. You don't want her face all banged up."

"Goddamn it, Ernie, you hit her first! Don't forget that," shouted the sergeant.

Bert walked slowly and deliberately over to the table and leaned down to face the other man.

"Let's get this straight, you silly ass," he said in a quiet and deadly voice. "You may be selling, but we're buying, and the money can dry up quicker than you can say, 'Aye, aye, Sir!' You got me?"

The man glared angrily at Bert for a long moment, then made a sudden move to get up from his seat. Bert quickly reached under the wooden table and flipped it over with a mighty heave, slamming the sergeant's head hard against the wall. I held my breath as he sank slowly to the floor in an unconscious heap.

Bert removed a dirty bandana from around his neck and stuffed it

191

in the man's mouth, then pulled some duct tape from his pocket and securely wrapped his face and hands.

"Paisley, are you okay?" he whispered urgently as he worked.

"Yes, yes . . . but what's . . . ?" I asked in a daze.

"Plenty of time for answers later. What happened to the girl?"

"He kicked her."

Bert finished tying up the sergeant and went to check on Ta'Ronda. He knelt down and gently examined her injuries.

"She hasn't made any noise," I told him. "She may be . . . "

"Yeah," he confirmed grimly. "She's dead."

"Oh, my God," I cried. "Oh, dear God."

Bert crossed the room quickly and pulled me up against his lean body. He held me close for a moment to muffle the sound of my sobs. Then he lowered his face next to mine.

"Listen to me, Paisley. We don't have much of a chance to get out of this alive, but a chance in a million is better than none at all. Do exactly what I tell you, and maybe we can make it. Okay?"

My voice quivered as I answered him. "Okay," I said.

"That'a girl!"

He went to the door and listened intently for a minute, then gestured for me to join him.

"I don't think anybody's out there. When I left the mess hall they were all inside celebrating."

He looked me straight in the eyes and smiled. "It's now or never. Are you with me?"

I nodded because fear had stolen my voice. I took a deep shuddering breath and smiled back.

"I love you, Paisley," he said abruptly. "No matter what happens, I want you to know that. I've loved you ever since the night I first saw you."

He smiled grimly and continued, "You were scared that night, too, but you were tough and sassy. I need you to be that tough now. Can you do it?"

For a response, I lifted my face up and kissed him firmly on the lips. That was all the answer he needed. He took my hand tightly in his and cautiously opened the door.

The room was empty.

Bert gestured for me to stay back as he edged around the wall to the window and peered out.

"I don't see anyone outside," he whispered. "But that could change at any moment. These sweethearts aren't exactly predictable. We'd better make a run for it while we can."

He grabbed a jacket from a peg on the wall and helped me put it on. The sleeves were much too long, but I knew I would welcome the longer length around my hips once we were outside. He found another coat for himself and turned to go back inside the room we had left.

Startled, I finally found my voice. "Where are you going?" I croaked. I was terrified of being without him even for a minute.

"The jerk had a gun. We may need it," he explained.

I heard him move the table off the man's body and turn him over.

"Damn!" came his muffled curse.

He came back to my side.

"Must have left his sidearm somewhere else. Fine soldier he is."

"Was he really in the army?"

"He wished!" laughed Bert softly. "He was cashiered out two years ago under a cloud. He was suspected of stealing arms, but there wasn't enough evidence. I've got the goods on him now, if I ever get to tell somebody, that is."

He patted me on the back. "I'll fill you in when we have more time. Gotta move now. Ready?"

I nodded once more.

Bert turned off the overhead light and opened the outside door. The clearing was empty, but we could hear laughter and loud voices coming from the mess hall. We skirted the edge of the woods and headed down the dirt road I had followed earlier.

The wind had died down and it wasn't as cold. Nevertheless, I soon had to stop and pull up the hood to my jacket. I took a minute to search the pockets and came up with some very welcome mittens. When I was ready again, we hurried on with the light of a full moon to guide us.

Without my watch I couldn't be sure, but it felt like we had been walking for over an hour. I was so tired I couldn't think. It was all I could do to put one foot in front of the other. When Bert stopped abruptly, I ran into his broad back and bumped my nose. Bert ignored me as he kicked up the dirt with his booted toe and walked around in a tight circle.

"What are you looking for?" I asked crossly.

"Your flashlight," he explained. "You must have dropped it earlier. I saw the shattered glass and the metal rim in the headlights of the four wheeler. That's how I found you before."

He knelt down on one knee and strained to see in the darkness.

"There! See it?"

He pointed to a bit of glass shining in the moonlight. It was the broken bulb.

"Okay, Paisley, where is it?" he asked excitedly.

I was too tired to understand what he meant at first. I shook my head and tried to understand his words.

"You would never have escaped empty handed. You're much too smart for that. Where did you hide your stash?" he insisted gently but firmly.

I tried as hard as I could to focus, but my memory was hazy and fleeting. Pictures formed and dissolved rapidly behind my eyes. Finally one image lingered.

"A . . . a big rock. There was a hollow tree next to it. I put it in there. Yes! I had food and a coke and . . . some other things. I can't remember what," I finished lamely.

"Which side of the road?"

I turned around and around trying to find something that looked familiar, but my head was full of stuff and nonsense. I couldn't think. It was such a silly thing not to be able to recall. I looked up at Bert in despair and bit my lip to keep from bursting into exhausted tears. I was so ashamed that I had let him down.

"That's all right, Paisley," Bert said softly. "It's okay. You stay right here. I'll find it."

"No! No, please!" I cried. "Please don't leave me. I'll never see you again, I know!"

I was ashamed of my weakness, but I had never felt so vulnerable. Bert was my lifeline. I had to stay close to him. I threw my arms around his waist and held on for dear life.

"Please!" I begged. "I know if you leave me one of us will die."

He held me for a moment while I calmed down. I buried my cheek in the rough wool of his jacket. Even in the cold I could smell the good clean smell of him. The winter wind had blown away the cigarette smoke and the violence and underneath was all Bert.

"Come," he whispered against my ear. "We'll look together, but we must hurry. We haven't much time."

We were lucky. Bert saw the big boulder almost right away, and then I was able to point out the hollow tree trunk. My knapsack and the two blankets were right where I left them. Bert opened my picnic packet and gave us each a sandwich. We wolfed them down hungrily and took greedy gulps of the coke.

"Tastes great, huh?" he laughed.

The food gave me a renewed feeling of energy. My fears abated and my legs and heart felt lighter. The rough underbrush was easier to walk through, and I even laughed when a limb broke, sending a rain of tiny icicles down on our heads.

Then we heard the rifle fire.

Bert knocked me to the ground and covered my body with his.

"Damn! I thought we had more time," he grunted.

We lay there on the frozen ground hardly breathing as we listened for another sound.

We didn't have to wait long. The sound of gunfire came again but from farther away.

"They're going in the other direction, back toward the lake and my cabin," observed Bert with relief. "That makes sense. The going is easier in that direction and help is closer. There's a ranger station at the dam."

"Then why are we . . . ?" I gasped as I tried to catch my breath.

"Because I hoped they would start looking the other way. I wanted to buy us some more time."

"What are they shooting at?" I wondered.

"Probably at anything that moves," he said as he helped me up. "Most of them are drunk and the rest are stoned."

As I brushed the dead leaves off my jeans, it suddenly occurred to me that something about Bert had changed dramatically. I grabbed his arm and turned him around so I could see his face.

"You can hear! You can, can't you?" I asked excitedly.

"We don't have time . . . "

"Answer me, damnit. You can hear, I know you can. You heard that man hit me and came to my rescue just in the nick of time. And you heard the rifle fire and everything I've said tonight whether you could see my lips or not. You're not deaf anymore!"

Bert smiled down at me and nodded.

"I had an operation. The doc only gave me a fifty-fifty chance. It didn't seem worth it before, but after knowing you . . . I decided to take a chance, and it worked."

He gave me a quick hug and a peck on the cheek.

"Now we have to make tracks. An hour, more or less, is probably all the head start we have."

I had a million questions to ask Bert, but I shut up and hurried along behind him. I was as anxious as he was to get as far away as possible.

CHAPTER THIRTY-THREE

Fleeing from enemies who were bound and determined to bring me back to their brand of justice was not a new experience for me. The big difference here was that during the revolution in San Romero, I had been driven to safety by a trusted family chauffeur in a comfortable luxury sedan.

Late one night under a bright tropical moon, we had raced across the mountains to a small airport on the coast. There we found a pilot willing, for an exorbitant price, to take Cassie and me to the safety of an island resort. We spent the last reserves of our cash and almost all of what my jewelry brought trying to get back to New York. It had been a harrowing, fearful time, but we were comfortable and warm. We stayed in the finest hotels, and when we had an appetite, we sated it in the best restaurants.

"I'll have the lobster salad and a glass of Chablis, please," I told the waiter. Only the waiter was Bert. He took me by the arms and shook me back to the present moment.

"Paisley!" he shouted urgently. "You've got to stay with me!"

I watched his face come into focus and shivered violently.

"Of course, I'm with you," I answered crossly as I tried to clear my vision. "Where else would I be? Cold, wet, and miserable is my favorite thing."

He grinned and touched my cheek with his rough fingers.

"You were having a fine old time there for a moment. You even told me to turn right at the next block and park in front of the restaurant."

"Don't be silly. Why would I say such a thing? But now that you mention it, I am very thirsty. Can't we stop for a minute and drink something?"

"We'll have to stop soon enough. It looks like snow. I'm afraid we're in for it. Be on the lookout for someplace we can hole up. Okay?"

I nodded my head and gave him the bravest smile I could muster, but with the wind blowing in my face, it was hard enough to see his broad back as he walked in front of me, much less a cave or some other place to hide.

Only an hour or so later we almost stumbled over something even better.

"It's a hunter's den," shouted Bert over the wind. "That's why we didn't see it at first. It's camouflaged."

He motioned for me to stay back while he crept cautiously forward and peered in the door of the small dugout. It was built against the side of the cliff we had been skirting for hours. The roof was made of tree bark and covered with brambles and vines. In the summer it would have gone unnoticed by even the most observant eye.

I watched anxiously until Bert reappeared and then hurried over to his side.

"Is it safe?"

"We'll just have to take a chance," he answered with a weary shake of his head. "I would have like to put a few more miles between them and us, but we need to rest and eat something before we drop in our tracks."

I smiled and hugged his arm. I knew he was being kind. I was the one who needed to rest. He could have gone on for hours.

"Allow me, madam," he said as he lifted the thick leather hide that served as a door to let me crawl inside.

Before I could stop myself, I tumbled head over heels down the small incline into the saucer-shaped depression that had been carved out of the earth. I lay there for a moment catching my breath and cursing Bert with what little strength I had left.

"Sorry," he laughed as he turned on the flashlight and saw my angry face. "I should have warned you about that first step."

He extended a hand and pulled me up to a sitting position while he pointed out the features of our new home like a proud real estate salesman.

"It's much bigger that it looks, and there's even a chimney of sorts in case we want to risk a fire. We'll be safe here tonight."

I looked around skeptically at the dark corners as I listened for a rustling sound in the dry leaves that carpeted the floor.

"How about critters?" I asked petulantly. "Spiders. I hate spiders."

"How about something to eat?" he asked, changing the subject. "You want a sandwich or an apple?"

"Oh! Sandwich, please!"

"Okay! Housekeeping chores first. Then we eat. Try to gather all the leaves over in that corner against the back of the depression and spread one of the blankets on top. I need to go find some wood in case it snows. Even those bad asses will stop for a snow storm, and we'll be warm and cozy."

"Let me go with you," I begged.

I was still terrified of losing Bert.

He took my outstretched hand in his and pressed his warm lips to my palm.

"I'll only be a few minutes, Paisley, I promise. Do you think I'd miss a chance to spend another night alone with you?"

And he was gone.

I closed my eyes and shut my mind against the irrational fears that assaulted me.

"Come on, Paisley Sterling, you big dummy. You have enough to worry about without borrowing trouble. He'll be back. He promised."

I busied myself arranging things the way Bert had requested. It was cold inside the little enclosure, but the absence of the wind made it seem thirty degrees warmer. I pulled down my hood and unzipped my coat. Bert had left the flashlight sitting on its end in the middle of the room. I picked it up and peered gingerly into the dark corners. I didn't see any bright, beady little eyes staring back at me, but I did see something that aroused my curiosity. I crawled over for a closer inspection.

The architect of our little abode had been very inventive. He had hollowed out shelves in the soft sandstone of the cliff that served as the back wall of the dugout. The bottom shelves were empty, but when I stood up and hunched over to peer in the back of the top one, I saw two large metal containers. I stood straight up in my excitement and banged my head on the roof, sending a shower of pine needles and bark down in my hair.

"What's going on in here?" asked Bert as he stuck his head in the doorway.

He crawled inside with an armload of kindling. I waited until he turned back around and pulled in several big logs before I told him.

"Treasure! I found a buried treasure!" I said excitedly. "Big containers full of something. They're too heavy for me to move. Maybe it's food!"

Bert laughed and crawled back to my side to inspect the treasure.

"You're right," he agreed. "They are heavy. But don't get your hopes up. I doubt we'll find tins of caviar and plum pudding."

"I'd settle for some pimento cheese and a cracker."

Bert lifted the first container down and carefully stripped the wax seal away with his knife. I waited breathlessly while he pried open the top.

"Son of a gun! When did you get to be a witch?" he gasped as he pulled out a large jar of Cheese Whiz, several cans of deviled ham, and a round metal container of crackers. We sat back and laughed in amazed delight. Bert opened the crackers and one can of ham with his knife, and we dug into our feast.

"We really should have finished your sandwiches first," he said while he munched, "but this was just too good to be true. Want some more coke?"

I nodded and he passed the bottle. The crackers made me thirsty and I almost drank more than my share. Bert tried to refuse the rest, but I insisted, so he finished it off.

"If it snows, we can melt some over the fire," I said with all the authority of my Girl Scout background. "Is there anything else in the tin? Chocolate mousse, maybe?"

"If there is, I'm finding another place to spend the night. It's not Halloween yet," he laughed as he tipped the metal container over and dumped the remainder of the contents out on the blanket.

"Well, what do you know! How about a box of Hershey bars instead?" he asked with a grin. "And here's some more matches and a compass . . . "

In spite of my joy and excitement with our treasure trove, I was so exhausted that I slumped over against his shoulder and fell fast asleep before he could finish his sentence.

I woke up hours later feeling warm and relaxed. A small wood fire burned merrily in the center of the dugout, its smoke wafting up through a hole in the roof and leaving our little hideout warm and cozy. Bert sat up against the hide door with his arms crossed and his chin resting on his chest. At first I thought he was asleep, but when I made a move to sit up he opened his eyes.

"Ah, Sleeping Beauty!"

"I bet!" I laughed as I tried to run my fingers through my tangled hair. Pieces of bark and pine needles fell out when I shook my head. I knew I looked like hell.

"Want some water? I melted the snow like you said."

"It's snowing? But it's so quiet?"

Bert smiled. "It's been snowing for hours. It's not exactly the blizzard I predicted, but it's enough to call a halt to any search party out looking for us."

I drank deeply of the melted snow, then poured a tiny bit on my shirttail and swiped at my face. I doubt if I accomplished anything, but I felt better.

"Hungry?" asked Bert. "You haven't had dessert."

"Shouldn't we ration things out? I mean, we might be here for days."

Bert looked uncomfortable. "I might as well be honest with you, Paisley. We won't be able to wait around for days. These characters can't afford to let us escape. They'll be hunting for us with a vengeance as soon as the weather's clear."

"But why? I couldn't even begin to tell the police where I was held prisoner. And I certainly don't know who those men were."

I looked up and saw his eyes darken.

"Oh, but you can! You're not one of them?" I asked in alarm.

"Of course not! That's the only stupid thing you've said to me since you asked me to pretend to be Leonard," he said almost angrily.

"So what were you doing there? Is that where you disappeared? Andy didn't even know where you were."

Bert smiled slowly and dangerously.

"Oh, yes, he did. He and Danny helped me. Andy got me a driver's license and a social security card, and Danny faked a jail record in the name I picked, Ernest Banks. I camped out in the woods for a week or so until I grew the beard back and got a nice woodsy aroma going. Then I struck out in the direction of the camp. Andy had a pretty good idea of where it was. He overheard a couple of drunks bragging one night after he threw them in jail. They were known militia members and . . . "

"Militia? What militia? I thought this was all about some maverick soldiers from Fort Morgan," I sputtered.

"Yes, and no," answered Bert carefully.

"Tell me about the 'yes'."

"About three years ago, that jerk back there at the camp, Sergeant Callard, got an idea of how to steal from the army. He sweet-talked Ta'Ronda Yancey into helping him.

"But she seemed . . . "

Bert held up his hand to stop me.

"She was bored with the army and anxious to get out. She was a young girl, pretty and ambitious. This man made her believe that they could make a fortune and then go away somewhere and live like kings."

Bert smiled sadly. "It's the same old story, but some women always fall for it. When she got scared and wanted to call the whole thing off, they had a fight and broke up. He experimented with the idea on his own, got caught, and was immediately given a dishonorable discharge. Ta'Ronda felt sorry for him and let him back in her bed when he had no place to stay. Finally, she agreed to do what he wanted when he threatened to spill the beans about their relationship. She could have gotten in big trouble for having an affair with a man who had a record of stealing from the army."

"Anyway, after Callard's bad experience, they decided they needed someone more knowledgeable who could hack into the computer in the Quartermaster's Office. Ta'Ronda came up with a young civilian from Morgantown who had a crush on her. Armed with a laptop computer and the hacker's expertise, they were in business in no time at all."

"And that was?" I interrupted.

"They ordered supplies—pots and pans, blankets, boots—you name it. Then they got the shipping papers and sent them by fax to several bases. They made fake transfers of the goods into each base's inventory electronically, received payment by changing the name of the shipping company to an address of their own, then deposited the money in an offshore account. After doing this several times over, they had quite a little nest egg. That was when Callard got the really big idea."

"And what was that?" I asked in excitement. I had forgotten the cold and the snow and our precarious situation.

"The militia. He decided to sell the goods to militia groups. After all, what could he do with a few hundred gross of pots and pans? And the crazies in these extremist groups believed fiercely in stockpiling goods for the coming battle against what they called the New World Order."

I was puzzled.

"I thought it was the Special Forces Underground? That's what Horatio said."

Bert nodded thoughtfully. "Smart man. I can see why he would have come to that conclusion. I had my suspicions, too, but as far as I could determine Ta'Ronda was the only active duty soldier involved after her boyfriend was cashiered. These militia guys are all loners, but they have similar politics. They used to belong to larger groups, but since the Oklahoma City bombing they've broken up into small individual cells and gone to ground."

Bert added another log to the fire and stirred the ashes underneath until the wood ignited. "During the last few weeks, I've met quite a few of them. Some of them are serious-minded people who are really concerned about the future of this country. They mean to protect their families at all costs, and they have no agenda other than arming themselves to the teeth. But the largest contingent hate the federal government. They believe they are being taxed into poverty and forced into menial, low-paying jobs while minorities are given special privileges. As far as they're concerned, they're already at war, and they'll stop at nothing to defend their rights."

"And these soldiers need arms and ammunition, am I correct?" I asked.

"Correct. And that's where Ta'Ronda's little computer nerd dug in his heels. He didn't mind stealing blankets, but he refused to help with the guns. That's when they ordered him killed."

"Oh, God, my laptop was his wasn't it?" I breathed.

"Yes," admitted Bert. "Callard put the word out that the hacker was an enemy of the patriots: a spy. Unfortunately, the executioner that the militia sent was also a petty thief. After he blew the hacker away, he took what valuables he could carry, including your laptop, and pawned them before he disappeared back into the hills."

I passed Bert a candy bar and took over the narrative.

"Cassie bought the computer for me. I wrote *Virtual Violence* using some of the information on the hard drive, including a line or two from that pathetic love poem . . ."

I stopped for a moment. I was stuck.

"Who read the book?"

"I don't really know," answered Bert. "But it doesn't matter. When Callard found out about it, he went crazy. He had no idea how much information was on the computer or how much Leonard Paisley really knew, but he had to get the computer back at all costs. Again, I don't know who, but someone brought the article in *Pen and Ink* to his attention. He sent out another hit man after Leonard, only this time, the target fought back."

"Thank God," I whispered. "I'm so sorry, Bert. I'm so sorry I got you all mixed up in this crazy mess."

CHAPTER THIRTY-FOUR

If we had been Cassie's age and in the bloom of romantic youth, we might have spent the night in other ways. But we were older, if not yet old, and content simply to lie in each other's arms in front of the campfire as we passed in and out of a light sleep. At times, as I felt him press against me, I felt the stirring of desire, but Bert was a gentleman of the old school, and I still had a ghost hovering at the edges of my memory. So we just held each other close and whispered throughout the night.

Bert told me that Ta'Ronda had been left behind in the camp the day I was captured. The others had gone to make an arms deal with several militia members who had come from as far away as Utah and North Dakota. When Henry dragged me back and dumped me in my cell, she waited until he went to join the rest, then brought me food and water. She meant to help me escape, but her loving boyfriend returned. When he discovered what she had done he beat her severely. Bert was sure she was dying from internal injuries even before Callard kicked her that one last time.

"How far is it to some relatively safe place?" I asked a little after midnight. "I mean, will it take us another day, or what?"

Bert shifted his weight and pulled me against his shoulder. He buried his face in my hair and nibbled on my ear instead of answering my question. As ticklish as I am, it was impossible not to laugh and squirm. I retaliated by tickling him back. We rolled around like two teenagers until we were out of breath and the edge of the blanket caught on fire. Bert doused it with some melted snow and got out the biscuits.

"How about a midnight snack?" he asked.

"Are you trying to change the subject?"

"Desperately," he smiled sheepishly. "The truth is, I don't really know how long it will take us."

He picked up a piece of unlit kindling and drew in the dirt in front of the fire.

"As near as I can guess, we are about here where this 'X' is. The lake is here and the hotel and marina over there. We're going in the direction of Wieuca City, which is about thirty miles that way." He pointed the stick away from the fire. "This is a wildlife conservation district, so we won't run into any farms or homes on the way. There's nothing but woods and more woods between here and civilization."

"Thirty miles," I gasped. "Thirty miles? That'll take me forever."

"I know," he answered solemnly.

"You're not planning on going without me?" I asked with alarm.

"Paisley, we have to . . . "

"Please, can we talk about this tomorrow?" I begged. "We're both too tired to make any really coherent decisions. Let's wait and see how we feel in the morning." I smiled up at him. "For all we know, the sun may come out and melt the ice and snow before we wake up. There may be snow plows on our doorstep clearing the path back to the hotel where Mother and Horatio will be waiting for us with pheasant under glass, hot sudsy baths, and champagne."

Bert laughed and gave me a gentle hug. "Now I know you're hallucinating."

"Well, maybe hot chocolate and a meat loaf sandwich."

"Sounds good," agreed Bert as he got up. "Why don't you try and get some more sleep. I got a big log for the fire. It's right outside. I'll be right back."

The part of me that Bert's body had been holding felt cold and empty. I realized I could get used to being by his side without much effort at all. I thought briefly about Dora Nick and all her lonely years in an empty bed.

"Poor thing," I muttered.

"Who me?" laughed Bert as he crawled back inside pulling a huge log behind him.

"Good grief!" I teased. "That looks like a squirrel condo."

With Bert's help I straightened out our blanket and leaf mattress, then we settled down for the night.

"I could get used to this," murmured Bert, echoing my thoughts. "You're a very warm and cozy woman, Paisley Sterling."

Some time later it occurred to me to ask Bert if the cigar band I found on the patio was his.

"I had to come and see if you were okay after the accident," he explained. "Ernie Banks had already established a habit of sneaking off on occasion. I made sure of that right away. They didn't think anything of it when I disappeared again."

"But how did you know what happened?"

"Ta'Ronda came to camp the night after your visit to Fort Morgan," he told me. "She was pretty shaken up. And she was coming down from a coke high. Callard found out about your visit. He made her tell him everything that happened."

Bert threw back his head and laughed. "What ever made you hit on her? I almost lost it when I heard about that," he chuckled.

"I did no such thing!" I protested. "That was all her idea. I just wasn't very dressed up that day, and she jumped to the wrong conclusion." I finished lamely.

"Well, the Sergeant didn't buy it either. He ordered Ta'Ronda to take one of the trucks from the motor pool and go after you. He had a friend who was willing to make any repairs the truck might need to cover up signs of the accident. He was furious when she came back and said you had escaped."

Bert pressed his lips against my forehead. "I borrowed one of the four wheelers and took the back roads into Rowan Springs. When I got out to your place by nightfall and didn't see any lights, I got worried. But then I saw the back door open and your wonder dog run out to . . . "

I laughed aloud. "My wonder dog! Great watchdog, too. She never even noticed you, even on the patio."

"Let's just say she was preoccupied," he chuckled.

"Bert?"

"Yes."

"I'm sorry about Murphy. He really was a great dog."

Bert was silent for a moment, but I could feel his muscles tense against my back.

"Yeah," he breathed. "He was a great dog, all right. And that's just one more thing that somebody's going to pay for before I'm through."

I hesitated to ask, but there was something else I needed to know. "Andy said you came into a large sum of money last year. Was that part of the ruse or is it true?"

"Don't tell me you're a gold digger?" he laughed, as he nuzzled my neck.

"You know better," I answered quietly.

"Yeah, I guess I do." He kissed my ear and continued. "Do you remember that little clapboard house we parked in front of while I told you about the guy who tried to kill me?"

"Back off the street? Sure. What about it?"

"That's where I grew up." He was quiet for a moment and then went on. "A company from up north made me an offer I couldn't refuse for the house and the twenty acres it sits on. Seems they couldn't find a better place to locate their big discount store."

I closed my eyes and drifted in and out of sleep several times before

I finally felt him relax against me. His soft snores ruffled my hair and tickled my ear but I didn't move for fear I would disturb his rest. This man really was my protector and my hero. I prayed for his safety as I enjoyed the shelter of his arms.

In the early hours of the morning, I fell into a very deep sleep. When I awoke my hero was gone.

At first I thought he was outside getting more wood, then I noticed a stack of kindling and logs piled up high next to the opening of the dugout. He'd left me well provided for, but he had left me. The rest of the biscuits and the candy bars were beside me on the blanket. What was missing was Bert.

I was furious. He had underestimated me again. Maybe I couldn't have made it to Wieuca City, but I would like to have been in on the decision that left me behind.

I angrily threw a new log on the fire as I considered my options. Somehow I wasn't that surprised that he had gone. I knew that to him it seemed the best thing to do, but he didn't know how abandoned and alone I felt.

I tried to calm down. All I had to do was wait until he returned. But patience had never been one of my virtues. I had to find something to keep myself busy.

First, I melted some more snow and had a meager breakfast of half a candy bar and a biscuit top. I saved the cheese and the bottom half for lunch. The other half of the candy bar, I reasoned, would make a satisfying dinner. Bert would probably make it to the main highway sometime today. Without me slowing down his pace, he would make pretty good time even in the snow.

I decided to take a bath.

I scraped as much snow as I could into the cracker tin and dumped it in the big metal container several times over. Then I pulled it closer to the fire. When the snow melted, I stripped down and wet my undershirt and wiped everything I could reach with the warm water. It felt heavenly.

I considered wetting down my hair but decided I might catch a cold waiting for it to dry. I settled instead for rinsing out the rest of my underwear. I wrapped myself in one of the blankets and stoked up the fire until it was blazing.

The bright flames flickered over the walls of the enclosure and illuminated the second metal container. In our original excitement at finding the Cheese Whiz in the first we had forgotten to open the other one.

This one wasn't as heavy, but I still had to pull and tug with all my strength until I tipped it over the ledge and onto the blanket. Bert had taken the knife with him but I found the top of the cracker tin under some leaves and used it to pry away the wax seal. I took a breath to calm my excitement and tried to open the lid.

The blanket I had wrapped around my shoulders slipped down to my waist with my exertions. I felt the cold air on my breasts before I saw the barrel of the gun push aside the hide over the opening of the dugout.

"Well, will you look at this!" said a smooth and educated masculine voice.

I grabbed the blanket and pulled it up to cover myself, then scrambled towards the back of the dugout.

"Nowhere to run, and nowhere to hide, little lady. You might as well calm down. You're in no danger—not right now, anyway," he added with a sneer.

The man pushed his way carefully inside, making sure as he entered that I was alone.

"So he really did go off and leave you by yourself. How very unchivalrous. A pretty girl like you can find a better man than that. I'm glad I got rid of him for you."

The man sat down in front of the fire and nonchalantly crossed his legs. He unzipped his hooded jacket and pulled it off while keeping the rifle aimed at me. Underneath he was wearing overalls made of the same funny material as the jacket. It looked a bit like tree bark and was in camouflage colors unlike any I had seen before.

"It's for hunters," he said, answering my unasked question, "deer, geese, that sort of thing. Hunting is my hobby, and my avocation. My vocation has become much too tame, thanks to the early end to the war and our unit missing out on the fight. Hunting fulfills my need for outsmarting my prey—tracking him down and making the kill."

I finally found my voice as I stammered, "Wha . . . what did you mean you got rid of him?"

"Oh, we're backtracking, hum? Miss him already?"

The man's narrow eyes gleamed in the firelight. He was clean-shaven with dark hair cropped close to his skull. It was impossible to tell for sure in the firelight, but I thought I could see a thin white scar under his chin, like someone had tried to cut his throat with a very sharp knife. He was not a large man, but he was compact and muscular. He looked dangerous and very much in control.

"Please," I insisted, "what happened to Bert?"

"Oh, was that his name? I never like to know, really. It's so much more fun to simply think of them as 'the animal.'"

He added nonchalantly, "I killed him."

My heart stopped. For a moment I felt as though my head would explode. Bert was dead? I had a hard time comprehending it.

"Are you sure? How . . . how?" I gasped as I fought back tears.

"Ah, the lady wants to hear the gruesome details," he said with a sly grin. "Always glad to oblige with that."

His teeth were big and very, very white. I found myself staring at them as he told me about the fate of the man who had been my only hope.

"This little place, humble though it may be, is mine, all mine. I built it a year ago just in case certain events should fall into place. As so often happens when one is forced to deal with fools, those events occurred slightly before their time; but never mind, thanks to prior planning I was ready. When I went to the camp . . . "

"You're one of them?" I interrupted with surprise.

He laughed. His white teeth glistened in the firelight.

"Not exactly. Let's just say I let them play at being soldiers and armed that rabble as long as it suited my purpose."

"Which was?"

"Patience, my lovely, patience. Don't you want to hear about your friend first?"

He reached over and put some more wood on the fire before he resumed his narrative.

And he ordered me to start getting dressed.

"Turn your back, please," I asked.

His harsh laughter ricocheted around the small enclosure and assaulted my ears. Then his dark eyes narrowed even more, and the points of his teeth gleamed as he clenched them.

"DO IT!" he barked.

My underwear was still slightly damp, but I struggled into it using the blanket as a screen. He watched my every movement with interest, but I could tell it was because he was enjoying my fear, not the sight of my body.

"He never even knew I was stalking him until the very last minute," he bragged as I zipped my jeans.

I stopped dressing for moment as his words registered. He raised the rifle with one hand and leveled it at my heart.

"Socks and boots, now. That'a girl. Left foot, right foot."

Then he sang out in a booming voice, "Left, left, left my wife and sixteen kids, right, right, right in the middle of . . ."

He stopped suddenly and thrust his index finger into the middle of his forehead.

"I missed the head shot. Damn! That doesn't happen often, I can tell you that. I have the trophies to prove it. Got him through the lungs. I could tell from the pink bubbles as he floated downstream."

"Downstream?" I whispered, my voice hoarse with unshed tears.

"Yeah," he said with satisfaction. "I let him climb all the way up the cliff. A mighty effort it was, too. He was a worthy prey, I have to admit that. Just as he pulled himself up over the top of the bluff, I called out. He saw me and stood up to run. That's when I squeezed off a shot. He fell over the edge and into the river. There are miles and miles of shoreline around the lake it empties into. With any luck at all, and I am a very lucky man," he grinned wolfishly, "his body won't be found until there's nothing left to identify."

CHAPTER THIRTY-FIVE

Controlling my emotions took an enormous effort, but I could not allow myself to break down in front of this man. I knew instinctively that it would give him far too much pleasure. I finished dressing and reached for my anorak, but he knocked it out of my hand with the rifle barrel.

"Not just yet," he ordered. "Finish opening that container first. We're going to need the goodies I left inside."

The container was on the edge of the blanket. I got up on my knees and pulled it closer to me. The top was almost off. One mighty tug and it came away in my hands and sent me tumbling backwards. The man leaned forward with anticipation to see the contents.

For one crazy instant I considered trying to grab the gun while his attention was elsewhere, but fortunately, my practical side intervened. This man was as dangerous as a cobra. I had to treat him with great respect and hope for a lucky break. He would not make a foolish mistake.

He watched me warily out of the corner of his eye as he reached inside and emptied the container. He lined up several jars on the blanket. Two were the size of Mother's pint canning jars, but the rest were smaller, and they were not glass but plastic.

"These are a hunter's best friend," he said, pointing to the smaller bottles. "This is raccoon urine, this one is fox. A few drops on the bottom of my boots and my scent is masked. Deer won't come anywhere near the scent of man," he explained smugly. "This is doe estrus. Drives the bucks crazy. They'll come running if they're anywhere in the vicinity. But it's really cheating. I only save it for when I'm bored. And this last one," he said, "is extract from the tarsal glands of a buck. Strictly illegal," he laughed. "Had a buddy of mine make it up for me."

He held the rifle up and insolently rubbed the cold barrel under my chin.

"Bucks are very territorial. Can't stand the smell of another male anywhere near their does. Sometimes I like to spread a few drops of this around just so I can see them go wild and fight each other," he confided. "It's a real high. None of that cocaine shit for me. I prefer a real primitive rush from the bottom of your guts."

His eyes glittered in the firelight as he talked. I sucked in my breath and held my chin still until he put the rifle down. If I had any chance of surviving at all it would be by staying as calm and reasonable as possible. Nothing would make him happier than for me to get hysterical and make a run for it.

"And this," he said, picking up one of the pint jars, "is the *piéce de résistance*. You know what Ricine is, little lady?"

I shook my head and tried to look uninterested.

"It's probably the most potent poison know to man. Castor beans," he laughed, shaking his head. "It's made from castor beans. Isn't that a kick?"

He held the jar up to the fire and watched as the glass sparkled in the flames.

"There's enough here to kill every man, woman, and child within a hundred square miles."

"Wha . . . what are you going to do with it?" I asked as calmly as I could.

"Put it in the dam reservoir, of course. How else could I get it into the homes of thousands of unsuspecting people so fast?"

I sat dumbfounded at the horror this man proposed so matter-of-factly.

"The area water treatment and distribution plant is a quarter of a mile away. Nothing they have can detect it, and there's not a chance it will get too diluted. It's six thousand times more powerful than cyanide. Four hours after I dump it, Mr. and Mrs. Kentucky and all their little kiddies will be dropping like flies!" he laughed with satisfaction.

"But why? What possible reason can you have for killing so many innocent people?"

"They're stupid," he shouted. "Stupid, stupid, stupid! They take men like me for granted all their lives until a war comes, and then all of a sudden, I'm cannon fodder. Kipling knew what he was writing about, '. . . savior of our country when the guns begin to shoot.' But right now I'm an embarrassment, part of a bloated military machine. They want to close Fort Morgan like they have so many other bases. Ruin my career like they have so many others."

He slammed his hand on the stock of the rifle.

"Well, not this soldier!"

He leaned across the fire, his eyes shining with wild excitement.

"You want to know how I'm going to stop them? Of course you do! And I'm going to tell you because then you'll have a real good reason to try and escape. You'll want to save the world, just like any red-blooded American hero. Like I did once upon a time, before I found out nobody gives a shit. And then things will get interesting between us."

In spite of all my good intentions I lunged across the fire and tried to grab the jar out of his hand. I felt the bright heat of the flames sear the top of my left thigh and screamed in pain. The man placed a booted foot on my chest and kicked me back against the wall of the dugout. I lay on the dirt, stunned and struggling for breath. The fabric of my jeans was singed and smoking on top of the burn on my leg. The acrid smell quickly filled the small space. I choked and sputtered.

"You see!" he laughed with satisfaction. "It's already started. I knew you were a live one. You'll make up for my having to shoot your friend in the back. You'll give me a run for my money!"

"They'll find you," I gasped. "They'll know it was you, and then they'll have even more reason to close down army bases that spawn crazy people like you."

He clenched his fist, thrusting it in the air.

"Go, lady, go! Give it to me!" he shouted, grinning savagely. "But you're wrong, you see. I've planned this for a very long time. Always have a contingency plan, that's one of the first things they teach you in Officer's Training School. When I heard there was a chance the base might be on the closing list, I started the ball rolling. I had looked the other way when Sergeant Callard and Lieutenant Yancey tried their flimsy little schemes to steal from the government because I knew sooner or later I would have a use for men with no morals or code of conduct. I kept them on the shelf just like I did this jar of Ricine until the time was ripe. Six months ago I began using them to spread disinformation through the militia."

He laughed again. "The federal government has no idea how vast this underground army is. These men no longer need to meet, or even to know each other to blow up gay nightclubs and abortion clinics. Communication is strictly thorough the Internet, which has no government regulation or watchdog committee. The only thing the militia really need is to be adequately armed. Callard found a way to do that, just like I knew a scumbag like him would. When the timing was right, I broke in on their little party. Clouded up and rained all over their parade. I like to think the mention of a firing squad was what brought them around," he smiled in remembrance.

"From that point on, they were mine. They were instructed to start sending information to the militia about an imminent attack from foreign terrorists. I purposefully left all the details vague and incomplete. Fear travels much faster when it has no shape. Sooner or later, in small towns all across the country, swarthy, poorly-dressed men who speak little or no English will be blamed for acts of sabotage like the one I'm undertaking here. Hysteria will sweep the land, and all the military bases will be put on alert. Bases that were scheduled to be closed will get fresh orders, and the American people will once more rely on their men at arms to defend them. We'll be heroes in uniform again instead of millstones around the neck of the Congressional budget committee, and as an added bonus, we'll get rid of all the foreign scum polluting our soil."

The contrast between his polished eloquence and his ranting and shouting punished my mind, and I shut him out for a moment or two. The burning in my leg had diminished somewhat and was now only a stinging pain. I reached down to rub it and felt two of the smaller plastic bottles under my knee. One of us must have kicked them during the struggle. My hand closed involuntarily over the bottles. If he didn't miss them, I would have something in my own arsenal. I almost smiled to myself when I remembered what Dad used to tell me: that I was full of piss and vinegar. I had the piss now, fox and raccoon; all I needed was the vinegar.

"Who are you?" I interrupted with a voice that was much calmer than I felt. "If you're going to kill me, my knowing your name won't make any difference."

"Ha! You got that right!" he laughed. "Burke, Captain Lawrence Talbot Burke, at your service, ma'am," he added sarcastically.

"Captain Burke? You're the one Ta'Ronda said was in charge at Fort Morgan. You're the Quartermaster."

"Right again, madam," he sneered.

He glared silently at me for a moment before he slammed the rifle hard into my ribs. I lay in the dirt retching and coughing while he hastily stuffed the plastic bottles and the pint jars into zippered pockets on each leg of his pants. Even in my agony I smiled because he failed to notice the two that were missing.

"Put this on," his said throwing the anorak in my face. "We have a lot of miles to cover. If you don't keep up the pace I'll have to shoot you where you fall. You know I'm going to kill you sooner or later. But just think—the longer you survive, the more false hope you'll build up. I'll get a real kick out of seeing that hope die in your eyes when I cut your throat."

"Is that what someone saw when they cut yours?" I whispered hoarsely.

The rage that bloomed in his eyes was terrifying. For one dreadful moment, I truly thought that I had gone too far by guessing right. Then the murderous light died and he shook his head and motioned for me to precede him as we crawled out of the hut.

He was right about one thing. Once I had faced him down, my sense of hope, false or not, began to grow. This man was a monster, but he had his own demons to fight. Maybe those demons could be persuaded to come over to my side.

CHAPTER THIRTY-SIX

Captain Burke set a brutal pace. His legs, however, were not as long as Bert's and I was just able to keep up with him. The rawness of the cold and the frigid bite of the wind were almost more than I could stand. To escape the misery of the present, I let my mind float back to better times and immersed myself in happy memories.

I relived a pleasant sunny afternoon in the flower-filled garden of a British friend in San Romero. We shared a pot of Earl Grey and wonderful warm scones dripping with clotted cream and the tiniest of strawberries in sweet jam. My imagination was so strong I could taste the hint of bergamot on my tongue and smell the jasmine that bloomed on the garden gate.

The memory of that fragrance reminded me of another, the cloying sweetness of a night-blooming cereus one New Year's Eve in another garden, this one in my own home, Hacienda La Buena Suerte. The house and patio were full of the joyful sounds of laughter as I swirled in the arms of my husband to the wildly romantic music of Spanish guitars.

We were surrounded by friends and family as we celebrated the happy promise of a year that was to bring us nothing but despair. But I didn't dwell on that. Instead, I recalled the delicious aroma of meat cooking over the barbeque and corn cakes baking in the outdoor oven. I recalled little Cassie's delighted giggles as she danced with her grandfather under the soft light of paper lanterns hanging from swaying palm trees. It had been a glorious night, and the pleasure I felt from the memory warmed my heart, if not my cold, tired feet.

I trudged doggedly behind Burke, ignoring the pangs of hunger in my stomach and the dryness of my cracked lips. I neither asked for, nor did I receive, any attention or concern from the man who pushed himself as hard as he pushed me.

We walked for hours, winding our way through the pine and cedar forest. Burke apparently knew the trail we were taking, because he never once hesitated or consulted a compass or a map.

I watched for even the slightest opportunity I might have to escape. Unfortunately, the growth of young cedars in this part of the forest was sparse, and the thin trunks of the pines offered little protection to hide behind. Most of them were smaller around than my waist. I would have to run from one to another much faster then I knew was possible if I wanted to avoid a bullet in the back from Burke's rifle. For the present, I put any escape plan on hold.

We had been walking almost six hours when Burke held up his hand for me to stop. I opened my mouth to ask what we were doing. He slapped one gloved hand over my lips and jerked me closer with his other arm.

"Up there." he whispered urgently, "up in that tree. Do you see the deer stand?"

I strained my neck backwards and searched all the trees within sight, but I could see nothing. I shook my head. Burke wasn't happy with my negative answer. He slapped his hand against the side of my head and twisted my face around and up so that my line of sight was forced ten feet or so higher. Then I did see it, a crude plank shelf about six feet square built out from a fork in one of the larger oak trees. It was carefully hidden in the branches so that I would never have spotted it if he hadn't been pointed out to me.

"We're going up," whispered Burke. "And make it snappy!"

I stared at the tree in utter dismay. I was already exhausted and footsore. Even in my younger days I had not been able to climb trees very well. My sister Velvet had been the monkey in my family. Now I would probably be shot for my lack of talent. Weary tears coursed down my cheeks as I pondered the unfairness of it all.

Burke shoved me roughly against the tree and placed my hands on the short wooden slats nailed to the side of the trunk. He stuck the rifle in the middle of my back and urged me painfully up the crude ladder one foot at a time. As I put my hand on one of the slats high above my head, it split and came bouncing down on top of us. I heard Burke's muffled oath. I smiled grimly. It must have hit him harder than it did me.

Fortunately, the missing step was one of the last ones, and I was able to pull myself up on the shelf without it. I lay there panting like a beached seal until Burke climbed agilely up beside me. He grabbed my collar and pulled me back up against the tree trunk.

"Not a sound," he whispered in my ear. "Someone has been following us for the last several miles. We'll wait here until the unsuspecting little Nimrods make their appearance."

I started to tell him he was a paranoid schizophrenic son of a bitch, but decided my life was worth more than the pleasure of a few carefully chosen epitaphs. Instead of cursing him, I took advantage of the unexpected rest. I tried to relax as much as I could, considering I was perched twenty feet above the forest floor on a flimsy wooden shelf with a vicious killer. I was almost asleep when he jabbed me painfully in the ribs with his elbow.

"Quiet!" he mouthed as he showed me a wickedly curved hunting knife. He held the knife underneath my ear and whispered with barely a sound, "Here they come. And remember, they're just militia scum, not worth dying for."

I strained to see through the branches of the trees. So far I couldn't see or hear anything. But even in the failing light of late afternoon,

Burke's trained eyes had picked up the two men picking their way carefully through the underbrush.

I saw their heads as they walked in and out of the swirling fog. They looked as though they were swimming in deep grey waters as the dense air flowed and eddied around them.

They were sitting ducks.

Burke raised his rifle and took aim as the first man stepped into the clearing beneath our perch. For one crazy instance I considered calling out a warning, but at that moment I recognized the man who had treated Ta'Ronda so cruelly. I bit my tongue and closed my eyes as Burke squeezed off two shots.

When I opened my eyes, the militiamen were nothing more than two heaps of crumpled clothing stained a bright and glistening red. I started shaking uncontrollably. Burke ignored me as he scrambled down the tree and ran over to bodies. He quickly searched their pockets and emptied out their backpacks. I heard him laugh as he dumped out the contents of the last man's pack.

"Hey, lady! Looks like you're going to have a hearty last meal after all. These bastards have all the ingredients. Get your little butt down here and help me set up camp for the night!"

How I got down that tree I'll never know, but afterwards, the muscles in my calves and thighs were quivering and my arms felt like strands of spaghetti. The will to survive is stronger, I suppose, than we are. I imagine that's the only explanation for the fact that I was still able to help Burke gather wood and start a blazing campfire.

Burke seemed sickly elated, almost triumphant. He laughed and hummed as he cut open some tins of food with his hunting knife and set them in the coals around the edge of the fire. The aroma of warming beef stew filled the air. My mouth began to water, and as much as I wanted to refuse my captor by not joining in the meal, I couldn't resist.

We sat around the brightly burning campfire and shared a delicious dinner of tinned beef stew and Vienna sausages like two old friends. Burke laughed when I licked my fingers and passed his tin of sausages to me.

"Here, I'm full," he said. "Finish these off."

I thought only briefly about the "full mongoose" being the slow one and wolfed down the last two sausages.

"You're pretty damned gallant for a murderer," I observed sarcastically.

"Officer and a gentleman, at your service, ma'am," he sneered.

"What about that?" I asked. "What about your oath to serve your country? What about your sacred duty?"

Burke grinned wickedly in the light of the flames. It wasn't a pretty sight. I shivered and crept closer to the fire and the warmth of the glowing embers.

"What about the respect I'm supposed to have?" he finally answered. "What about the flag waving and the parades and the admiration in other men's eyes? What about having a country worth saving? What about having leaders who are above reproach?"

He picked a stick out of the fire and lit a cigarette with the burning end.

"I decided when I saw how the Desert Storm vets were treated that all bets were off," he answered softly. "One of my best friends . . . "

He threw the stick back in the flames.

"Never mind that, he said brusquely. "I'm not here for your entertainment."

We sat in a quiet, almost companionable silence. It was strange, but I no longer felt threatened by this man. He said he would kill me at the very last minute and I believed him. I knew until we arrived at the reservoir I was safe, so I persisted with my questions.

"Why the militia?"

He stared at me angrily.

"I thought you were going to shut up," he barked.

"You said you wouldn't kill me until later. I believe you'll keep your word. Humor me now, and I promise I'll put up a good fight when the time comes."

Burke threw back his head and laughed aloud. "You're really something, lady. I like you." He screwed up his face and did a fair imitation of Bogart. "Where have you been all my life?"

"Staying as far away from men like you as I possibly could," I blurted out without thinking.

He stared at me angrily and then laughed again. This time the laughter had an edge that made me realize I could go too far despite his promises. Then his face grew serious as he stared into the fire and answered my question.

"The militia poses the greatest danger to the very fabric of this democracy than any in the history of the United States. The formation of small unidentifiable cells of guerillas intent on disrupting industry and communication is quite possibly the most perfect military maneuver against a central government. The militia are practicing guerilla warfare at its best. And they have the advantage of fighting with the fervor of fanatics. Most of them are very religious and devoutly believe that they have been chosen to defeat the ungodly."

"And who are the ungodly?"

"You, me—anybody who's not like them. Jews, blacks, foreigners, and homosexuals mostly. And abortion clinic docs," he added.

"Gee, I've never been called 'ungodly' before."

"Yeah, they're a pious and unforgiving lot."

"Not unlike Captain Lawrence T. Burke," I snapped.

"Captain Burke, pleased to meet 'cha."

The booming masculine voice came out of the darkness beyond the glow of the fire. Burke made a move to grab for his rifle. A flame burst in the night. Burke screamed and drew back a bloody hand.

"Don't think you want to try that again, buddy," said Burke's assailant as he stepped into the firelight. "Whoa, you two look as cozy as two peas in a pod. Nobody'd ever guess you was enemies." He grinned slyly, "Or are you bosom pals, now that the little lady is all alone?"

I sat and shook while I fought to control the nausea that threatened to bring up the hot sour liquid at the back of my throat when I saw his face in the firelight. It was Henry, the man who had captured me three days ago. Burke was a known entity. As crazy as it sounded, I knew I could count on him not to dispose of me until we reached the end of our journey. This man was unpredictable and volatile—a live grenade.

Burke sat very still with his wounded hand held tightly against his chest. Henry pulled a dirty handkerchief out of his pocket and tossed it to him.

"Here, buddy, wrap that around your hand. I'll need you to help bury my friends after you feed me."

Henry shrugged off his backpack and hunkered down to warm his hands in the flames. He laughed and pointed at his knapsack. "Here I am loaded down with enough money to burn a wet mule, and I ain't got nothing to eat. What's for dinner, sport?"

CHAPTER THIRTY-SEVEN

Burke was unable to open the last two remaining cans of food with his injured hand. When Henry got tired of waiting for my poor efforts, he grabbed Burke's hunting knife and attacked the cans himself. He didn't wait to warm the food but swallowed the beans that were to have been our breakfast cold and congealed.

"Ah! That really hits the spot," he laughed, wiping his mouth with the back of his hand. "Got any coffee?"

"No!" answered Burke abruptly. "What we had, we got from your idiot friends."

"Whoa, buddy! Careful how you speak of the dead. They might just be waitin' for you on the other side."

Henry shifted his weight on one knee and peered through the darkness to the heaps of clothing that had been his compatriots.

"Burial detail comin' up right up, guys."

He turned back to Burke and grinned slyly.

"You know all about that don't you, buddy? Hear tell your best pal, old buddy, old friend for years, comes home from Desert Storm with some kinda' weird brain disease. Somethin' the docs don't pick up. When he ain't feelin' so good, you take him in, only he wakes up one night and tries to cut your throat. Thinks you're some kind'a raghead or somethin', and damn near splits you from ear to ear. If you hadn't got hold'a your sidearm he'd be somewhere makin' baskets and you'd be pushin' up daisies. Boy," he said shaking his head, "that must have been some bloody mess. You bleedin' like a stuck hog with his brains splattered all over the bed."

Henry stopped and spat in the fire. "Is it true they found you two naked together?"

Burke didn't move a muscle. His only physical response to the other's man's jibes was a wildly pulsing vein in his temples. I was beyond being shocked by anything either of them could say. This was worse than any nightmare I had ever had.

I closed my eyes and tried to wish myself elsewhere. Then I sighed and took a deep breath. The situation was as real as it gets, and I had to stay with it if I wanted to remain alive.

"Got a shovel?" asked Henry.

Burke shook his head.

"Then you two had better get busy picking up rocks. Don't want them coyotes having my pals for dinner. That's the least I can do for them considerin' they helped me make off with the money from the arms sale."

Henry stood up and slapped his free hand against his thigh.

"Damn! I'm might' near a millionaire, what' ya think of that, honey?" he asked me.

"I'd say that's a lot of money for a few guns and ammunition," I answered softly.

"And two sidewinder missiles. Don't forget the missiles. Have to thank Captain Burke here for that. Right, Capt'n?"

Burke clenched his teeth tightly. I watched his jaw muscles bunch up and waited for the explosion I dreaded. When it didn't come I tried to defuse the moment.

"Wha . . . what coyotes? You said something about coyotes. Surely we don't have anything like that here. Don't they live out west somewhere?"

"They did until the winter of nineteen and seventy-eight. One of the worst winters we ever had. Froze the Mississippi River clean over in two or three places. Them coyotes was starvin' over on the western side. They crossed over on the ice and stayed after the thaw. Screw each other more than rabbits, they do. Now we got more coyotes than deer this side of the river. Damn scavenging bastards eat up all the quail and pheasant. A fellow can't hardly find anything to hunt no more. I shoot 'em ever' chance I get."

Henry lifted his rifle and followed our every move as we searched the area around our campfire for rocks to cover the bodies of the men Burke had killed. Rocks were scarce on the level ground under the trees, but I stumbled on a gully twenty feet or so away from the camp. In periods of heavy rain it was probably a good size stream. The water had carried and deposited stones of all sizes down to a narrow mouth that disappeared between two large boulders.

The snow hadn't melted in the gully and my hands were soon stiff and unfeeling from digging the rocks out of the frozen ground. Burke must have been in much more pain with his wounded hand. He staggered and groaned with each step.

Henry unceremoniously shoved the bodies of his two friends close together and directed us to start piling rocks on top of them. Slowly the burial mound grew. I was only able to carry two rocks at a time and Burke had all he could manage carrying one.

I lost count of the number of trips I made to the gully and back. I was beyond caring whether or not Henry shot me and was about to sit down for a rest when Burke stumbled and fell. I stopped and bent over to rest my hands on my knees while I tried to catch my breath. Burke lay still and unmoving. I straightened up and made a tired effort to lift his shoulder.

"Cut that out! If the son of a bitch can't get up let him lay there and freeze to death. Some tough guy soldier he turned out to be," Henry scoffed, his rough words making angry white puffs in the frigid air. "Guess all that crap about him being a fag was true."

Henry sauntered over to Burke's prone figure and poked him in the back with his rifle.

"Just the same, as much as I liked these good old boys he killed, he did make it possible for me to keep all the money for myself. Maybe I ought'a let him have a clean shot through the heart, a present from one hunter to another."

There was no fight left in my body. I was past caring or protesting. I had reached the limits of my endurance. He could kill Burke or he could kill me. I sank down in the snow and let the words of a Spanish prayer soothe my soul.

Henry propped his rifle against a tree stump and dropped down on one knee next to Burke. He unsnapped the holster of his pistol with his right hand while he tried to turn Burke over with the left. I sat and watched the two as I would have actors in a play. I was as detached and uncaring about their future as I was their past.

I didn't even flinch when Burke flopped around on his back apparently lifeless only to rise up swiftly and smash the rock he had concealed in his hand against Henry's temple. Henry made a small sigh and fell heavily on the cold ground, his dead eyes open and staring dully at the night sky.

Burke got up to his knees and spat in Henry's bloody face, and then smashed him again and again between the eyes. I didn't start crying until I heard the bones in Henry's face crack.

Burke knelt over his enemy's dead body and searched him. Finally he struggled to his feet and staggered over to the dying fire.

"Here," he cried hoarsely, "come here and help me put more wood on the fire or we'll never last the night."

"What does it matter?" I sobbed. "You're going to kill me anyway."

"Yeah," he grinned, "but remember there's always the smallest chance that you might get me first. Life," he laughed hoarsely, "is full of surprises. Just ask that good old boy over there."

Burke was right. I still felt the tiniest kernel of hope deep within my heart. I said one more *Salve Regina,* remembering how sweet and pure Cassie's voice had sounded when she sang it at her First Communion, and pushed myself up from the ground.

For twenty minutes I hobbled around the clearing picking up dead limbs and branches. Burke helped me kick over a big hollow tree stump we would put on the fire before going to sleep. It was big enough to keep us warm throughout the night.

"Our main problem," Burke said seriously, "is food. You're about all in, and I need your strength for tomorrow."

"Well, gee thanks for thinking of me," I answered crossly.

Burke went on without paying any attention, "You'll have to carry the vermin's body to the reservoir."

He ignored my startled gasp and continued with his tirade.

"I couldn't have planned it better if I'd tried. Old Hank's body is going in the drink with a smashed jar of Ricine in his pockets and that knapsack of money on his back. I'm sure his ugly face is well known to the authorities. This way, there won't be any doubt the militia is responsible for all the deaths. The National Guard and the regular army will be put on full scale alert for the next fifty years! If I work it right, I may even get a promotion. I can tell the FBI that I suspected Yancey and Callard all along and followed them to the camp. From that point on, I can borrow your story and pretend to have been the prisoner who finally escaped and risked his life to keep at least one bottle of Ricine from going in the river."

His grin was wicked and feral, showing all of his huge teeth.

"Hell, I'll be a bitchin' hero!"

CHAPTER THIRTY-EIGHT

Before Burke finished pinning imaginary medals on his chest, I interrupted to burst his manic bubble.

"And just how am I supposed to carry the dead weight of a two hundred pound man another ten, or five, or even two miles, when I can hardly make it out to the bushes to pee?"

"I'm going to get you a venison steak for breakfast," he announced with an even bigger and more insane grin. After you eat your fill of roasted deer meat you can carry Henry, and me, to the dam and back," he laughed.

I didn't exactly jump up and down, clap my hands, and sing "a hunting we will go," but I did join in his enthusiasm for a big juicy venison steak. On that cold dark night in the middle of the forest, I was as looney a tune as he was. I wasn't too happy, however, about his plan to build a sled using the fresh deer hide and two long poles. I liked it even less when he told me I would drag Henry's body on that sled to the river, but the delicious anticipation of meat cooking and sputtering over the campfire seemed somehow more important. And to make me even more agreeable, Burke surprised me with a present.

"Here," Burke said as he dug his uninjured hand in his pocket. "I think these are yours."

He held his hand over mine and dropped my Rolex and my other jewelry into my palm.

"Where did you . . . ?" I gasped as I slipped my wedding band back on my torn and dirty finger.

"Henry," said Burke, pointing at the stiffening body at the edge of the clearing. "They were in his jacket."

Burke spat in the fire. His spittle danced and sizzled in the embers.

"Once a thief, always a dirty rotten scumbag. Henry was the executioner they sent to kill Ta'Ronda Yancey's hacker boyfriend. He started unraveling this whole mess when he stole the computer and sold it to the pawnshop. You can thank him for your short life span."

"You forget," I said with a tired smile, "just like another Southern lady once said, 'tomorrow is another day.'"

Burke thought that was very funny. He rocked back and forth on his heels and laughed manically.

I was tired—bone tired and very hungry. My stomach felt like a giant, gnawing, empty hole. I brought the conversation back to breakfast. I wanted to be sure Burke could make good on his promise.

"So how do you catch a deer?" I asked innocently.

Burke went into another paroxysm of laughter. I was getting tired of being his straight man and told him so.

He wiped his eyes and shook his head.

"Catch a deer! Hunt! You track and hunt deer. Actually, in this case, I think they'll come to us. Somebody knew enough about the habits of the deer in this vicinity to build that stand here in these oaks."

He reached over and picked up a couple of acorns from the base of the tree he was leaning against. "Acorns. Deer love acorns. They practically can't resist them. I imagine if we hadn't made such a ruckus here today they would have shown up to graze. They know very well if they don't hurry the squirrels will get them all."

"But you said they won't come near the scent of man. We have three dead men and two live people. How are we going to get them to ignore that?"

Burke was unusually quiet for a moment.

"That has been worrying me. But I think I've come up with a solution."

He looked up at me with cold dead eyes.

"We'll uncover Henry's friends and leave them as far from the clearing as we can drag them. The coyotes will take it the rest of the way. Deer are used to scavengers. They won't sense anything strange about that."

I groaned when I thought of the macabre work ahead of me. And Burke had another even more disgusting task in mind.

"And you can pull Henry up to the deer stand. I have enough rope. What I don't have is enough raccoon or fox urine to cover both our tracks. You'll have to stay up there with him until I bring down a deer."

"You've got to be kidding," I breathed. The world whirled and danced in front of my eyes. "You're insane!" I whispered. "I won't stay up there with a dead man, not even for a minute! You can't make me," I finished feebly.

But of course he could.

I stumbled over to the impromptu burial mound of Henry's two friends. Then I remembered that Henry had worn gloves. I marched deliberately over to his body, pulled the suede gloves off his stiff dead hands and slipped them on mine. They had fleece inside and felt great. I smiled grimly and bent to my task.

Kicking and tossing the rocks to one side, it took me much less time to uncover the bodies than it had to cover them up. When I finished, I called to Burke to help me pull the corpses away from the clearing. At first he didn't answer. I called a second time. He got up slowly and stretched before he came to join me. He had been asleep! I could have made a run for it. But where would I run? And how far would I get without food or water? I sighed and resigned myself to whatever fate had in store for me in the company of this man—to the bitter end.

I tugged and pulled until I managed to get the smaller of the two men back out of the clearing and well away from the light of the fire. Together, Burke and I dragged his larger companion over to join him. This time, without hesitation, I helped Burke search their pockets for anything that might prove useful to us. Burke found a two candy bars, and I found a pamphlet from the Mount Pisgah Baptist Church denouncing the fiends who kill unborn babies. It was wrapped around three marijuana joints.

We abandoned the two militia men to their fate with the coyotes and staggered back to the warmth of the fire. With my last ounce of energy, I helped Burke push the hollow stump on the flames, then collapsed on top of the blood-spattered jacket I had taken off the larger of the men.

Without a word, Burke offered me half of one of the candy bars. I was, after all the best pack animal he had. I barely swallowed the last bite before I fell into a deep and dreamless sleep.

At some time during the night, I awoke to the sounds of gnashing teeth and cracking bone. The coyotes growled and fought each other for bits of flesh and sinew. I shuddered and tried to put what was happening in the forest out of my mind. After a while I succeeded when exhaustion overtook me and I slept again.

Burke woke me before dawn the next morning. He'd rigged a primitive pulley using a rope and the fork in the tree above the deer stand. He ordered me to start climbing. Without a word of complaint I followed his instructions and pulled on the rope while Burke guided Henry's cadaver the twenty feet to the stand. Despite the freezing temperature, I was soon sweating with the exertion.

I was also worried about the two bottles of animal urine I still had tucked in my pockets. Burke thought he had the urine. How was I going to make the switch? It was as important for me that he succeed in his quest to kill the deer as it was for him. I had to think of a way to exchange the bottles.

When Henry was safely tucked away and tied down to one corner of the flimsy shelf high above us, we melted some snow from the gully in the Vienna sausage tins. Burke shared another candy bar with me while we drank our hot water.

When he finished eating, Burke unzipped his pockets and handed me the bottles he had been carrying around. His hand was swollen and throbbing with infection. He wanted me to open the bottles and help him apply the liquid. He must have been in considerable pain, because he closed his eyes and leaned back against a tree. I thanked God for the opportunity so easy offered and quickly tucked his bottles away. I fished the others out of my pocket and broke the seals. Then I set about dabbing and drizzling the contents over his boots and lower legs.

The stuff had a strong, unpleasant musky stench, but Burke didn't seem to notice. His face was flushed and feverish. I wondered if he would drop in his tracks with fever and infection so I could slap him with a rock like he had Henry. I guess I stopped for a moment to enjoy thinking about it because he opened his eyes and slowly brought the rifle up until it was resting on my cheek.

"Don't get any cute ideas, lady. It'll take a lot more than a little fever to knock me off my feet. One false move from you and all bets are off. I'm very creative. It won't take me long to come up with another plan when you're just a memory."

He pressed the rifle hard into the soft skin of my cheek and kicked my feet out from under me.

"Save some of that urine for the back of my heels," he ordered.

He stood up and turned around from me to finish. When I was done with his boots there was still some liquid left in both bottles. I stood up and drizzled the rest over his back and shoulders. I took great pleasure in covering him with piss.

The pale winter sun was making a weak entrance over the horizon when Burke made me climb back up the tree.

"Stay there," he hissed, "until I come back for you. Don't move even if you hear a shot. With my hand . . . I might be a little off my marksmanship. A wounded buck can be very unpredictable. I don't want to have to worry about you getting in the way."

And off he went, the mighty hunter, to fetch us some breakfast.

It was cold up in the tree even though I hunkered down as far as I could out of the wind and the occasional flurry of snowflakes. I tried to imagine that they were fireflies, that I was watching them from the patio on Meadowdale Farm on a balmy summer evening, but the sight of my stone-dead companion spoiled the ambience.

For the first time since Burke appeared in the dugout I was alone and had the luxury of mourning Bert. It was too cold for tears, but I mourned. I thought of all the things I wished I had said, all the things I wished we could have seen and done together.

When Rafe disappeared, my greatest sorrow was that he didn't get to share my life with Cassie. She brought such joy to my existence. He would have reveled in her triumphs and valiantly protected her from all harm. He would have loved being her papa.

The emptiness I felt with Bert's death was different—it was for the future that might have been. And now, somehow, I knew there would never be another man for me. I had my chance with these two, one every two decades of my life, and that was it. There would be no third man when I was sixty. I would have no Horatio to laugh at my silly jokes and flatter me extravagantly when I was wrinkled and grey. Nora Dick and I would have more in common than my own Mother and I did. I think Nora realized that when I went to visit her. That snowy December afternoon she had seen in me the ghost of her youth, the last gasp of fading desire. That's why she had sympathized instead of encouraged.

"Oh, God," I begged, "Let me live and carry it off half as gracefully as Nora."

CHAPTER THIRTY-NINE

The morning grew colder as the minutes passed. The snow flurries got thicker and closer together. I looked over at Henry and cursed him for being cold and dead. I needed the warmth of a live human being. I considered ignoring Burke's orders and climbing back down to warm myself by the dying embers of the campfire, but I was too afraid to risk it.

I huddled back against the tree, seeking its protection from the icy blast of freezing wind. My body went into spasms of involuntary shivering. The planks of the stand swayed and shook with each seizure and left me breathlessly wondering if the shaky structure would come apart and send me hurtling to the ground.

Burke would have no use for me if I broke my leg. He would shoot me on the spot like an injured horse. Nevertheless, I had finally decided to risk ignoring his orders to seek the blessed warmth of the fire when I heard the rifle shot.

"Damn! He did it!" I shouted exultantly, then whispered, "Bring home the bacon, you sorry piece of shit."

I crawled as close to the edge of the wooden shelf as I dared, listening; but silence lay on the land thicker than the new blanket of snow. All I could hear was the occasional fall of a forgotten dry leaf as it spiraled to the icy ground.

For what seemed like hours, I agonized over what to do. Not knowing what had happened was the stuff of my nightmares.

I had no idea how far away Burke was when he fired the rifle. Sound carried a long way in the cold, that much I knew. With the trees almost bare and the absorbent layer of snow on the ground, it might possibly travel even farther. There was nothing else to do. I steeled myself to wait.

It didn't take long. I heard a scream in the distance and then the sound of pounding hooves. I heard the rifle fire once more, then saw Burke staggering through the woods. He lurched drunkenly from tree to tree, circling each one before going to the next. It took me a moment to figure it out. Something was chasing him.

The big buck was huge. His antlers looked like a hayrack and his shoulders and haunches were enormously broad and muscular. He was a creature of wild and spirited beauty. But in spite of his size, he was all power and grace, and he was definitely on the offensive in the battle with Captain Burke.

Burke frantically circled the tree trunks as the deer circled him with casual contempt. The terrified man hesitated, then made a break for the clearing. The buck followed at a slow and deliberate pace. Burke grabbed a smoldering branch from the fire and held it in front of him like a sword. Ignoring the flame, the deer stood on his hind legs and attacked Burke viciously with his forefeet. One razor-sharp hoof caught the edge of Burke's eyebrow. Bright red blood poured freely down his face. I screamed and Burke turned his blinded eyes toward me. He raised his arms up in supplication as the buck lowered his antlers and ran him through the middle of his body.

Unable to tear my eyes away from the horrible sight, I watched the deer shake Burke like a rag doll as he struggled to rid himself of the man's torn and bleeding flesh. With one final mighty toss of his head, the buck sent Burke tumbling head over heels across the clearing. He pawed the frozen ground and snorted angrily. When he was sure his prey was broken and helpless, he turned and raced off into the silent white shroud of the forest.

I sat frozen on the edge of the platform hardly daring to breathe, yet unable to look away. Burke's legs jerked violently several times, then stilled as the snow around him turned a bright and hideous red.

I finally closed my eyes, and with a great shuddering sigh, admitted to myself that Burke was dead and I was free. There was no sense of elation or joy associated with my liberation, only a great weariness.

I turned around and crawled over to the tree trunk in preparation to leave my flimsy perch. Just as I secured a foothold on the first crude rung of the ladder, the deer stand swayed one last time and began to break up. I hugged the tree tightly as planks rained down upon me. Henry's side of the shelf was the last to go. He followed, stiff and unbending, in an awkward diving half gainer. I tried to duck out of the way, but his frozen legs caught me on the shoulder and tore me away from the ladder. We landed side by side beneath the tree, two wingless snow angels, one breathless and the other beyond breathing.

For one moment I considered lying there beside Henry for eternity. I was so very tired. I hadn't moved since I fell and I didn't know if I could. It would be so easy, I thought, to just close my eyes and go to sleep. Nobody would blame me. I had fought a good fight. I was the last one left. I had won. Raggedy Ann, armed with nothing more than raccoon piss, had managed to outlive them all. I smiled slowly. It was just too good a story. I had to live to tell the tale.

With wobbly knees, I got to my feet and brushed the snow off. The fire was completely out except for a few hot ashes. The knowledge that I had no matches spurred me on in search of fuel.

First I piled up the planks from the deer stand. I tried to break them into smaller pieces to use for kindling, but it was no use. And there was nothing smaller within sight. But I did see Henry's knapsack.

He hadn't been kidding about the amount of money he had gotten from the arms deal. There was money to burn, and that's exactly what I did. A stack of twenties helped fan the ashes to a healthy and respectable flame. Three thousand dollars later, I had a lovely, roaring fire.

I gathered up all the wood I could find without venturing too far into the woods. The coyotes would be waiting around in their eagerness to finish off Burke and Henry. I didn't want to run into them before dinnertime. That brought another problem to mind. I didn't want to be anywhere near the all-night scavenger buffet. Henry and Burke had to be moved.

Henry's body was the heaviest. I tackled him first. Burke was still warm to the touch. I shuddered with repulsion when my hands brushed his flesh. With considerable effort, I managed to drag them both a safe distance from the clearing and me.

I turned my back on the bodies and then remembered the Ricine. It was too dangerous to leave unprotected. I trudged back to Burke's body and unzipped his pockets. Both pint jars were inside and still intact. I gingerly picked them up and took them back to the campfire. Henry's knapsack seemed the best place to put them. I opened it and marveled once more at the stacks and stacks of bills inside.

I tucked the Ricine safely into one corner of the bag and decided to add the bottles I had switched on Burke to the stash. Might as well put all the rotten eggs in one basket, I thought. When I pulled them out of my pocket, I noticed each had a small round label on the bottom. I turned them over. One label read, "Raccoon Urine," and the other "Fox Urine."

I sank down to my knees in horror. If these bottles were correctly labeled, I had doused Burke with doe estrus and the tarsal gland extract. It was no wonder the buck had attacked him! The two confusing scents must have driven the animal wild. And I had poured the entire contents of both bottles on Burke. I had killed him as surely as if I had stuck a gun in his ear and pulled the trigger.

I had a hard time deciding whether to congratulate or condemn myself for what I had done. Ultimately, torn between the two, I decided to have a hot drink and think about it later.

I heard the distant sound of the helicopter when I was melting my second cup of snow in the sausage tin. I anxiously searched the sky above the clearing but saw nothing. Knowing the campfire would be the only way to signal anyone in the air, I piled on more wood. Soon the flames were higher than my head and reaching eagerly upward. I piled on even more branches and sticks as I prayed for the aircraft to come my way.

Forty minutes later my hoard of firewood was almost spent and there was no sign of anyone or anything. The fire had dwindled down, and there was barely enough wood left to last me the rest of the day, much less all night. My goose was cooked. I didn't think I had any tears left, but suddenly my cheeks were wet. I gave in to my disappointment and cried bitterly.

The first time I heard Cassie calling me I thought I was hallucinating. I raised my head and wiped my face on my sleeve. Then I heard her voice again—a pure, sweet, lovely sound coming from the depths of the forest.

I stood up and opened my mouth to shout back. I didn't care if I was imagining things. If I had lost my mind then let me go all the way and howl like a banshee in the wind.

"Cassie!" I called. "Cassie, where are you?"

Again I heard her clearly. Her voice was excited and full of joy.

"Mom! Oh, God! Mom! Wait! Wait! We're coming!"

I sank back down on my knees and sobbed with relief. That's how Cassie found me when she burst into the clearing with Danny Hall close behind.

"Oh, Mom! Thank God you're alive. Oh, Mom!"

She threw herself on me. We tumbled over in the snow, hugging each other. We laughed and cried and rolled over and over like two rambunctious puppies in our happiness.

Finally Cassie sat up and grabbed my hands in hers.

"I bet you're starving to death!"

"You sound like Gran," I laughed. "But you got that right!"

Danny knelt down beside us and examined my face.

"Are you hurt, Mrs. DeLeon?" he asked.

"All over," I laughed, then shook my head and smiled. "No, Danny, I don't think so. Not really, just some bruises here and there. But I am very, very tired and hungry."

He helped Cassie lift me up and looked around the clearing.

"Looks like you kicked some butt," he marveled.

"We saw the bodies back in the woods. Did you . . . ?" asked Cassie with raised eyebrows.

"Only one," I answered her unspoken question. "And honestly, that was an accident. I didn't know the urine from the estrus."

Cassie looked at Danny and shook her head.

"We'd better get her out of here as quickly as we can. Let's not wait for the others. They can take care of the dead guys. Let's get Mom back to the hotel."

"Ohhh, hotel! How wonderful! Mother and Horatio are still at the lodge? They have a lot of food there. Let's go," I agreed happily.

"Yeah," grunted Danny, as he cocked his head knowingly at Cassie. "The sooner the better. She's just this short of around the bend."

"Just around the bend," I asked. "Is that all? Well, let's get started. Come on Cassie! Don't be the cow's tail," I laughed.

CHAPTER FORTY

My feet moved and my legs followed, but I don't remember anything of our trek out of the woods. Cassie told me later it was only about a forty-five minute walk to the trail where she and Danny had left the jeep they borrowed from the forest rangers. That forty-five minutes is erased from my memory bank forever.

I wish some of the other things that happened to me in the woods would go away. But even after I was checked over by the doctor, after I had been assured over and over again by everyone I loved that the nightmare was over, I still remembered.

That first night the hotel doc gave me something to make me sleep, but it didn't keep me from dreaming. I awoke at three in the morning, screaming with fear. Burke's hands were around my throat again. I could smell the musky odor of the doe scent as he poured it over my body. And the buck was running, hooves pounding in the snow. Only this time he was coming for me, not Burke, but me. I screamed.

"Darling, it's all right," crooned Mother softly. "You're safe now. You're with us. Cassie and Horatio are here, and we'll all protect you. Nothing else is going to hurt you."

Her soft hands brushed the damp hair back from my forehead and massaged my throbbing temples.

"Go back to sleep, dear. You need to get your strength back. You've nothing to fear ever again."

She was wrong. I kept myself from screaming again, but Burke and Henry waltzed through my dreams all night, threatening me with death and eternal damnation.

"I'm waiting for you," screamed Burke, his eyes wide open and filled with his own blood. "I'm waiting for you in Hell. You can try to forget, but I won't! Not ever!"

I finally pulled myself out of the tumbled, sweat-soaked sheets when I smelled breakfast. I spent a long time under the luxuriant warmth of the hotel shower, soaping my hair over and over again with Cassie's apple-scented shampoo. The bathroom was full of steam when I climbed out of the tub, and I studiously avoided looking in the fogged-over mirror as I wrapped myself in the big, thick terry cloth housecoat hanging on the back of the door.

I dressed quickly in warm fleecy sweats and joined the others in the living room. Horatio was sitting in front of the fire with a clean fresh cast on his leg. Danny and Cass were perched on the stools at the breakfast bar smiling and talking while Mother hovered over the stove, deep in culinary bliss.

I sat down quietly beside Horatio, took his hand and held it to my cheek. I closed my eyes and thanked God I was back. My old friend turned and gently pulled me into his arms. He held me while I cried without making a sound.

Mother made a huge breakfast, and we unanimously decided to eat in front of the fire so Horatio could be with us. Danny and Cassie carried plates of tender apple pancakes dusted with pearl sugar, sunny yellow scrambled eggs, crispy bacon, buttered grits, and country sausage into the living room. Mother followed with a basket of crusty angel biscuits and two racks of hot Texas toast.

I thought at first all I would be able to manage was a cup of tea and a biscuit, but I was mistaken. The more I ate, the more I wanted. Ultimately it was Danny who brought it to my attention that I was making a pig of myself.

"Wow! You sure can tuck it away," he marveled.

"Danny! Don't be rude!" chastised Cassie.

I burst into tears.

Danny's big kindly face crumpled as he watched me in horrified embarrassment.

"Oh, Jeez, Mrs. DeLeon, I didn't mean to . . . "

"That's okay, Danny, she's just tired," said Mother as she led me back into the bedroom. She must have called the housekeeping staff at some point, because the bed was freshly made with crisp, clean sheets and another comforter. My very own down pillows from home were piled in a welcome nest against the headboard. I sank gratefully into the warm softness and slept deeply and dreamlessly for the first time.

When I awoke again it was after dark. I could hear the voices of strangers in the living room. I slipped on the clean clothes Mother had laid out for me and pulled my hair back with a ribbon.

My legs felt much stronger and my mind was almost clear. It suddenly occurred to me that I hadn't said anything to Danny about his stepfather. Maybe, I thought in dismay, he didn't know. I hated to be the one to have to tell him that Bert was dead.

I opened the door a bit to peek out and see who was there. It wasn't Danny. That was a momentary relief. I opened the door the rest of the way and went on in to join the others.

Mother and Horatio were seated side by side on the sofa in front of the fire. Horatio held his arm protectively around Mother's shoulder. Cassie was standing stiffly in front of one of the sliding glass doors that opened to the balcony. She had her back to the two men who were questioning Mother and Horatio, but it was clear she was listening intently to their every word. As I entered the room she whirled around to face them.

"You're crazy!" she shouted angrily. "My mother would never be a part of anything like that!"

"A part of what, Cassie?" I asked softly.

The two men stood abruptly and tried not to look embarrassed at being put in their place by a twenty-year-old slip of a girl. They were wearing dark suits, plain white shirts, and black ties. The only thing they needed to complete their outfits, I mused, were dark sunglasses.

"And you would be the 'men in black,'" I joked as I held out my hand. "I'm Paisley Sterling DeLeon. Is there something I can do for you? Besides confess to crimes and misdemeanors, that is?"

The taller of the two men grinned awkwardly as he shook my hand.

"Special Agent Stern, ma'am," he said. "And my partner here is Agent Roberts."

He pulled up one of the armchairs and offered me a seat.

"I know you've been through a great deal, Mrs. DeLeon but you must understand we have a lot of questions we have to ask."

"Who is 'we,'" I asked carefully.

"FBI, ma'am. Federal Bureau of . . . "

"Okay," I interrupted. "And just why is the FBI interested . . . oh, because of the Ricine."

I might as well have slapped them both with a wet mop. Their jaws dropped and they both turned white as a sheet. They looked so comical I had to laugh.

"Paisley, dear," asked Horatio earnestly, "did you say Ricine?"

"Yeah, two pint jars full of the stuff. Burke was going to break the glass and stuff it in the dead militia guy's pants before he dumped him in the reservoir. But it's okay. I poured the tarsal gunk on Burke and the deer killed him. The Ricine is in the knapsack with all the money from the sale of the sidewinder missiles."

I turned to Cassie and asked, "You and Danny brought the knapsack back didn't you?"

She was staring at me with as much surprise as everyone else in the room, but she quickly recovered and opened the door to the balcony.

"I stuck it out here," she said. "It was filthy."

She bent down to pick up the dirty knapsack but Stern, moving with the speed of light, got there first. He lifted the bag gingerly by the strap and motioned for Roberts to help clear the coffee table.

They both donned latex gloves and carefully examined the exterior of the bag.

"It's okay," I laughed. "There's no bomb in there or anything. Just money and that white stuff. Believe me. I searched it from inside out looking for something to eat."

They turned and looked at me like I had done something dreadful.

"I'm sorry," I stammered. "The money's all there. Oh, except for the three thousand dollars I used to start the fire."

Horatio threw back his head and laughed. The sound of his genuine amusement filled the room and cleared the air of suspicion. Agent Stern sat back in his chair and started laughing also. Soon Roberts was wiping his eyes and holding his sides.

I looked from one to the other in consternation. My feelings were hurt. I had attempted to be as open as I could. God forbid I should ever be accused of stonewalling a federal government investigation. I sat there in acute discomfort trying my best not to cry while they rocked back and forth with laughter.

My feelings must have been transparently etched on my face because Horatio reached over and held my hands while he struggled to control himself.

"My dear, Paisley I promise you have done nothing wrong. As a matter of fact you couldn't have done a better job of clearing yourself of any wrongdoing if you'd hired a seven hundred dollar an hour Foggy Bottom lawyer. Am I right, gentlemen?"

"I'm afraid you're right, sir. She couldn't be that ingenuous and be guilty of anything. Please accept our apologies Mrs. DeLeon," said Stern as he made a quaint little half bow from the waist. "But you must realize we are very much in the dark here. We thought we were investigating a simple case of fraud. We had a tip from someone in the

Quartermaster's office at Fort Morgan that an enlisted man and an officer were involved in a scheme to misappropriate funds. We're here because you went to see that officer a week before she vanished. Now you've put a new light, er, several new lights, on the picture. Stolen missiles, deadly poison, the militia, and domestic terrorism; that's quite a lot to swallow all at once."

"Especially from a little lady who makes her living writing mysteries," added Roberts with a sly wink. "Are you sure this whole thing isn't some kind of publicity gimmick?"

"That's quite enough, gentlemen," announced my elegant little mother. "My daughter has been through a dreadful ordeal. She doesn't need to sit here and listen to innuendo and outright insults. She needs peace and quiet to recover from the terrible things she experienced, whether you believe her or not."

She stood up and opened the door. "Now if you will please excuse us."

Stern and Roberts looked at each other and shrugged their respective shoulders. My mother had given them no other option. They had to leave or serve me with a warrant. Apparently they weren't in any position to do the latter so they left, knapsack in tow, without further ceremony.

Stern paused in the doorway and turned to give me a final warning.

"Be careful, Mrs. DeLeon. You just might want to keep this story to yourself. I'd be very cautious about speaking to anyone else if I were you. Someone just might believe you."

"Good bye, gentlemen," said Mother firmly as she closed the door in their faces.

"Horatio," Cassie asked, "what's a Foggy Bottom lawyer?"

We stayed in the lodge one more day, then packed up and headed for home. We stopped along the way and rescued Aggie from the hotel kennel. Mother explained that when I didn't return, Aggie had made a nuisance of herself by barking and howling all night. I was quite touched by this tale of canine affection, but when we picked her up she ignored me completely and sat on Cassie's lap all the way home.

Even on that cold, rainy, winter day, Meadowdale Farm had never looked more beautiful to me. Mother's friend and sometime housekeeper, Mabel, had opened up the house, shopped for groceries, and fixed a wonderful luncheon for us in front of a roaring fire in the library.

"Oh, my," I sighed as I relished the warmth and comfort of the room I loved. "This is what kept me alive, the thought of being here in front of this fire just one more time."

"Oh, darling, what a terrible time you must have had! I get quite upset when I allow myself to imagine what you must have gone through."

Mother dabbed her dainty lace handkerchief at the corner of each eye and filled my plate high with baked ham, baby peas, and mashed potatoes.

"Here, dear," she said handing the loaded dish back to me. "You're thin as a rail."

"I am?" I asked with surprise. "Am I really? Well, in that case, please pass the butter."

Later that night when we were relaxed and content and all alone, I broached the subject of Bert's death with Cassie.

"Danny knows," she said. "It's strange. I thought he would be devastated, but he got over it very quickly."

She sat down beside me on the sofa and put her arm around my shoulders.

"I think I was more upset than he was."

"How did he find out?" I asked her.

"I don't know," Cassie answered shaking her head as she lay back so that Aggie could hop up in her lap.

"Who told him?" I wondered aloud. "Captain Burke told me himself that he killed Bert. How could anyone else have known?"

That question kept me awake half the night. I carefully reviewed every word that Stern and Roberts had said back at the lodge. Finally I became convinced they knew no more about Bert than they did about anything else.

Around three in the morning I came to a conclusion. The only person who could have told Danny that his stepfather had been shot was Bert himself. I knew it was crazy, and I couldn't tell a soul, but I had a feeling that Bert Atkins wasn't dead after all!

EPILOGUE

For the next few days, Mother and Cassie took on the role of palace guards as they politely but firmly turned away all curious visitors. The one exception to the rule was Horatio, who showed up every evening with a fresh tidbit of gossip. The rumor mills were working overtime with speculation about what happened during my adventure in the woods.

But all good things must come to an end, to coin a phrase, and on the sixth day, the Country Club gossip was all about Jim Bealour's ten-pound "premature" baby who bore an uncanny resemblance to his new bride's former fiancé. I was old news. It was safe to venture out once again.

Cassie had already gone back to school to prepare for her last round of classes. The next time I saw her she would be wearing a cap and gown. It was hard to believe my baby was graduating in June.

The weather was changing rapidly from winter to spring. Some days it seemed Mother Nature couldn't decide which was which. Perhaps that was why I was so restless and irritable. I found myself quite unable to sit still long enough to write, and I was peevish with Mother and the dog. On these occasions she would patiently tell me I needed some exercise to walk off my demons, then call Horatio to come and rescue her.

One half-blustery, half-sunny afternoon after they left for Wieuca City, I finally decided to take Mother's advice. I spent ten fruitless minutes trying to put Aggie's sweater on her, but after she nipped me twice, I closed the French doors in her face and shut my ears to her incessant barking.

"You had your chance, dog," I muttered as I stomped angrily down to the orchard. I didn't get far. Andy Joiner drove up and circled on around the driveway to meet me. He saw the scowl on my face and held up his hands when he got out of the car.

"Peace!" he laughed. "Maybe I'd better come another day."

"Sorry, Andy," I said trying to force a smile. "I've just been out of sorts lately."

"Yeah," he answered shifting uncomfortably from one big foot to the other. "I, eh, heard about what you went through."

He looked me straight in the eye. "You're a pretty tough cookie, Paisley Sterling. I'm not sure I could'a handled what happened half as well as you."

"Thanks, Andy," smiling for real this time, "that means a whole lot to me."

We both pretended to examine the clouds for a moment. Then something about what he said clicked in my mind.

"Hey, how come you know anything about what happened to me? I haven't told anybody but the FBI, and they thought I was making the whole thing up."

In my excitement I grabbed him by the front of his jacket and tried to shake him. I shook myself more than I moved him, but he got the message.

"Whoa there, girl. Calm down," he laughed.

"Bert is alive, isn't he? Danny knows it, and so do you!"

I smacked him on his big beefy shoulder with my open palm.

"Tell me!" I begged as bright tears flooded my eyes. "Please, tell me," I whispered softly.

Andy held my face in his big hands and smiled.

"Paisley, honey, let's just say it's a great day for a walk, maybe back down the lane and over to your Grandad's old fishing hole, the one by the big willow."

"Oh, thanks, Andy!" I laughed wiping away the tears. "Thank you so much! You'll never know . . . "

"And you won't either if you don't get a move on," he said with a grin.

I took off running before he even got back in his car.

The ground was still wet in some of the shadier parts of the lane. My sneakers were soon heavy and caked with mud, but that didn't slow me down a bit. I flew past the hollow oak and the little pond, then cut across the field to the big pond and the spillway on the other side where my grandfather had once made a name for himself by catching a trophy-sized bass. I shaded my eyes against the capricious sun and scanned the valley below before climbing down the rocky hillside. I could see the willow tree from the top, but there was no one in sight. I tried to keep from screaming with disappointment as I made my way with reckless abandon down the hill. I lost my footing and slid the last five feet on my butt before coming to a halt on the soft mossy bank beneath the willow. I lay there panting and out of breath. That's when I heard his voice.

"That was some entrance, Paisley Sterling. Bet you can't do that again."

"Bert?" I whispered. "Where are you?"

I sat up and looked around. The new growth of the willow tree hung down around its trunk like a Southern belle's lacy petticoat. I pushed some of the delicate branches aside, but I still couldn't see him anywhere.

"I swear if this is some kind of joke, or if you're just a ghost, I'll kill you Bert Atkins!"

"That's my girl," he laughed as he jumped down out of the tree and landed by my side.

"That's my girl," he whispered hoarsely as he took me in his arms and held me tightly.

"Oh, Bert," I cried. "I thought . . . "

"I know," he answered, his breath warm against the soft skin of my throat. "I know."

I finally pulled away from his arms so I could see his face.

"You look terrific for a dead man!" I laughed. "What's with the tan?"

"Vacation in sunny Florida," he answered as he wiped the mud and moss off my cheek and place his lips on mine.

"Hey," I finally protested, after a very long and satisfying moment. "Time for that later. You've got some questions to answer, mister!"

He held my face the way Andy had, and looked into my eyes. That's when I noticed the pain and sorrow deep in his.

"Wha . . . what's going on, Bert? We do have time for that later, don't we?"

"That's entirely up to you, Paisley," he said. "But first, ask some of your questions."

"You're not dead?" I laughed. "For sure?"

"Honestly," he answered, kissing me lightly once more.

"How come?"

Bert sat back against the tree and pulled me into his arms. "After I left you in the dugout I headed back to the lake. I knew I was taking a chance, but it was the quickest way to find help. I had no idea I was being followed until I heard the guy shout. I was standing on the cliff trying to decide which way to get down when he shot me. That solved my problem," he laughed. "I went head first."

He kissed my ear and continued with his story.

"I was lucky. There were two kids fishing from a boat near the bank. The guy who shot me obviously didn't see them or he would have killed them, too. The kids saw me go in the drink and paddled over to fish me out. Somehow they got me to the ranger station. From then on it was a given I was going to make it. They flew me to St.

Thomas Hospital in Nashville and dug the bullet out. That's when the men from Alabama came for a visit."

"You mean from Washington—the FBI, don't you?" I asked.

"No," he answered shaking his head. "This is a different bunch altogether, lawyers mostly, and some civil rights activists. They've had their eye on the Klan and other extremist groups for quite some time now. They thought it would be safer for me to disappear for awhile."

"And here you are," I said happily as I hugged him.

"Here I am," he smiled. "Now tell me what's up with you. How are Cassie and your mother? And that vicious little mutt?"

"Fine, fine, and vicious," I answered showing him the most recent dog bite.

"And guess what? Pam says I can be Leonard now, for real. No more pretending he's you, or anybody else."

"I guess that makes two of us who have a new job," he said quietly.

"What job?" I asked with immediate concern. There was something about him that told me my worries weren't over.

"Let's walk around some," he said instead of answering me. "You're shivering. It's cold under here."

We walked hand in hand beside the meandering little stream that fed the pond and the fishing hole, then lost its way in the meadow beyond. Here and there wild iris, lily of the valley, and even an occasional daffodil poked dainty heads up in search of the afternoon sun.

Bert stopped and pulled me into his arms.

"These men, let's call them watchdogs, want me to go back undercover and infiltrate some other militia groups out West," he said finally.

"Oh, Bert, no, please don't go," I murmured, knowing somehow he would in spite of me.

"It's important work, Paisley. And I'm an old warhorse. It feels good to be back in the traces."

"Let someone else do it!" I said angrily. "Let somebody else get shot and left for dead."

"Okay then, will you marry me? That's the only thing that could keep me from going."

I whirled around and stomped my foot.

"That's not fair!" I cried.

"Look, I'm not one of the characters in your books, Paisley. I can't run like the wind or ride like the devil. When I get shot I bleed, and it hurts when I cut myself shaving. I get constipated. Sometimes I even have bad breath, and I wake up in the morning looking like hell. But I love you. I promise I'll love you for what's left of the rest of my life. You are all the warmth and smiles and laughter I've ever missed out on. I crave the sight of you. A glimpse of that rag mop you call hair is enough to get me through the worst of days. I cannot imagine the joy of having you by my side for twenty-four hours, much less a lifetime. But that's what I'm asking. I want you to marry me."

I slumped down in the soft grass and covered my face with my hands.

"That's the most beautiful proposal I've ever had," I said when I regained control of my voice. "It's the most beautiful one I've ever heard of, but . . . "

"Oh, God, but what?"

"I'm not free, Bert. Something in my past is still holding me prisoner."

"Cassie's father?"

"Yes. Until I know, until I'm sure . . . until then, I can't promise you anything. I can't promise myself anything."

He knelt down beside me and stroked my cheek with his rough, calloused fingers—a touch as gentle as the softest feather in an angel's wing.

"I knew," he sighed.

"I know," I whispered

His lips were warm and sweet and wet with my tears. We pulled apart reluctantly, then he smiled and walked away.

I didn't call him back.

Leonard would have been proud.

www.ingramcontent.com/pod-product-compliance
Lightning Source LLC
Chambersburg PA
CBHW031218020726
47499CB00002B/631